IN THE CAGE
WHERE YOUR SAVIOURS HIDE

MALCOLM MACKAY was born in Stornoway on Scotland's Isle of Lewis. His *Glasgow Trilogy* has been nominated and shortlisted for several international prizes, including the Edgar Awards' Best Paperback Original and the CWA John Creasey (New Blood) Dagger award. His second novel, *How a Gunman Says Goodbye*, won the Deanston Scottish Crime Book of the Year Award. Mackay still lives in Stornoway.

MALCOLM MACKAY

IN THE CAGE WHERE YOUR SAVIOURS HIDE

HEAD
of ZEUS

An Apollo Book

Printed and bound in Great Britain by
CPI Group (UK) Ltd, Croydon CR0 4YY

Head of Zeus Ltd
First Floor East
5–8 Hardwick Street
London EC1R 4RG

WWW.HEADOFZEUS.COM

For my father

PROLOGUE

A drop of dirty rainwater fell from the guttering and landed with a splash in the open eye of the dead man. He lay with eyes wide and mouth open, arms close to his side and legs together. The body had lain there for three hours and not a soul had cared to notice. The alley was narrow and unlit, with large bins pushed against the walls on both sides. Navigating from one end to the other was an assault course and that was what had slowed him down and killed him.

The dead man had run into the alley at ten past one in the morning, gasping, bleeding and limping. The ground was wet and he slipped against a green industrial bin placed beside the plain red rear door of a struggling restaurant. His hand reached out instinctively and hit the top of it with a thump, sliding it backwards a fraction, feeling the thick raindrops that had settled on it wet his palm. He pulled away and the lid slid shut with a hollow knock. Running was already beyond the man with the knife wound, and now he had to weave between bins and boxes stacked against bare brick walls. The effort ensured that twenty-five seconds later he was on the ground, dying.

A little before two o'clock in the morning a waiter came out of the back of the restaurant and pushed open the lid of the bin a dying hand had touched. He held two plastic shopping

1

bags filled with food scraps, the bags knotted at the handles. He slung them into the bin in a looping movement and pulled the lid tightly shut to deny the rats a meal. He took a cigarette from his pocket and lit it, standing by the bin for two or three relaxing minutes, ignoring the familiar, rotting smell. A shout from inside the building, a woman's voice, the waitress he gave a lift home to each night. He dropped the cigarette on the ground and stubbed out the orange glow with his shoe, blew out the last mouthful of smoke and walked quickly back into the restaurant. He said he saw no body in the alley, that there was light enough to spot it so it can't have been there.

At twenty past two a police car sped down Somerset Street and past the end of the alley. Its siren knifed the silence, its lights flashing blue into the darkness, bouncing off the walls and briefly down the alley. The city had many emergencies for its police to tackle, and no one had realised another victim was lying, waiting to be discovered, nearby. From the alley, beside the body, you could hear the siren fade away into the distance, looking for a new horror. They wouldn't have to search long.

At four o'clock in the morning another man entered the alley from the Morti Road end. This one was walking more slowly, carefully, picking his way and watching his footing with unnecessary care. He went past the bins and saw the body lying flat, so he stopped. He moved slowly beside it and nudged the still arm with his boot. He knelt down and slapped the face gently, held a hand over the nose to try to feel breath. There was nothing. His medical expertise exhausted, he stood and took his mobile from his pocket and called the police. Two and a half minutes later sirens were loudly announcing their return. The dead man had been found and reported, and now the investigation would begin.

1

WE'LL START BEFORE the obvious point because the real beginning of this story comes a couple of days earlier than that. Instead of opening with the gorgeous dame walking into the office on Cage Street we'll instead go to a flat on Haugen Road, over in the Bakers Moor district in the east of the city.

There were forty people in a room that could hold twenty, in a flat that housed six and was designed for three. That's always the way on the east side of Challaid, too much life for the space. The music was loud and indistinguishable from the general racket, shite, to be succinct; the crowd packed so tight it was hard to tell who was dancing and who was waving for help. It was hot and, boy, was it sweaty, the movements slow. A young couple were kissing with the passion of people who had uncovered a new art form and wanted to perfect it, fast. Darian Ross stood back against the wall by the door, on his own, and watched.

Girls in vest tops and shorts and boys in T-shirts with unwitty slogans printed on the front, shimmering brows on blissed faces.

A constant and aimless sway of bodies in the absence of actual dancing.

A pill passed discreetly from one hand to another.

A shout and then a bottle breaking, the crowd pausing in anticipation of a violent follow-up and then carrying on, disappointed, when they realised it wasn't coming.

Someone was trying to make themselves heard close by and failing, the music screaming and the babble of voices always rising in the battle to be heard above it. This was what other people's joy looked and sounded like. A gap just large enough for him to raise his hand cleared and Darian took a sip from his warm beer can.

His eyes never wavered, fixed on the same couple.

The girl had black hair in a bob and big teeth but he couldn't see the rest of her. They were deep in the crowd, Darian catching occasional glances of their heads as they looked into each other's eyes, the man doing all the talking.

He was older than her, older than most of the people in the room. She and they were teenagers; the man she had her arms around was twenty-seven. Brown hair combed back, average height, an ordinary, clean-shaven face and small, dark eyes that always seemed to have a light trapped inside them. Not a lot to look at, but his charisma held him above the ordinary mass of boys that usually chased her.

Two young girls had offered Darian a body to lean on earlier in the evening when there had been more room to approach but he had turned them both away, not interested. The only person he was there to see was the man with the unremarkable face. As the crowds filled the flat and the temperature rose the light had faded from the room, too. Darian was handsome, light brown hair, feminine features, large brown eyes and full lips, six feet and slim with an intense look. In the dark he could lean back against the wall by the door and play the detached observer, still just young enough at twenty-two to slot in and not look like a creepy bastard. He'd picked his spot to make sure anyone who left had to parade right past him. More coming than going, and it had reached the point where a couple arrived and instantly decided that being crushed in a sweaty crowd was not actually the best available option for a Friday night. In this city there were always, always better options.

The beer in his can was flat and had lived long enough to rise to room temperature but he didn't notice. Darian sipped from it only so that he wouldn't be the only person standing still. In this room the man not moving was the man who stood out, so he'd occasionally nod his head self-consciously to the thudding music he hadn't yet identified. He found his excitement in silent moments, but this crowd was looking for something else. Most of them wanted more from life than peace and quiet, and one of them wanted everything.

Darian lost sight of the couple for a few seconds, a wave of bodies rising in front of them. Where the hell did they go? Shit, lost them. No, wait, there, he saw them again. Picked them up, walking towards the door beside him, politely nudging past partygoers to reach the exit. The ordinary face leaning down to speak into the ear hidden by dark hair. She smiled, buzzing, eyes wide and too alert, looking forward to being somewhere else. They managed to escape the scrum and passed Darian, out of the flat.

He let them go and counted slowly to ten, then counted a second time to make sure he had it right. He put the beer can on the floor for someone else to kick over, spun off the wall and walked out through the door, not looking back at the crowd that had barely noticed his presence and didn't spot his departure at all.

THE CHALLAID GAZETTE AND ADVERTISER

14 January 1905

32 DIE IN TUNNEL COLLAPSE

Tragedy struck Challaid yesterday morning with a major collapse in the rail tunnel being dug under the Bank district of the city which killed thirty-two men working at the site. It is believed the men drowned when the tunnel ceiling collapsed and mud and water poured in from above, filling the tunnel and preventing escape. A large rescue operation began immediately but no survivors have been retrieved, and it has now been confirmed that bodies will not be recovered until the tunnel has been drained, which may take several weeks.

Concerns had previously been raised regarding the digging of the tunnel as part of the rail extension with unions arguing the boggy land close to the docks was unsafe. The project, funded by Sutherland Bank, has been controversial since its announcement, with the tunnel proposed as an alternative to an above ground line, reducing disruption in the city centre during construction and afterward. Lord Sutherland, chairman of the bank, has stated his shock and sadness and added his hope that work can begin again on the tunnel in quick order for the good of the city.

Glendan Construction – who are building the rail line from Barton to Whisper Hill – have confirmed that thirty-two of their workers are missing after the collapse but will not confirm the identity of the men until families have been informed. It is thought that most or all of the men were from Challaid and Glendan has stated that its senior engineers were leading the tunnel excavation at the time.

Further questions have been raised about the proposed underground rail system that would connect various parts of the city not served by the new main line. The underground designs are before the council planning committee and it was hoped construction would begin next summer with parts open to passengers by 1908. This is now likely to face delay while the safety of all proposed lines is assessed.

KING BEGINS TOUR OF CALEDONIAN STATES

His Royal Highness King Kenneth IV yesterday docked in the port town of New Edinburgh in Panama for the first day of his three-week tour of the Caledonian states. King Kenneth, travelling without Queen Margaret, was greeted by large crowds happily waving saltires and Caledonian flags, with all suggestions of unrest in the region surrounding his visit proved false.

King Kenneth will give a speech to parliament in Panama City on Monday and will attend a banquet in his honour on Tuesday in the city. His tour will continue north to Costa Rica and Nicaragua. It is the longest visit by a reigning monarch to Caledonia in more than seventy years and comes against the backdrop of growing demands for full independence for the three states. Recent elections in Costa Rica saw the independence party finish second with almost thirty per cent of the vote. The Scottish government has denied his majesty's visit is a reaction to the rising volume of the independence movement, and have reiterated that the visit will boost trade and opportunities for both Scotland and the Caledonian states.

2

DARIAN LEFT THROUGH the open front door and made his way to the stairs. He could see them ahead, both pulling on coats as they moved out of view, walking side by side, leaning against each other out of lust and a need for balance. The stairwell they skipped down was dark, streetlights coming through the full-length windows giving a dull orange tinge to the deep grey surroundings. Darian lurked at the top to play voyeur, listening to them go down together.

The girl said, 'Hold on, I can't see properly.'

A squeal followed as the man said, 'Don't you worry, I got you.'

She sounded too young to be playing this game. She started to giggle and that noise was smothered quickly by a kiss on the landing a floor below Darian. Thirty seconds passed before it turned back to movement, shoes clacking on bare concrete stairs as the couple moved further down. Darian kept up the stalk, making sure they couldn't hear him, walking slowly on the balls of his feet. He only needed to be close for this early part of the journey, just until he was sure his guess was right.

He was on the first-floor landing when he heard the front door click shut behind them. Darian sauntered down, pushed it open and stepped out into the cold, clear night. They were, as we said, on Haugen Road, dirty lamplight showing the four-storey flats on either side of the long street, their dark brown brickwork hugging the shadows tight, the road curving downhill towards Bakers Station. One man, he looked middle-aged, was walking up the street, and seemed to be struggling to keep his feet on a flat pavement inconsiderately not designed with the stumbling drunk in mind. The young couple had crossed the road and were walking down towards the station, the man with his arm tight around the girl. Darian stayed on the other side and walked more slowly than them.

It was a careful process, staying far enough behind to make sure his footsteps couldn't be heard. He didn't need to stay close now, but it was hard to walk down the hill to the station any slower than the lovey-dovey, hands-on couple were going without tying his feet together. They went into the brightly lit, century-old, grey stone station at the bottom of the road ahead of him, so now he could take his time, let them get ahead, let them disappear. They entered through the large arch to the concourse and Darian followed slowly, dragging his fingers along the bumpy surface of the stonework on the outside.

The couple used their travel cards to get through the barriers and hopped onto the next train heading north to Whisper Hill. Darian was, technically, working, so he went to the machine and bought a ticket with money he could claim back the cost of with a rare proof of expenses. The purchase killed four minutes; made sure he missed the train north they were on but got him to the platform in time for the next.

A short detour from the tale here, but anyone who's ever been to Challaid will know the leading pastime of the populace is not football or camanachd or the theatre or, unfortunately, books or any other noble pursuit, it's complaining about the transport system. Ignore the stadiums and grand halls and libraries the other hobbies occupy, nothing can compete with the scale of people whinging about travel. This is a port city, founded over a thousand years ago as a fishing and trading town, or so your history teacher would have you believe, and centuries later boats remain the only vehicles we're any good with. The roads are clogged because we're a long but narrow city, U-shaped round the end of a sea loch, and because the rail system is a calamitous joke. We have no underground trains, and a single line running round the city above ground.

Look, we all know the reasons; a lot of people died when the original line was being built, probably more than was ever admitted because immigrant workers were never properly counted, and the companies involved were tone-deaf in their response. People protested against further development. It was dangerous back then, and by the time engineering skill caught up with public demand to make building an underground system safe it was prohibitively expensive. We're a reasonably rich city, but there's no appetite to spend the many billions something that big would now cost, so instead we complain. It's cheaper. There had been a suggestion in recent years that a monorail should be built, running over buildings instead of trying to dig under them. Funnily enough this idea had met with little support from communities who would have trains rattling above their heads every ten minutes and the odds of it ever happening ranked somewhere alongside the chances of everyone in Challaid being provided with a jetpack.

Darian was on the next train up to Whisper Hill, the carriage a mix of people silently annoyed with the others who were drunkenly loud. He was content to let the couple get ahead of him. It took fourteen minutes before the train stopped at Three O'clock Station in Whisper Hill and Darian got off. He walked out through the eastern exit of the sprawling station, each expansion adding a new architectural twist to the last stop on the city line, a glass and steel frontage on old brickwork on the east side of the tracks, a long, thin, white-panelled extension on the west and the back end of the building twice the height of the front.

There was a time, probably, when Whisper Hill would have been attractive. The hills, the narrow stretch of moor and then Loch Eriboll; who wouldn't find that pretty on a rare day of summer, midges the only pollution? Now this area of the city was dominated by the large industrial docks built in the thirties around an inlet, and the 'engineering marvel' of Challaid International Airport built on top of Whisper Hill itself, the hilltop mostly levelled to accommodate it. No one in the last century has put the eyesore area on a postcard.

The lights up the steep hill shone bright, and Darian walked that way. Along Drummond Street, the long road that ran from the docks to the airport, the first half flat and the second a steep climb out of the tangle of concrete and up the heather-clad hillside. Darian turned right before he reached the bottom of the hill to walk down Gemmell Road, a narrow street with ugly brown three-storey flats on each side. This was low-cost housing built for people working the docks in the thirties and forties. Short-term housing for temporary residents. It was the sort of area, buildings tightly packed together, a squash of inhabitants with a high turnover of tenants, in which a person with secrets could live a life unnoticed.

Darian knew he was looking for the second building on the left; he had spent time on Gemmell Road already, and went in through the front door and up the stairs to the first floor.

There was no need to creep around now; they would have been inside the man's flat for more than five minutes.

Darian pictured them, kissing intensely, hurried, all that energy bottled up since meeting at the party cracking the glass with its intensity now.

Tension racing wild as soon as it was let off the chain.

Clothes being pulled off as they moved into the bedroom, onto the bed.

The girl underneath, that was the pattern.

The man licking and then biting, the girl getting scared as he forced her to roll over.

She would try to push him off, slap him, and he would ignore her.

When she moved too much for him, made his mouth's work too difficult, that was when he would reach for the knife, that's when he would want blood.

Darian stood outside the front door, eyes closed, trying to calculate the time that pattern would take to play out. There was a scream from inside, quickly muffled. Darian took a step back and kicked, aiming for the lock of the front door, knowing how cheap and feeble such fixtures were. It was the smash and grab burglar routine; kick, damage, repeat, the same methodical impact taking three kicks before the door cracked open. Darian was into the corridor and pushed open a door to find a bathroom, pushed open the next one to find his target.

A lamp was on beside the bed, showing the walls painted a dark blue, the bedside cabinet and a wardrobe opposite, no other furniture. The girl with the black bob was sitting up on the pillows, her eyes wide, a single drop of blood tickling down her left breast. The man, Darian knew his real name was Ash Lucas, whatever he was telling the girls, was standing at the foot of the bed, naked and excited. He had a large silver knife with a serrated edge in his hand and he spun to face the door when Darian walked in.

It took a glance for him to see it all, to understand that the pattern was indeed being repeated. Not pausing because delay gave the knife an advantage, Darian took a step towards Lucas and swung hard with his right fist, aiming accurately for the bridge of the nose. He hit the smaller man hard but he didn't hear the crack he was hoping for. The tactic was to hurt the bastard, and fast. Lucas stumbled backward, gripped the knife harder and reeled forward to his front foot to try to make a thrust at Darian. A second punch caught Lucas around the left eye, Darian's longer arm jabbing over the knife before he danced a step away.

That punch hurt both of them, Darian's index finger cracking, but he didn't show it, didn't react to pain in a fight. Lucas dropped sideways onto the bed. Darian took aim, his boot this time, the girl shouting as Darian stamped down on what we'll chastely call the man's excitement, scuffing down the skin. Lucas opened his mouth and instead of screaming he gasped loudly for breath as his eyes bulged, dropping the knife onto the floor. Darian picked it up and pointed it at Lucas.

He said quietly, 'Got you, you piece of shit.'

He was about to say something reassuring to the girl when she bolted across the bed and out of the room, scooping up enough of her clothes in a bundle to cover herself as she ran down the hallway, struggling to dress as she hopped and stumbled out through the broken front door.

Darian shouted, 'Hey.'

She didn't come back and he didn't chase, couldn't leave Lucas unguarded. Another punch, this one to make sure Lucas didn't kid himself by thinking he had the same freedom to run his victim did. Unlikely that he could have moved fast anyway, hunched over and crying quietly as he was, hissing through his teeth. Darian took his mobile from his pocket and scrolled down through his contacts. He knew the nearest station was Dockside, and he called his contact there.

3

HIS CONTACT CAME round in minutes in a police car with another uniformed officer. They used to say that all the toughest cops in Challaid were based at Dockside station because Whisper Hill was by far the shittiest area, populated by people who saw violence as another form of exercise. It might not be as brutal now as it was in more casually violent times gone by, but the Hill remained the home of the darkest nights in town.

It was two reassuringly large coppers who stood in the bedroom doorway of the flat, looking at Darian standing over the prisoner. Darian's contact was PC Vincent Reno, a barrel-chested bruiser in his thirties and the sort of honest rogue who made the ideal friend in the force. Vinny had a wide, smiling face, pale skin prone to flushing red when he was talking energetically as usual, and he looked like he'd been born in the uniform. Darian didn't know the other cop, he was very young and quite tall, narrower than Vinny, and looked like he'd borrowed his uniform from his father to play dress up.

Vinny was looking down at Lucas, relishing his discomfort, pleased to see the smudge of blood under his nose mingling with tears. He looked at Darian and said, 'So this is how Darian Ross spends his Friday nights, is it?'

'Aye, very good. There was a wee girl with no clothes on as well, but she did a runner.'

'Happen to you a lot, does it?'

Darian gave him the classic don't-push-it-too-far-pal look, and Vinny knew him just well enough to take the hint. Knew him enough to know this was a mixed blessing. Darian had no business chasing after this now-naked bastard, not legally, but Vinny was among a group of coppers who knew exactly what sort of arsehole Ash Lucas was, what he had been getting up to and getting away with. He'd take any chance to put a stop to it, even a bloody awkward one.

Vinny said, 'Right, get some clothes on you; I'm not looking at that ugly wee willy of yours all night. We'll take you for a drive to the station.'

Lucas looked up at him through teary eyes and, with spit on his lips, said, 'Fuck you, I need to go to the hospital.'

Vinny smiled and said, 'That's not really for you to judge, that's for me to judge. They won't have much room for you at A&E in the Machaon on a Friday night anyway, better off trusting yourself to doctor professor Reno. That's me, by the way.'

Lucas groaned a lot as the younger cop threw a random selection of clothes at him to put on and Darian and Vinny stood in the doorway and watched. Vinny wasn't gentle as he led Lucas down the stairs and out to the police car. Challaid cops seldom are. It was a short drive, nobody speaking a word in the car on the way.

Whisper Hill rattled past them, gloomy and menacing where the high buildings faded above the lights, figures walking through a welcoming night in search of easily found fun or fleeing from the amusements of others. Countless stories that would never be told. They went down past Three O'clock Station and left onto Docklands Road. It was a long street filled with large, irregular buildings, on one side the backs of the huge warehouses whose fronts looked onto the dock itself and on the other a line of large buildings intended to serve shipping in other ways; among them the much-needed police station. They drove up the side of the whitewashed block and round to the walled car park at the back.

Vinny led Lucas by a well-gripped arm to be booked in, shouting happily to the sergeant at the desk, 'Ash Lucas, assault and attempted rape. Suffered a few cuts and bruises to the face, but I believe most of the damage was done to the, uh, front of his rear end. He'll live, just at a higher pitch.'

Before the smirking sergeant responded the young cop, still remaining nameless, put Darian into an interview room to await interrogation. If the young cop looked nervous it was because he knew this might turn out to be uncomfortable for Darian. They all knew who he was, knew who his father was, and they knew what Darian was doing for a living.

He sat in the small, windowless room, just the table and two chairs on each side of it, and waited for eight minutes. He ran his finger along the ridge in the light blue table top where someone had tried to gouge something – likely a name because people are stupid enough to do that – on it but had stopped before they'd finished an identifiable letter, maybe a p or B, presumably after being caught.

The detective who came into the room introduced herself as DC Angela Vicario. He didn't need the name to see her ancestors had sailed across from one of the Caledonian countries, but her accent was purest Challaid so she was a few generations rooted. The young PC came in and sat silently next to her, but she didn't bother to introduce him either. Poor bugger seemed doomed to never get a namecheck. That told Darian this wasn't going to be a formal interview with a witness but a casual chat among people who could help each other out. He'd never met her, she looked too young to have worked with his father before things went sour, so he had no idea what her approach would be.

DC Vicario had long dark hair, tied back, black eyes and a large mouth that smiled easily at him. The Hispanic look was quickly overwhelmed by the Challaid accent when she said, 'I'm not sure I should thank you for a gift like Mr Lucas, like a cat bringing a half-eaten mouse to my door.'

'It's the thought that counts, and I thought getting him off the streets was a good idea.'

'Why don't you start by telling me how you ended up in his flat, booting him in the unmentionables?'

'I was at a party in Bakers Moor, house party. I noticed him there with a girl, remembered that the company I work for had been hired to track him down regarding money he owes. He and the girl left the party together and I went after him.'

'All the way to his flat?'

'All the way.'

'You didn't manage to catch him up between a party in Bakers Moor and his flat on Gemmell Road, protect the girl before the attack began? Must have taken a series of remarkable quirks to prevent you, falling down open manhole covers, shoelaces tied together, that sort of thing. Did you take the train or did you decide it was such a nice evening you would walk?'

'Him and the girl must have been on the train ahead of mine.'

'I see. So you got to the flat...?'

'I got to the flat and I heard the girl shout as I reached the front door. I didn't know what to do, call you guys and wait or try to help on my own, but I decided I should try to help. I kicked open the door and went in, stopped him from attacking her with a knife. Then I called you.'

DC Vicario nodded and smiled again. 'Could you identify the girl if we find her?'

'I think so. Young, mid-to late teens I would guess, black hair in a short bob. I'd know her if I saw her. The party was on Haugen Road, the flats on the left just where the road straightens on the way up. Someone there should be able to identify her.'

'And you just happened to be at the same party? What are the odds?'

'You never know your luck.'

'Are you still working as a private detective with Sholto Douglas?'

'We're a research company, not private detectives.'

'Right, because private detectives have a long set of rules they have to operate by, like not kicking in doors, stamping on cocks and arresting sexual assault suspects. Research companies have a little more leeway.'

'Douglas Independent Research, down on Cage Street in Bank, that's us.'

She looked like she was enjoying this now, the two of them batting back and forth and ignoring the young PC beside her. She said, 'So you have someone hunting Lucas for money?'

'We were asked to research his whereabouts, if he had left the city. Just happened to spot him at the party and I'm glad I did.'

'I'm glad you did, too. I'm sure you'll be called to give evidence, probably be interviewed a few times more before then, but you can go.'

Darian got up and walked out the way he had been led in, to the car park at the back. Vinny was leaning against the wall just outside the door, smoking a cigarette, a San Jose by the smell of it. He dropped it on the ground and crushed it under his boot, reached into his pocket and took out a packet of mints.

Darian said, 'Last time I spoke to you you'd quit smoking.'

'Last time you spoke to me all was quiet on the western front.'

His ex-wife lived over on the west side of the loch, in case that comment needs some explanation.

Darian said, 'You see much of the boy?'

'Every weekend, we all get on all right, it isn't as bad as all that. I wouldn't weep if someone threw her in the loch, but... You need a lift up to the train station?'

'Thanks. You need to wait for your ten-year-old pal?'

They had started walking across to the police car they'd arrived in, a Volvo that was probably the most expensive thing anyone had ever trusted Vinny with. 'Nah, I'll run you up the road and come back. He doesn't need to work anyway, that one, he's a Sutherland.'

'Not an actual one?'

'An actual fully functioning one of the bastards, and not some distant wee branch at the bottom of the family tree either, mainline. Wanted to be a cop instead of a banker, whizzed through training and into the force, got sent here.'

'You're pulling the piss out of me. A Sutherland and they sent him to Dockside.'

'I reckon it's what the family wanted, put him somewhere they think is the arsehole of humanity, hope it scares some sense into him and he goes screaming back to the family bosom. The kid's all right, he'll stick it out.'

'Won't be too hard if he's working next to you with your effort avoidance techniques.'

Vinny, aghast, said, 'Are you insinuating I don't work hard? Do you remember that gathering of wee fascist fuckwits with goofy haircuts they had and only six people showed up? Do you know how hard I had to work to come up with an excuse to belt the leader of that rabble? Don't tell me I don't make an effort.'

Darian said, 'You smacked him? Won't that get you another complaint?'

'Oh sure, people like him are always the whiniest, and the disciplinary panel will file it straight into the shredder. We're getting more and more of those pricks crawling out of the internet and into daylight, bunch of half-witted, shrieking virgins. Let me tell you something, Darian, punching a fascist in the face will ever be prosecuted in this city.'

He was right. Our city lost almost a third of its young adult males in the Second World War, and on top of Stac Voror we built a tower that can be seen from every corner of Challaid as a constant reminder. Out beyond the mouth of the loch, a few miles to the east, you can still see the metal mast of the *Isobel*, a destroyer docked in Challaid during the war and sunk by a German U-boat as it left with two hundred and six men lost, the ship wedged in the rocks underwater with the radio mast breaking the surface, a maritime grave untouched by man and left to nature, a reminder of the danger of worshipping power and identity more than the rights of the people. Many of the young men who fought in the war came back to a broken city, an economy held together by the women they'd left behind, and few jobs available to them, so a lot were fast-tracked into the police service, itself a struggling mess at the time. They could easily have slipped the other way and fallen in love with the uniform, seeking to protect those who aggrandised their power, but instead turned their violent power against those who tried. You can accuse, accurately, the woefully corrupt Challaid Police Force of many, many, many indiscretions, but forgetting their history is not one of them.

Vinny dropped him in a no parking zone outside Three O'clock Station and Darian rode the train down to Bank. It was an eight-minute walk up Fàrdach Road to his flat on the corner with Havurn Road. He was moving slowly, full of himself after what he considered a good night's work. Fàrdach Road is on the edge of the Bank district, which is the city centre and full of old-money businesses and pubs, clubs and venues, but this little knot of residential buildings was usually peaceful.

It was an expensive place to live, even a flat as small as Darian's, and it was unusual that a young man on his own could afford to buy there. The flats were old and sturdy, all well-maintained three-storey, sandstone blocks with large bay windows and ornate black railings out the front. Darian was able to afford his place because of the ugly way his family fell apart, but more on that later.

He lived on the top floor, right on the corner of the building, and from the living-room window he could see the long sea loch, and the lights of the city up both sides of it. It had a living room, a tiny kitchen, a bathroom and one bedroom; the smallest flat on the block because it was on the corner.

It was as much as he needed, living alone. The furniture was cheap and basic and there was little enough of it to make the floor look work-shy. The living room had a couch, a chair that didn't match and a TV. That was it.

Darian had always wanted to be a police officer, but he couldn't follow in his father's footsteps because of where they stopped. If things had been different, well, that's not a sentence there's much point in finishing, is it, because things weren't different. There were still moments, like that night, when the good outweighed the bad, and he believed the future, while not the one he had hoped for, could belong to him.

The Private Security Industries Act 2004

This act states that all companies/individuals involved in private investigations should be licensed. Under this act you will require a PSI licence from the domestic security office of the security department of the Scottish government if you are involved in any surveillance, enquiries or investigations that are carried out for the purposes of:

- gaining information about any individual or about the activities or whereabouts of any individual; or
- gaining information about the circumstances in which property has been lost or damaged.

Anyone involved in providing contracted private investigation services will require a licence. This includes employees, employers, managers, supervisors and directors or partners of private investigation companies.

According to this Act, the following activities will not require a licence:

- activities solely for the purposes of market research;
- activities solely concerned with a credit check;
- professional activities of practising solicitors and advocates;
- professional activities of practising accountants;
- professional activities of journalists and broadcasters, and activities solely relating to obtaining information for journalists and broadcasters;
- activities solely relating to reference to registers open to the public; registers or records to which a person has right of access; and published works;

24

- activities carried out with the knowledge or consent of the subject of the investigation.

PENALTIES

The penalty for operating as an unlicensed private investigator will be:

- upon summary conviction at a Sheriff Court, a maximum penalty of twelve months' imprisonment and/or a fine of up to £10,000.

The penalty for supplying unlicensed staff will be:

- upon summary conviction at a Sheriff Court, a maximum penalty of twelve months' imprisonment and/or a fine of up to £10,000;
- upon conviction on indictment at High Court or Sheriff and jury trial, an unlimited fine and/or up to seven years' imprisonment.

4

DARIAN ROSS MIGHT have been the only person who enjoyed the commute to work in Challaid, or at least admitted it. A short walk down to the crowded Bank Station, making his way through the bustle of bleary-eyed miserablists at half-eight. Onto the train and east through the tunnel, off at the next stop, which was Glendan Station. That was the closest stop to the tunnel where all those people were killed digging it, so they claimed they would name the station in honour of those lost. Their choice? The title of the company the dead men worked for, that had sent them to excavate in treacherous conditions with no thought for their safety. Apparently the people of influence who picked the name couldn't understand why none of the families accepted their invitations to the opening. Anyway, that was also the closest stop to Darian's work, and it was a twelve-minute walk through the morning to Cage Street. On a nice day, admittedly rare, the stroll through busy streets could be pleasant.

Here we'll talk a little about what Darian did for a living. He was, in truth, a sort of private detective, but if you asked him about his job those would be the last two words that would fight their way through his lips. He worked for a man called Sholto Douglas, a former detective now running

Douglas Independent Research. How Sholto had managed to last fifteen years as a detective was one of the great many mysteries he never solved, and he was relieved to get out of it. Now he was in a single-room office on the second floor of a building in need of repair on a narrow old street in the city centre, pretending his company limited itself to market research and credit checks.

When he started Darian asked Sholto about the fact he was a private detective dressed up as something else and nearly provoked an aneurysm. Sholto growled and said, 'It is research, really, when you think about it. That's what all of police work is, or detective work, or whatever you want to call it.'

Then the conversation would switch to who was to blame, and while Scotland hadn't had a proper war with England since the Trade Wars of the eighteenth century, Sholto was all for kicking off another.

'And the licences, and the restrictions, they're all nonsense anyway, just there to stop you doing the work. They only did it because the English put the same stuff into law so they thought they had to copy it. Just copying another country because they couldn't think of anything better to do with their time, that's all it was. Bloody English. Bloody Scottish government. You look at the two laws; they're almost identical except ours are harsher. Also, it's Raven's fault... Don't get me started on Raven...'

Raven Investigators was a large firm of private detectives based in Edinburgh and with offices in our own fair city who were raking up more muck than a landscape gardener. Their respect for the law was considered inadequate, so the law was tightened hard and Raven Investigators shrank accordingly.

Companies like Douglas Independent Research existed so that people who couldn't afford the shiny corporate professionalism of Raven had someone to pester small-scale criminals for them, or that's how Sholto liked to present it, anyway. So that was the not exactly noble world of half-truths and delusions that Darian walked into each morning, including this Saturday.

Sholto was at the office before him, which wasn't always the case. Darian had a key for the days when his boss was late. He used to be DC Douglas, and he had struggled to escape the comfort of the marital bed and get in to work those days as well. The one piece of timing he got right was retiring early before they invited him to do so, and that left him as a man in his late forties with nothing to get up for. He started Douglas Independent Research, and needed someone to help him, someone young enough to do most of the heavy lifting. Sholto had worked with Darian's father, so he knew him already, knew he had wanted to be a cop, so offered him the job. He never said it out loud, but there were probably days he regretted it.

Both of them spent too much of their lives on Cage Street. Darian turned down onto the short and narrow pedestrianised street, slipped in between two larger ones. There were three buildings on each side of the walkway, and the office was in the middle on the right as you went down. It had all become quickly familiar to Darian, a place of comfort, the grey three-storey building with the entrance to the stairs at the side.

Their office was on the top floor.

The ground floor was a Chinese restaurant, The Northern Song. It was owned by Mr Yang and Darian and Sholto lived on his rather fine grub.

Mr Yang and his family lived in the flat on the first floor, the other room on the first floor an office for an entertainment agency that never seemed to be occupied and can't have been entertaining anyone but the taxman with its creativity.

There were three small offices on the top floor. Sholto's not-quite-a detective agency was the first door on the left at the top of the stairs, and the third office was occupied by a data services company that had no nameplate on their door but had told Mr Yang they were called Challaid Data Services, which didn't expend much of their imaginative powers. The room in between had never been occupied in the three years Sholto had been there. He and Darian occasionally heard people from the data company coming and going from it, and it sounded like they used it as a storeroom.

Darian had asked, 'What does a data services company need to store?'

'I don't know. Data, I suppose.'

They bumped into the three men from that company in the corridor often enough and they were all polite and likeable fellows in their thirties, well dressed and groomed. If ever there was an issue with the building, those three were happy to chip in and prove themselves good neighbours. One day, Darian was going to have a deeper look at them and their work, try to figure out who they really were and what they were up to, but there were so many other more urgent things to do first. Taking a look at the owner of the building could be one of them.

The building was owned by Randall Stevens, a man in his fifties, no more than five feet tall. Darian had never met him, or even seen him, he never visited the place. Sholto was half- sure he'd seen him at a distance once, but he'd never spoken to him. Apparently, he lived in the Cnocaid district, somewhere near the Challaid Park football stadium, and took his money from this and two other buildings. Didn't seem like enough income for the house he had, but Darian hadn't dug any deeper. If he'd just Googled the name he might have realised something was amiss, but he didn't care to look when there were cases already on his desk to tackle.

Darian went in the side door and up the stairs, in through the office door to see Sholto at his desk, reading what looked like a good old-fashioned letter.

Darian said cheerfully, '*Madainn mhath.*'

'Is it?'

'We got anything interesting today?'

He didn't mention Ash Lucas because he wasn't supposed to be chasing after the man. People came to them and asked for their help but Sholto, with the wisdom of many years dodging difficult cases, didn't always choose to get involved. There were cases, like Lucas, which he felt should have been left to the police and would risk his cover as a 'researcher' if they got involved. Sometimes Darian would accept that, sometimes he wouldn't, and Ash Lucas had been a target he couldn't stop himself aiming at.

Sholto put the letter down and looked at him. He was sitting at a mess of paper that everyone assumed had a desk underneath but you could only ever see the legs; there might have been nothing but a gravitational miracle holding up the paper, laptop and phone. He was just inside the door on the right, a short bald man, grey hair at the sides. He was chubby in a way that filled in all the worry lines he ought to have had, and he always tried, and just as often failed, to dress well. He wore a shirt but it was typically too small or badly tucked in, or he'd have tied his tie on wrong so the thin half was noticeably longer than the wider half. Darian's desk was a less frantic affair, over by the window, looking down onto Cage Street.

Sholto said, 'Nothing exciting, just back to the south docks. Take a look at the warehouses again; see if you can find them importing drugs or people or plotting the downfall of decent society, something like that.'

Darian scoffed. 'They're not importing drugs. They're trying to run a legal business at the old docks and Glendan just wants to push them into the loch so they can build more flats normal people can't afford.'

'Yeah, well, abnormal people need places to live as well.'

Darian sighed and Sholto sat and stared at him, not saying a word. He struggled to understand what Darian's problem was. A small, family-owned, long-standing company was refusing to sell its two warehouses at the south docks, the last buildings down there still used for their original purposes. The rest had been turned into flats and trendy waterside bars years ago. Glendan, the building company, wanted to play with those last two buildings, but the Murdoch family had been there since they arrived in the city a hundred and fifty years ago and weren't in the mood for budging.

Douglas Independent Research was investigating it because some rich and powerful people had told them to, not because there was any suspicion of a crime. They were acting as intimidators, not investigators. Challaid was a city founded as a trading port in which authority was granted only to those who knew how to look the other way, and it had been occupied by an assortment of Vikings, pirates, mercenaries and crooks in the centuries since. The modern world had reached Challaid, but it hadn't changed it.

Sholto was a man who went to church every Sunday morning with Mrs Douglas, and she went every Sunday night and to a bible study on Wednesdays as well. Sholto seemed to feel his mortal soul didn't need such a deep cleanse, just a regular wipe down. He was a person without malice, but he needed to make a living.

'Just go and watch them, they might surprise us and we need the money.'

Sholto always thought they needed the money. The last big payday had been three months before, £46,000 for three weeks' work. They had been hired by Challaid FC to go down to London and investigate a player they wanted to buy and whose team were suspiciously keen to sell. The two premier league clubs in the city were fairly regular customers. In this case Challaid were planning to spend big money on a twenty-three-year-old called Arthur Samba and they wanted to know what sort of human being went with the footballing talent.

Darian did most of the work, being young enough to move in the same circles as the target without looking ludicrous, and he stumbled across some alarming behaviour, even by the standards of a professional footballer. Sholto delivered the dossier to the club and assumed they would pull out of the deal. Instead they used the revelations to knock the fee down from £4 to £2.8 million. Saved themselves a fortune for the sake of a forty-six-grand investigation, and now they just had to hope that when they inevitably sold the troublemaker on, the buying club wouldn't be as curious as they were. That's how 'research' works.

Darian left the office and walked down to the old docks on the south bank. The new, much bigger ones, up in Whisper

Hill, had been built for modern industrial ships in the 1930s, but there had been some sort of dock on the south bank of the loch, they said, since the city was founded.

The sort of history lessons you get in primary school will tell you the city was founded by warriors, regrouping at the loch before they defended their fair lands from invading Norsemen or other enemies.

The sort of history lessons you get in secondary school will tell you it was founded by a group of Hebridean pirates who needed safe shelter from which to raid boats sailing to Ireland or further north.

The sort of history lessons you get in college will tell you Challaid was founded by groups of Highland and Norse traders who needed a safe bay to exchange goods, and the city grew from there.

The last is the most likely but nobody knows because we're a thousand years old and the first thing you lose in old age is memory. The one thing every story agrees on is that the south bank was the original port.

Boats still landed there, Darian could see them from the glass-fronted café he stopped at twenty yards along the dock from one of the Murdoch warehouses, but they were mostly yachts. Pretty white things that rich people played with because other rich people did, and few of the well-to-do liked seeing two big ugly brick buildings right beside their dock otherwise lined with sleek architectural show-offs. Those old buildings belonged up in Whisper Hill these days. Darian liked the dirty things for their defiance, for the way they summed up what the south docks had always meant to Challaid. That was why he made so little effort to watch them. The owners were doing nothing wrong that mattered, but the hope was that he or Sholto could spot a molehill that Glendan could spin into a mountain. It wasn't work to be proud of.

5

IT WAS THE middle of the afternoon when Darian started to walk back to the office. The only things going in and out of the two warehouse buildings were the employees, only a handful and all of them Murdoch's. They'd had a shipment the day before, and Darian was sure they had another two on Monday, but it was always small drips of the tide of goods that washed into Challaid. There was a persuasive economic argument that they should sell the warehouses to Glendan and move up to Whisper Hill. It would be easier and cheaper for them to do business in the bigger docks and without a major property developer poking them in the side every day, but their bloody-mindedness was amusing.

When he turned the corner onto Cage Street, Darian saw the man standing just outside the door to The Northern Song, eating one of Mr Yang's spring rolls. Darian had never met the man in the suit and wannabe smart coat, but he recognised what he was from a distance and who he was when he got closer. DC Alasdair MacDuff, a young detective working in the anti-corruption unit at Cnocaid station, and where he went you could be certain DI Folan Corey was a few steps further ahead.

It should tell you all you need to know about our city's

commitment to tackling corruption that the unit dedicated to the task had only a dozen or so officers and was led by a detective inspector instead of someone more senior, a man allowed to run the unit in whatever way pleased him and the people of influence in Challaid. There had been a time, back in the late nineties, after the Three O'clock killings, when the force made a very public effort to clean up its act, but that was a long time ago, and old habits had returned.

Darian didn't acknowledge DC MacDuff, a tall and plain man, light hair cut short and small features. He seemed awfully hungry, leaning against the wall by the restaurant doorway. He was waiting for someone. Darian went in the side door and ran up the stairs, stepping into the office to find Sholto behind his desk looking red-faced and angry, a man in his forties sitting across from him with wavy dark hair, beady eyes and an easy grin. The guest was DI Corey, now and always in control of his conversations.

He looked at Darian and said, 'Ah, you must be the young Ross, I can see the resemblance. I knew your father. He seemed like such a good man. It's actually you I'm here about.'

'Oh, why's that?'

The dirty look Sholto gave Darian was the opposite of encouraging.

DI Corey, legs crossed, hands in lap looking comfortable, said, 'You were involved in the arrest of Ash Lucas, I'm led to believe, which is strange given that you're the employee of a research company.'

The mocking tone of the last two words made Sholto visibly wince; he wanted no part of anything in the world that would blow his thin cover. He was an ex-detective who could be convicted of running an illegal business, and was now faced with the sort of former colleague who would take cruel pleasure in making that happen.

'I was asked to find out about his finances, for that I had to find out where he lived. I just happened to be at the same party as him, ended up outside the flat and heard the girl scream.'

DI Corey's attitude blunted every clever thing he had to say. If your intelligence lives behind a sneer it's unlikely to be quite as sharp as you think. He smiled happily and said, 'All just a big happy fluke, huh?'

'Good luck and good timing.'

'Odd thing, though, that you wouldn't be able to find his address without following him home. I'd have expected better of you. I mean, what the hell sort of research is that? We're getting very close here, dangerously close, I think, to straying into police business, and I'm sure neither of you would want that to happen.'

Sholto said quickly, 'Of course not, course not; we go out of our way to avoid anything that might interfere in an active case. I know how it works, Folan, don't worry, I know.'

'You know, but does your boy here?'

'He knows.'

Darian stood uncomfortably beside his desk. He was being talked about rather than to, mockingly by Corey and angrily by Sholto, and that raised his hackles. He should have said nothing but instead he said, 'I'm surprised you have any interest in Lucas, Detective. Last I saw of him he was at Dockside, being well looked after. I'm not sure I see how a rapist fits into the anti-corruption unit's remit.'

Sholto's eyes were wide now, and he was sitting bolt upright. Terror was the one workout his posture ever got.

DI Corey remained impassive when he said, 'There are a lot of things about my department, about policing and about this city, that you do not understand. I know you want to hate me because I'm a detective, and we were the ones who put your father away, which means we absolutely must be the bad guys. All of us, all the time. It's going to come as a grievous shock to you when you realise that even those of us who aren't terribly pleasant are still trying to do a good job for the right reasons. Some people have a lot more value than you realise.'

'People like Lucas?'

'Even the worst people have the ability to do good. You're young, you're idealistic, you're ignorant, and because of that you made a mistake. I'm a forgiving man, but I expect a higher level of professionalism from this office in the future or we might have to ask some questions about whether your behaviour on the street matches the description on your registration sheet. No more mistakes.'

Darian said, 'I'll learn.'

'Too late for learning, boy, you learn before you leap. You jumped into the Lucas situation because you thought you knew it all, thought you were doing what us dim-witted policemen and women couldn't, and now Lucas is back out on the streets. He won't go to trial, and the only way he ever will is when a police officer, a senior police officer, gets involved. Someone like me.'

'Someone like you.'

'Yes, and not someone like you.'

'What's wrong with someone like me?'

'Apart from the fact you're not a cop and never will be? You're an idealist. A hero. The saviour of the downtrodden, bringing justice to all those in peril. You go chasing after bad guys and to hell with the rest of it, right? You give your life to being something noble. That's fine, I'm not mocking it, there's nothing wrong with wanting to be someone's hero, we're all arrogant enough to want that at some point. Thing is, this city doesn't need people to be heroes, it just needs them to use an ounce of common sense now and then. Real police work is about something less gallant. It's about doing the dirty grind that people think you should be doing anyway, about doing work nobody ever finds out about so they curse your laziness because they're ignorant of your efforts. It's about keeping your head down and your mouth shut when ignoramuses shoulder-charge their way into your business and spoil years of effort. It's no place for heroes.'

'I'm not trying to be a hero.'

'You are, and you'll keep on trying, I know you will. It's written all over your righteously offended face. But you will learn, just like Sholto here learned, back in the days when he used to spend his life hiding in an office at the station instead of hiding in this one. You'll become like him, looking to get through another day without tripping up, praying for no fuss, no challenge. Your ambition will shrink to fit your talent and position, and when people come here looking for your help, for you to be their saviour after exhausting every other option, you'll pretend you're not home. You'll learn, all right. I do not expect to bump into you again.'

Without looking at either of them he walked across the office and out, down the stairs where his acolyte MacDuff was waiting for him. Darian looked at Sholto and Sholto looked like he wanted to sprint down the stairs after his former colleague and boot him up the arse, but he didn't have the courage or agility. Instead he looked furiously at a spot on his pile of papers until he calmed down enough to talk, although it still came out as a voice raised high.

'You went chasing after Lucas when I said not to, when I told you to stay away from him.'

'He was attacking a schoolgirl with a knife, and Corey's let him go.'

Sholto was a decent man, so he hated that he was shouting at Darian instead of DI Corey, but his voice would never have the strength to attack the cop. He said, 'Don't you understand what this could mean, going up against a man like Folan Corey? I'm not saying you crapped the bed here, but there is an awful lot of crap all over the bed you were using. He is dangerous. Every cop can be dangerous to us, but him a hundred times more than the rest because he'd enjoy it.'

'I didn't know he had a connection with Lucas, and I still don't understand what the connection is. How can you be relaxed about him letting Lucas out when you heard what Lucas has done before?'

'I'm not relaxed, don't say I'm relaxed, do I look relaxed? Never been less relaxed in my life. I'm at best a heartbeat and a half ahead of a coronary right now. I know what Lucas did, and he should be locked up for it, but he must be valuable to Corey. Him, Corey, he's the sort that has a thousand dodgy contacts up his sleeve, anyone he needs help from falls on the floor as soon as he shakes an arm. That's why I could never make it and people like him always can. He'll have Lucas on the rack now, willing to do anything for him.'

'That's not...'

'I know it's not right, you don't have to tell me, but it's how it works round here. This city, it's always been the same, always about the least worst people getting out on top. Just promise me, Darian, promise me you'll stay clear of Corey from now on, and from Lucas. Corey's good at what he does, and what he does isn't for you and me. '

He paused and didn't say anything.

'Darian.'

'Fine, I promise you.'

Whisper Hill

He had lived on the hill all his life and he didn't know how long that had been, but he was certainly an old man now. His parents, oh, they'd died when he was young and that had left him alone. He had wanted a different life, back in his youth when he would watch the town from the hill with envy. Down across the loch there was a world of activity, people running along cobbled streets, boats sailing out to sea, noise and chatter.

He could see that it had changed over the years, the routines of the place different now. He remembered when he was a boy and the boats used to go out first thing in the morning but now they waited until afternoon. He always saw them leave when he took his break. He lived the way his father had wanted the family to live, separate from the people, alone.

He followed the same routine each day, getting up around sunrise to scavenge on the hill, going through the forest on the far side looking for things to eat. He always walked the same route, checking traps he had laid for small animals and taking a separate bag for vegetables. He had been doing it for more years than he remembered. The old man would get round to the front of the hill in the afternoon where there was a flat stone among wind-stunted trees that had a clear view across the loch. He liked to sit there for a few minutes, maybe eat a piece of fruit, and watch the town.

Then he would return to his shack on the far side of the hill, a single-roomed small wooden building with a stone chimney.

There was a time when it had been clear of the trees and had a small garden around it, but not now that he wasn't strong enough to cut them back and they had overwhelmed the plot. They didn't threaten the shack yet, but they kept it in deep shade. Not that he minded because the dark, the trees and the hill itself, these were things he knew, they were reliable and constant, and he had lived his whole life among them. He trusted them, and he trusted nothing else. He pulled the ancient, filthy blanket around him, lying on the floor of the shack, and thought nothing of the life he led.

———

The boy had always been intrigued by the wind, but nobody seemed to know anything about it and that troubled his inquisitive mind. He asked his parents and his grandparents, he asked his teachers and his neighbours, and none of them knew. That couldn't be right. How could all these grown-ups not know the answer to such a simple question? Where does the three o'clock wind come from? They knew about the rain and the tides and the sun, but they didn't know about the wind.

On Saturday he was going to walk around the harbour, over the moor and take the track up to the hill. He had been before with his friends, but this time he was going alone. He gathered a few things in a bag, slung it over his shoulder and set out. He didn't tell anyone else, he was too smart for that because they would try to stop him. Little boys weren't supposed to go onto the hill alone; they had all been told that. His teachers and his parents had said it to him in that stern tone they used when they actually meant something.

It was fun, getting through the streets and past the harbour

43

and out round the bay, sneaking down backstreets, hiding behind trees, making sure nobody saw him. Not just an expedition of discovery but a secret one. He was glad he was on his own; it was so much better this way, more dramatic. He didn't want to have to share the credit when he found out where the wind came from.

He pushed on into the trees, slowed down by branches and bushes nobody had had the good sense to cut a path through. Maybe he would suggest that when they were all marvelling at his soon-to-be discovery. It did make the truth of the wind, whatever it turned out to be, all the more special that he'd had to fight his way through the trees to get to it.

———

The old man had made his way round the front of the hill and up towards the stone where he took his daily rest. It was getting harder to keep this pace and he knew in coming years he wouldn't be able to make the walk every single day. That thought filled him with fear. He had never found rabbit burrows near the shack; they were all on this side of the hill. He could get some mushrooms nearby, but even they required an effort he might one day not be capable of.

He sat on the stone, letting the relief of rest sweep through his weary muscles, and he opened the bag to see what he had collected so far. One dead rabbit that he would skin back at the shack, a few berries and some mushrooms he'd made the effort to gather today, having not done so for a couple of weeks. He took some of the berries out and wiped them clean on his dirty shirt. He put a couple in his mouth and looked down the hill and across the harbour at the town.

The boats were idling in the harbour with their sails loose, waiting for wind, and the old man could just see the movement of people in the streets, more than usual. There were days like that, a few a year, where there seemed to be an awful lot more people running around the town. From the top of the hill you could catch a glimpse of one end of the large town square, and you could see the celebrations. They held them every year in the winter, you could see the fire barrels and decorations they had up. It was nice to see them happy and it made him feel warm.

He took a deep breath and sighed because all this happiness belonged to other people. The boats in the harbour shot forward, sails billowing against the wind that carried them out to sea. He couldn't hear it from so far away, but there were even a few cheers followed by laughs from the jovial crowd.

This was what he enjoyed, sitting on the stone, watching the town spring to life and become the sort of busy place he had always dreamed of being a part of. He'd had his five minutes of rest and it was time to go. As he stood he heard a rustle in the trees that made him pause, thoughts flashing automatically through his mind. It sounded too heavy to be any of the animals he usually encountered here, the old man knew he was the largest thing living on the hill. He was uncertain, a little afraid, when he watched the boy step forward.

———

He came close to the edge of the clearing, walking on soft moss, and saw the man. He hadn't sat down yet, coming from the opposite edge of the clearing and walking across to the stone. He looked old and had white hair that appeared dirty and long, and he had deep lines on his face. He looked like the boy's grandfather if the boy's grandfather didn't wash for a few months.

This old man could be dangerous, some sort of wild man. What a wonderful thought! Fighting through the trees and encountering a wild man in the woods, a chance to prove his courage. He knelt down beside a tree and watched, waiting for the man to do something wild, except he didn't do anything. He sat on the stone like a normal old person, and then reached down into a bag. The boy watched as the old man pulled some berries from the bag and started to slowly eat them. Wild men didn't eat berries slowly, they ate birds with their wings still flapping, ripping them apart with broken teeth and eating the feathers as well. This was just some old man the boy had never seen before.

Then he sighed. From his spot in the trees, the boy could see the old man do it, could see the dying leaves on the ground rustle in front of him as the wind ran down the hill and across the harbour. The boy grinned happily. He had found the wind. He studied the old man, watched him sit there staring down at the town. He only took a few minutes to rest and watch, and then got up.

This was the moment, time for the hero to confront his discovery. He stepped out of the trees and stood a few feet from the old man, looking up at him with a smile on his face.

'Hello,' the boy said.

'Hello.' The word sounded uncertain coming from the old man who wasn't used to speaking out loud, or speaking to other people. The last conversation he'd had was, well, he didn't know how long ago but it was decades, certainly.

'I saw you,' the boy said, 'I saw you sitting there and making the wind. You did, didn't you? You made the wind.'

The old man looked at him, afraid of the boy and what he was saying.

'I don't. I just sit there. It's not me.'

The boy took a step forward, moving to the stone. He looked back at the old man and out across the harbour to his home town.

'Can anyone?'

The old man looked at him and shook his head slightly as the boy sat on the stone and looked to the loch, smiling. He put his bag down and cleared his throat and then suddenly the boy blew out hard. Leaves kicked up on the hill and the few boats still tied in harbour rocked on the sudden waves.

With a grin on his face, the boy was about to say something joyous when a hand grabbed him and pulled him roughly off the stone.

'Careful. You have to be careful.'

The boy paused and looked up at the frightened old man. 'I understand. Too much wind and you damage things, too little and it's not useful. Yes, I understand.'

The old man nodded, relieved.

'Okay,' the boy said. 'Is it just you?'

The old man nodded again.

'I can help you. I can come up here with food and clothes because you really need them. I can blow the wind sometimes, but mostly I'll leave it to you. And you're old, so you have to stop working soon, because that's what old people do. Then I can do it. Yes! I can do that, and it'll be our secret, I won't tell anyone.'

The old man smiled gently, and nodded again. There was someone to take over from him, to give the town the wind it needed. He didn't want to be responsible for ending it. There would be clothes, the boy had said he could bring him new clothes, and maybe even a new blanket. All these years he had sat on that stone and delivered the wind, and it had finally brought something back.

6

NOW, THIS IS the point where the damn sexy woman walks into the private detective's office looking like five feet five inches of pulp-novelesque seductive trouble. Her name was Maeve Campbell, she had long brown hair, dark eyes, a small mouth and when she smiled her cheeks dimpled. She was wearing a dark blue skirt under a dark coat and she sat with her pale legs crossed in front of Sholto's desk. He cleared his throat and his dirty mind and welcomed her.

'How can we help you, Miss Campbell?'

She tried to look decorously sad when she spoke, but there was too much anger and it spoiled the impression. She said, 'My boyfriend, my ex-boyfriend, I suppose, was murdered, about a month ago. The police have been investigating, but they haven't found anything and I'm certain they won't. They don't want to. I do. That's why I'm here.'

Sholto said, 'I'm very sorry about your, uh, ex-boyfriend, but I don't think there's anything we can do to help you. That's a police matter, it has to be left to them. We can't interfere with that sort of case, a murder inquiry; it would be criminal for us to do so.'

She scowled and said, 'There is no inquiry to interfere with; they've given up on him. Not that they broke a sweat in the first place, because they don't want to find the person who killed him.'

Darian asked, 'Why wouldn't they?'

Maeve looked across the room at him, Darian sitting behind his desk at the window. She appraised him in a heartbeat, a woman who always knew what her best chance looked like. He was seething, the kind of anger that would trick a smart person into making misjudgements. Darian wanted to do the right thing, to bring a morsel of justice to a city that wallowed in a lack of it. He was too good a man to avoid bad decisions. The fire of anger inside him had cooled, but he was still hot to the touch and Maeve Campbell touched him.

He had taken the train up to Three O'clock Station in Whisper Hill that morning to tell the woman who had hired them to catch Lucas that her attacker was untouchable, thanks to the Challaid Police Force, a hellish conversation.

It's worth a detour to point out that the names of the station, the hill and that district of the city, the furthest north-easterly side of the loch, came from an old folk tale about Bodach Gaoith. It started as a story from the late seventeenth century, before it was updated in the nineteenth, fleshed out a little. That's the version local kids get spoon-fed in primary school. The moral, they're told, is that being adventurous is good and the elderly have great knowledge and much to offer. A better message might be to keep a closer eye on your children before they wander off and meet weird men up a hill.

It's also worth mentioning that the story first became popular when Scotland was trying to create its own little empire in Central America, and came back into fashion when we were thinking of war in the early twentieth as the three Caledonian countries were gaining independence. Through that prism the message that bold adventures are a good thing looks a little more cynical, doesn't it?

Maeve said, 'My… ex, his name was Moses Guerra; he was involved in some things. He was a crook, that's the truth of it, and his crookedness was probably what got him killed. He was the sort of criminal who made money for people who want the world to think they're saintly, and that's why the police don't want to dig any deeper. The bones of credible people are down there, and they don't want the scandal of finding them. They brought in the anti-corruption unit and they did a damn good job of shrinking the investigation until it was small enough to focus only on me.'

Sholto was already shaking his hands in the air in front of him like a man in a foreign country who couldn't verbalise his distress. 'No. No, no, no. I'm sorry, but that's not an investigation we can have any part in. That's a case that only the police can handle, and any other research or investigative company will tell you the same. I'm sorry.'

Maeve looked at him and then across at Darian, the target that mattered. 'It was clear from the start they weren't interested in catching the killer. A Detective Inspector Corey has been leading the investigation, and all I've had from him are sly hints that he thinks I was involved. That's what he's aiming for, to persuade the world that I was the main suspect but never actually arrest anyone. It keeps people's eyes focused on me and off the truth.'

'What did your boyfriend do?'

'Ex-boyfriend. We had split up, although, I suppose, there was still a chance for us. Moses handled money, took in dirty cash and rehabilitated it. He was a sort of accountant, but not really, he wasn't qualified, just talented, and he used qualified people to add legitimacy. He connected people in possession of money they shouldn't have to people who'd take a small cut of it to make the rest look like it, always belonged to the original owner. He dealt with real accountants and businesses and banks. He was the point of contact for the people needing to use the service; they'd deliver to Moses and after a long journey of cleansing it would be filtered back to the original person by him. It was Moses who created the network in the first place, and it seemed to work. He met a lot of people that way, a lot of people who are more important than this city cares to admit.'

She had turned in the chair to face Darian now, Sholto behind her still waving his hands as if semaphore was making a comeback. Darian said, 'There are a lot of people fitting that description. Why does Corey think you might be responsible?'

'He doesn't. Moses and I had an argument, I hadn't seen him in a couple of weeks, Corey has tried to make that tiff seem big enough to kill a man. I'm convenient, that's all. My greatest crime was proximity to the victim. Corey doesn't have to prove I've done anything wrong, he just has to persuade enough people with innuendo that I probably did so they have an excuse to stop looking elsewhere. I get to be the clichéd femme fatale so he can cover bigger beasts' tracks.'

Darian nodded, both to her and to Sholto behind her. 'That's a very serious accusation. I'm sorry, Miss Campbell, but a murder investigation really is a police matter and if we were to get involved we would be breaking the law ourselves. You can make an official complaint about the current investigation and try to force a change in the investigating team.'

She had an angry smile now. 'So you won't help me? A man

is murdered and nobody gives a shit about finding out who did it? My God, this is some city, it really is.'

Maeve got up and walked quickly to the office door. She stopped as she opened it and looked back at them both, thinking of something clever and cutting to say, but the anger that filled her and Darian both, it smothered things like wit. She slammed the door behind her as a petulant alternative.

Sholto started speaking as soon as the door stopped rattling. 'Now you listen here, Darian Ross, please. You are not to go after her, you are not to get involved in anything, and I mean anything at all, that Folan Corey is at the heart of. That woman, she's only going to lead you down the road to ruin.'

'I know.'

'You know, yes, you do, but knowing is only half the battle. A young man, all hopped up on justice and anger and seeing a vixen with legs up to her arse and dark eyes that weepingly tell you she needs your help, you're likely to make a poor choice. It was a long time ago, but I've been there before and the scene hasn't changed a bit. That woman is grief in nice packaging, and you stay away.'

Darian smiled and said, 'I hear you, Sholto, don't worry. I'll stay away from her and I'll stay away from Corey.'

7

A FEW HOURS later Darian went looking for Maeve because he wanted to get at Corey. He lied to Sholto about it, sure, but that was a frequent part of their working relationship and Sholto would have been disappointed in him if he hadn't. They lied to each other because the truth was the sort of whiny goody two-shoes that got in the way of a useful arrangement. They were a generation apart but making money from working together, and whatever motivated one shouldn't weigh overmuch on the conscience of the other. Darian lied about Maeve because lying was best for business. And let's remember, when all this happened Darian was twenty-two, so while he may have been intelligent that didn't mean he was at all wise.

Finding out where a person lives isn't hard; there are so many companies and local government agencies that hold people's addresses and however much they say they'll protect people's privacy, their defences are only as good as the will of their lowest paid, most disgruntled employee. One call to a contact at the council and Darian had her details from the electoral register – Maeve Campbell, twenty-seven years old, living at 44 – 2 Sgàil Drive, Earmam, Challaid. Darian, thank goodness, had a knowledge of the city that would make a taxi driver's jaw drop, every street and almost every building. A good memory and a nerdish dedication to studying the detail, that was why. He knew Earmam, the region on the east side of the loch full of low-cost housing, people packed upon people, and he knew Sgàil Drive, a street whose name had started as a joke among the builders putting up the flats there.

He got off the bus at the corner and walked down to her building, three blocks of flats on each side of the road, all in a cross shape that might have been part of the architect's graveyard humour. Hers was on the left side of the road, directly under Dùil hill, too close to the incline to be able to see the standing stones, An Coimheadaiche, above. He went in through the red front door and up the cold staircase because the lifts had stopped trying. These were buildings thrown up in a hurry and on the cheap within living memory, using a slice of land that had previously been considered inappropriate for development and had since proven that initial judgement correct. He knocked on the door to number 44.

Maeve opened it and looked at him, no surprise in her expression. She had known Darian would come trailing after her when she left that office, whatever he had said and no matter how long it took him to find her.

She said, 'Come in.'

Her flat was much more a home that Darian's. It was cared for, and there was the ticklish sweet scent from a candle. The living room and kitchen were the same room, a living area some lying estate agent would describe it as, and there were two couches that were different shapes but had similar blankets tucked carefully over them. There was a small bookcase with a TV on top of it and a vinyl record player that was supposed to look old but had a USB slot on the front of it sitting on the floor under the window, a row of albums lined up beside it. The light was on already.

She said, 'Excuse the darkness, the sun doesn't climb the hill until late and then it comes all of a sudden before it runs away and disappears in the mid-afternoon. You get used to the dark, eventually. Can I get you a drink or something?'

Darian said, 'No, thanks. You know why I'm here.'

Maeve smiled a little because her dimpled little smiles could go a long way. She was strikingly pretty and knew it. She had changed since she was at the office, now wearing black trousers and a grey jumper that seemed shapeless, but when she sat on one of the couches and crossed her legs it still sent a confident ripple round the room.

Darian sat opposite her and said, 'I need to know everything you do about what happened to Moses Guerra.'

'Then I will tell you everything I know. He was stabbed outside his flat on Seachran Drive in Bakers Moor, chased from there to an alleyway between Somerset Street and Morti Road and killed. The police have found nobody they're willing to call a real suspect and one they've decided to imply is a suspect because they're lazy fucking liars. Moses helped people hide money, like I said at your office, so he spent time with plenty of law dodgers who had the ability to make a thing like this happen. He knew them and their secrets.'

'Do you have anything that would prove the sort of work he did, who he was working with at the time he was killed?'

'Come on, Detective...'

'I'm not a detective, I'm a researcher.'

'Fine. Come on, researcher, men like Moses don't keep a paper trail for a jury to walk along, you should know that, whatever you say you do for a living. Once he'd read something that told him what he needed to know he would shred and chuck it. Only just stopped short of burning the shreds and eating the ashes. No phone messages, emails, anything of that sort about work, he was too paranoid about online security. You won't find anything about his work which in itself should prove he was doing things worth hiding, but it's why he was killed and it's why the police did nothing. They're protecting the people he worked for, and even if they weren't, people with Moses' reputation don't get the same treatment. A second-generation Caledonian with his biography, there aren't many who will pretend he mattered. Well, he mattered to me.'

'In which case he matters to me.'

Maeve looked at him sceptically. 'I think you say things because you think you ought to, not because you mean them. It's automatic, the way you say it.'

'I mean it. Moses might have been a criminal, but nobody deserves to spend their last seconds in fear, lying in an alley, knowing they're a breath away from the end. I'll try to find out who did it, not just because you asked and because you're paying me but because the person who did it shouldn't be out there thinking they can do it again. Even in this city a dead man deserves at least a scrap of justice.'

'Good.'

That helped convince the employer of his commitment, always good to nail down early on, so Darian shuffled back to the awkward questions. 'His personal life?'

'He wasn't on social media, didn't send texts unless they were very ordinary things, and even then he shuddered when he sent them. He had a small group of friends and most of them were people who moved in the same narrow circles he did, so they're not chatty sorts. The police have dug into it, I know they've tried to talk to anyone they thought would admit to being a friend of Moses, but they only got the minimum required by law in reply. Nobody wants to incriminate themselves, or others, which doesn't leave them with much to say.'

'What sort of person was he?'

'Not the sort of person to jump into a hole without knowing there was an exit route at the bottom, or to pick a fight with anyone, not even one he could be a hundred per cent sure of winning. He was passive. We met at a party, we had mutual friends who introduced us, and I liked him. He didn't ever wear a mask. All the actors you get in this city, trying to pretend they're tougher than they are or smarter than they are or more dignified than they are. So full of shit. He was open.'

'Were your mutual friends criminal types as well?'

'I know a lot of people and some of them are on the shifty side of the tracks. If you know a lot of people in this city then you'll have friends your minister wouldn't love, but it doesn't make you a bad person.'

'How long were you and him together?'

'Six, seven months. Long enough for it to matter.'

'But you weren't living together.'

'Are you in a relationship?'

'No, I'm not.'

'I'm sure you've been in a relationship where having your own space was as important as sharing it with the other person. Just because you like being on top of someone doesn't mean you want to live there. I liked him a lot, might even have loved him. I think I did, and I'm fairly sure he loved me back, but it wasn't the sort of relationship that made you rush for a marriage licence. Moses understood that, although he didn't always agree with how hard we should press the accelerator. He wanted me to live with him and I wasn't ready. It was one of the reasons we had a falling out.'

'He was older than you?'

'He was, but not much and I don't think that's why he was in more of a hurry. He spent his life around people who thought might was right, thought they could be tough and dominant and everyone else would fall into line. It wasn't his natural way, but it was still hard for him to shake it off, even in a relationship where it wasn't needed. He didn't like pushing things along, but he thought he had to, thought that was how it worked.'

'What do you know about his family?'

'Very little. He was second-generation; his father came from Caledonia in the mid-seventies, got married, had a kid, got divorced and didn't see his son again. I think his mother's alive somewhere, but I couldn't point her out for you if she stood right in front of me. He was an only child as far as I know, although I suppose his father might have created a half-sibling or two. He had left his family behind and didn't want to look back, not even to see his parents, forward all the way.'

'Sounds a bit brutal.'

'No, brutal would be the wrong word for him, he was sure. Moses decided that you had to live life moving in one direction and I liked that, the certainty of it. He was always honest about it, that he would never let the past put up a barrier around tomorrow. It was one of the things I thought I loved about him, his honesty. It was a positive thing, I thought.'

'You thought?'

'Perhaps he was denying himself too much, but that was his choice. He didn't like any of his past so he wanted to pretend it wasn't there anymore. Maybe it's the equivalent of a child closing their eyes and thinking the world has disappeared.'

'You said you loved his honesty.'

'Said it and meant it.'

'When you came to our office you called him a crook, but he can't have been much of one if he suffered from honesty.'

'I've known a lot of people in my life that weren't honest. Some were just built to be liars from the ground up, others were like you, honest in bits while trying to hide a lot of the truth as they went along. Did you tell your boss, Mr Douglas, that you were dropping in to visit me at home? Did you get my home address from an above-board source, because I didn't give it to you? There are different kinds of honesty. Moses was genuine. I called him a crook because he was, but he never lied to me or to himself about it. You're lucky if you don't realise how rare that sort of honesty is.'

'I know how rare it is.'

'Then I'm not sure why I'm sitting here trying to explain it to you.'

Darian paused, realised her tone had grown a steel spine and decided that if he was in for a penny he was in for a pound. 'Was he rich when you started your relationship?'

'I was actually under the impression he was a lot poorer than he turned out to be. Is this your strategy, to come in here and try to coax something juicy out of me with petty insults, rile me up until I spill my guts? DI Corey tried the same thing, with a lot more skill I might add, and got nothing, because I have nothing to give.'

'Are you looking to hire me to clear your name or to catch who killed him?'

'Both. Catching the killer will clear my name.'

'It could be expensive.'

'You tell me when the cost starts to hurt and I'll tell you when to stop.'

'It could take a while.'

'I have some money, and I want to know.'

Darian had heard that sort of thing before, an investigation started while the raw emotion of loss pained someone into desperate action, but the hurt dulled and people began to move on with their lives. No matter how much a person meant to them, a life can't be lived standing still waiting for justice to be done. People wanted to know more about a dead relative, their financial affairs, their relationship with a woman who shouldn't have been in the will. People could be passionate with grief, but that's rarely a long-term motivation, and clients often grew out of the investigation they'd started and cancelled the contract early. They wanted the battles of their past in the history books, not raging alongside them. Sholto called it the distance clause, the dead becoming less important the smaller they got in the rear-view mirror.

He said, 'How long will you be mourning him?'

'Just as long as he would have wanted me to. No looking back, remember. I won't be wearing black into my thirties, but I won't forget him either, which is why I won't let you walk away from this when the going gets tough. You're going to find the person responsible; I'll make sure of that.'

She gave him the names of some of Moses' friends and the few people she knew worked with him. It was an unimpressive mob, some of whom were familiar to Darian and most could be safely ruled out straight away. Petty conmen that had found their way into Douglas Independent Research's files, low rate and non-violent, the only money they were interested in the easy kind. Killing a man did not make for easy cash. That left him with a shortlist to investigate. Armed with that, Darian walked to the front door. Maeve opened it for him, the two of them standing face to face, holding eye contact.

She said, 'I wonder why you wanted to know when I would stop mourning.'

Darian walked out of the flat.

8

BEFORE FOLLOWING THE trail of breadcrumbs Maeve had thrown his way, Darian had to bake a few of his own. The first trick in avoiding the police was to get all the information he could about their investigation into Moses Guerra's murder. It had been handled by DI Corey, which meant Cnocaid station, so he called up his senior contact there.

A good investigator makes sure they have someone in each of the six police stations in Challaid, preferably more than one. Darian didn't often pay them to talk, it's important you understand how it worked. There were rare occasions where money changed hands, but typically it was a favour for a favour, one scratched back for another. Darian did things for these cops, typically gathered information they couldn't reach, which helped their own investigations along, so they did the same for him.

His senior person at Cnocaid was DC Cathy Draper, a woman in her early forties and one of his earliest and most willing contacts. Her story is for another time. For now we'll mention only her very small role in the story of Moses Guerra, meeting Darian to provide information, and to gain a favour from him by so doing.

Meeting with DC Draper was an elaborate operation, Darian assumed because she worked in the same station as

Corey so had more reason to be careful than most. It was early in the morning, half past six, and she wanted to meet in the back office of Siren's record store on MacUspaig Road, just north of Sutherland Square, so it was only a fifteen-minute walk from home for Darian. It meant he had to get up at an ungodly hour. The fact she wanted to meet there, the back office of a record store run by an incalculably dubious former record company boss, was cause for surprise, but not necessarily concern. Cops were entitled to keep strange friends, too. She would have parked out front on the long, shop-filled street, just about the only time of day you could find a spot in the whole Bank district. Darian cut down the alley from the back and went in the side door, next to the entrance for From Cambalu, a clothing store that sold the finest, handcrafted items twelve-year-old Indonesians could produce.

She was there ahead of him, in a windowless storeroom filled with plastic containers, looking nervy, a small, tanned woman with short, dark hair. Her arched eyebrows and downturned mouth gave the look of a constant frown, and mood often matched appearance. Contacts all had to be handled differently. Someone like Vinny was a pal; you could joke with him, chat about shared interests and family matters, have your meetings somewhere you could get a drink and relax. Others, like Draper, had to be handled like a bottle of nitro-glycerine, so there was no sarcasm in his voice when he said, 'Thanks for meeting me.'

'You shouldn't be sniffing around Corey.'

He had mentioned that he needed to know about Moses Guerra to make sure she was armed with the right information when they met. 'I'm not; he's finished with the Guerra case.

I know Corey took over the murder investigation and didn't get very far, and I need to know exactly where he did go with it.'

'It's still his case and you're still taking a risk.'

'It isn't through choice, trust me.'

'I should be staying away from the bastard, too.'

'You work with him.'

'He'll crush you, if he finds out. That's his way with people who go against him. You and your family. Anyone he can get at you through, he will. He's smart, as well as dangerous.'

'I'm not going after Corey, just whoever killed Guerra. The worst I'll do with Corey is annoy him, not attack him. I need to know what he found out about the killing.'

She sighed but didn't try to discourage him further; it wasn't in her best interests. 'He didn't find much, but he doesn't always look for much. He has his own priorities. I know Guerra was a lifetime criminal, but he stood close enough to legality to get away with it. They found connections to very clean financial people that didn't go far. They decided it was probably the girlfriend. She knew about the money and wanted some.'

'They talk to anyone interesting?'

'Nobody in Guerra's building heard anything, and they don't think it started inside the flat. Might have been someone jumped him outside when he arrived home and he ran for it, ended up dead in an alley when that same someone caught him up a few streets over. He didn't get far. There was a waiter, the restaurant backs onto the alley, he said the body wasn't there when he went out for a smoke, but he must have been lying, body would have been there for a couple of hours by then.'

'That's it?'

'That's it from me. I wasn't on the team. I'm not one of Corey's people. He has his own group in the anti-corruption unit, cops that are all loyal to him. Mostly younger detectives, they owe him their rapid rise. Even when they're moved out of his unit to other stations or leave the force, they're still Corey's detectives before they're Challaid Police Force's.'

'It's not a lot.'

'It's more than you'll get from anyone else. No one inside his unit will talk to you. They're a team, and you're an outsider. They don't even talk to other cops, so your family connection won't help. Corey will hammer you for sticking your nose in, and he'll hammer me twice for helping.'

'I know. I owe you one.'

'A big one.'

'Fine.'

The thought of another favour acquired seemed to satisfy DC Draper and she left through the front of the record store. Darian left by the side door and went to the office, first one there, for another day of watching warehouses that had nothing to show him.

A BRIEF REVIEW OF THE CALEDONIAN EXPEDITION – SCOTLAND 1698

Just two months before the voyage, at that point referred to as the Darien scheme, was due to depart from Scotland, the Sutherland Bank made a late decision to invest heavily in what had before been viewed as a fanciful lowland idea. The then chairman of the bank, Lord Niall Sutherland, added significant funds and four additional ships to the five planned. He also appointed Alexander Barton, a man previously accused of piracy but who claimed to have been a privateer, to lead the expedition with Thomas Drummond. The nine ships left in 1698.

There remains much debate about what happened when the ships arrived in what was to become New Edinburgh. It is known with certainty that two weeks after arrival Drummond was dead, and Alexander Barton was declared commander of the remaining group. It was he who made the decision that the previously chosen site of New Edinburgh was inappropriate for the group's intentions, and that they should move inland. At this point the differing intentions of the original group of five ships sent by the Company of Scotland and the four sent by the Sutherland Bank became clearer. The Company of Scotland had sought to take and hold the land that would allow the passage of goods from the Atlantic to the Pacific, with ports on either side of the narrow stretch, while the Sutherland Bank had given Barton and his chosen crew orders to take much more.

The exact movements of Barton and his men in the months that followed is still unclear, but that they survived by establishing a defensive base further inland while ranging out to pillage local villages seems clear. While the settlers from the original five ships who stayed behind faced starvation and disease in New Edinburgh and saw their numbers dwindle fast, Barton and his men expanded their land grab, and gained new members from the indigenous population. While the stories of the time suggested those local Indians joined with them as a preferred alternative to Spanish rule, there is better evidence, in the form of large graves, to suggest Barton and his men gave them little choice. By the time Barton returned to New Edinburgh he had a small army, well fed and with a stable base inland, which they named Fort Sutherland, and had reached the Pacific coast and founded Port Isobel, named after his own wife. It is not disputed that they could have returned to New Edinburgh sooner with food and supplies, but chose not to. They argued this was impractical and would have put their own success at risk and by the time they did return the population of New Edinburgh had dropped to fewer than a hundred.

From this point forward the remaining members of the original five ships joined forces with Barton, accepting that his ruthless ways were their only opportunity for survival. The build-up of his army continued until barely a village covering the route from east coast to west wasn't under their control, as men were pressed into service. The New Edinburgh project, that was to have been the centrepiece of the original plan, was practically abandoned by Barton. He led his group from coast to coast, and although many lives were lost in the jungle it was, many said, fear of Barton that pushed them on. By the time the second expedition arrived, seven more ships, this time all funded by the Sutherland Bank in Challaid, Barton had achieved what he set out to do. On his return to Scotland he was knighted by the King in Edinburgh and lived well, the Sutherland family rewarding him generously. That he was successful only because of his cruelty towards the local population was written out of history at the time.

More ships sailed to Caledonia, bringing more settlers and boosting the population of Scots. New Edinburgh was developed and linked with Port Isobel on the Pacific coast via Fort Sutherland. Towns and villages were built along the line of what would become the Caledonian trade route. Scotland would expand throughout Panama and north into Costa Rica and the south of Nicaragua, creating what we now know as Caledonia. In the centuries since 1698 the bloody role of the Sutherland Bank and Alexander Barton have been romanticised, as has the often shocking behaviour of Scottish troops in Caledonia, but the links forged in those early years remain.

9

THE DOWNSIDE OF hiding his clandestine work from Sholto was that he had to spend all day on the Murdoch warehouse case. But working the Guerra case at night meant seeing the scene as it had been a month before, when Moses stumbled into it to his death. Darian started at the block of flats on Seachran Drive where Moses had lived. It's a narrow and short road, made skinnier by the cars parked there, long rows of flats along both sides. It's in Bakers Moor so we're not talking about the heights of luxury here, but it's a neat enough street, the four-storey buildings relatively modern and well kept.

It was after ten o'clock, earlier than Moses had been killed but still dark and cold enough to make sure conditions matched. DC Draper had suggested Moses was jumped on the doorstep, probably getting out of his car, and had run for his life, not quite fast enough. Darian stood and looked at the door to the building Moses had called home and understood why he hadn't gone that way. A gate leading to steps leading to a locked door, a man without a second to waste would have to go another way. From the flat where he had lived to the alley where he died was a five-minute walk, two minutes if you were running to try to keep up with the life that was seeping out of you. Darian tried to track the route a man with death at his heels would use.

He walked to the corner and across the road to confront the first conundrum. If Moses was just looking to create distance then he would go over the fences and round the backs of the houses there, cut across their gardens and save time. That meant running into unlit gardens, going where nobody would see him, where the potential killer would have no witnesses to his crime. Surely if he thought he was going to die he would stay in the bright areas where someone would spot them and help him. Darian shook his head; he needed to think like Moses, the career criminal. What was he carrying that night that he might want to hide?

Darian went through the gardens, trying to keep to the most logical route of a desperate runner, keeping his head down so the occupants wouldn't realise a young man was skulking across their property and think they were about to be burgled. Now he was on Somerset Street, and the alley where Moses bled to death was in view, but so were better places to run. Again, Moses had chosen the one route where he could be sure he wouldn't be seen, by the attacker and by other witnesses. He had passed many buildings on the way where he could have found help.

The alley was unremarkable but for the fact that a man had died there a month before. It's a narrow stretch behind buildings, a shortcut from Somerset Street to Morti Road, but it was mostly a place to store bins, boxes, crates, filth and rats. It was a place to hide, not a place to run. Darian walked down to where the body had been found, far enough away from either end to have been missed by people walking or driving past on adjoining streets. Not so well hidden that someone standing in the alley could possibly miss it.

'I must have missed it.'

Darian and the waiter were standing in the alleyway. He was in his mid-twenties, dark skin and dark eyes, nervous about this conversation. He was wiry and his movements were all sharp and jerky. His name was Benigno Holguin and he was taking his ten-minute break to speak to Darian. It took five of those minutes for Darian to explain who he was.

'Are all the lights that are on now on at two o'clock in the morning?'

'Yes.'

'So if you stood here…'

'I did stand here, for my cigarette. I come out with bags for the bin, I put them in the bin, I stop here to have cigarette, two, three minutes, I go inside.'

'So if the body was there you would have seen it, you couldn't have missed it.'

Holguin shrugged.

Darian said, 'They think he may have been dead before two o'clock, so the body should have been there.'

'I said this to the policemen, the body was not there, it must have come just after, I don't know. They must have their time wrong. I thought this was finished.'

Darian could guess why he was so worked up. 'Where are you from?'

'El Roble, Costa Rica.'

'How long have you been here?'

'Ten months. I have two months to go, I said that to the detective, he said this was finished and it was okay.'

Holguin was two months away from a fast-track dual

passport, Caledonian and Scottish. Anyone from two of the old colonies, Panama and Costa Rica, can get a dual passport after twelve months working in Scotland. Used to be you just had to live here for a year but some bored politicians with fear to spread got that changed to twelve months of legitimate employment.

That was going to change again soon enough, a clamour to keep people who wanted in out, blame them for things that couldn't yet be their fault. It would go to two years of employment. It was already much harder if you came from Nicaragua, because we only ever had the south of it, it was the last colony we captured and the first we gave up and the people spent the entire time in between fighting for their freedom.

For every good-hearted soul we sent across there was a murderous thug like Gregor Kidd or a scheming conman like Joseph Gunn, dark stories too long to tell here. Knowing what Kidd did to the people of Sambu you might wonder why any immigrant would want to live in a city that named one of its largest streets after him. The way we treated people in Caledonia, many think they should all get a dual passport if they want them, but it's more complicated than that. Once he had a Scottish passport Holguin could go anywhere in the EU, he didn't have to stick around if he didn't want to, so those tighter limits were on the way. He was two months from all of Europe opening its arms to him as a fellow citizen, and a man like DI Corey could put a stop to that.

Darian said, 'You couldn't have missed it, could you? Come out and looked the other way the whole time? It was near the wall so...'

'No, I don't think... No, I am not blind. I would have seen it, but it wasn't there. They say he died before then, I say no, he must have come here after. He was not here. Why is this not over?'

Darian tried again to reassure him, not wanting the waiter to go running for comfort to Corey or any other cop from the anti-corruption unit. The longer they were in the dark about Darian's work the fatter his slim chance of success got. He said, 'It is over, it is, I'm just trying to work out everything the police worked out. I don't think there's any chance of them wanting to speak to you again. Thank you, Benigno.'

'Okay.'

Darian let Benigno go back into the restaurant, working for less than minimum wage for a year because Challaid pretended he would be rewarded at the end of that time. Men like Corey were itching to use his vulnerability against him. His status as a Caledonian was a weakness. Challaid only existed so our boats could trade and raid with the Scandinavians and Irish, so they were our first immigrants, then the Caledonians and the Polish and anyone else we could make money from. They gave to our city and it mostly took from them.

Our past teaches us as many bad lessons as good ones. In this city we have a problem understanding what's telling us to change and what's telling us to stay the same. It comes, probably, from our desperate need to remain distinct, different from the Scotland of the Anglicised south and from the world beyond. We hang on to our language and our culture, our sense of difference, because we know these things to be good, but we allow that to spread to areas where cosmopolitan modernity is, frankly, a hell of a lot better. People in the south whinge incessantly about our Gaelic road signs, but it's the old prejudices underneath that pose the real problem here. We don't like outsiders unless we're dominating and exploiting them.

Darian left the alleyway, hoping Holguin wouldn't get caught up in any of this, but not sure. People like the waiter, a bystander who didn't deserve to suffer, were the first to take a hit because they didn't see it coming. Darian made the long walk down to Glendan Station and went home. He knew more about Moses Guerra's death, but he didn't know any better.

10

HE WAS LATE enough turning onto Cage Street the following morning to know Sholto would be there before him. It was wet and cold because this is Challaid and you can assume that any time the weather isn't mentioned it was drizzly and there was a nip in the air. Darian could feel the water trickle down the back of his neck because he wasn't dressed for it, which is a sign of stupidity in a city where the rain and wind stand beside death and taxes as life's certainties.

A man was standing across the lane, pushed back against the wall of the Superdrug store opposite The Northern Song. He had the last bite of one of Mr Yang's breakfast dumplings from a foil tray and stayed where he was, staring ahead and pointedly not looking at Darian. Darian pointedly didn't look back and went in through the door to the stairs and up to the office. Sholto was, as expected, there first.

Darian walked across to his desk by the window, looked down into the lane and saw the man still there, seemingly nailed to the spot. He said, 'There's a man…'

Sholto interrupted him. 'I know there's a man watching the building, and I know who he is and I know why he's here.'

'Who is he?'

'That's Randulf Gallowglass, stupid bloody name, and he used to be DC Gallowglass along at Cnocaid station, one of the anti-corruption team. He left the force, I don't know why but probably because he was the baddest egg in the carton, got elbowed out, and he's now doing work for Corey, off the books. Right this very now he's standing across the way because Corey will have told him to. That's Corey's old-fashioned version of a warning shot, Gallowglass the bullet that lets you know that he knows you're working for Maeve Campbell and he wants you to stop.'

'Oh.'

'Oh, aye.'

Darian looked down at the man in his thirties, light brown hair and a square face, big ears sticking out the side of it, a tall and blocky frame. He said, 'He does work for Corey?'

Sholto sighed and said, 'Yes, he does. Corey's very loyal to any cop that works with him, anyone he considers a protégé. There's a whole generation of them that he made sure he taught, and he keeps them all around, somewhere between apostles and bodyguards. They hero-worship him to a laughable degree. If he tripped up an old lady in the street they would hail him for inventing gravity. Just because a man like Gallowglass is outside the force doesn't mean the string from the back of his head to the end of Corey's finger has snapped. Never mind him, come away from the window and look at me.'

'What?'

'What do you mean what? You went wandering off after the Campbell girl, all googly eyes and bulging trousers, and you're digging about in that Moses fellow's bones.'

'You knew I would.'

77

Sholto shook his head and said, 'I thought this time some of my good sense might have rubbed off on you. How many hundreds of times have I told you not to get involved with a client?'

'It's less than fifty so, to the nearest hundred, none.'

Sholto huffed and said, 'Well, that's because I should only need to say it once, and even then you should have guessed it before I opened my mouth. We should be swerving around Corey like he's poison, and that Campbell girl isn't much healthier for you. You know they think she did it.'

'Do you think she did it?'

'I don't know who did it, it could have been her. Recently split up with the man, knows where he keeps his money, bloody hell.'

'Why would she be waiting for him out on the street, though?'

Darian was getting excited and Sholto wanted to put a stop to it. 'Never mind trying to talk yourself into believing her innocence. Never mind any of it. Could have been King Alex in his castle in Edinburgh that did it for all I care. Moses Guerra is dead and buried up in Heilam, it's not our case and there's every chance we'll never know who killed him. I've seen enough investigations like that, too many suspects and too little evidence; they never amount to anything but wasted sweat. It's not worth the dust up your nostrils that poking around in his background will get you.'

Darian paused for a second and said, 'How do you know he's buried up in Heilam?'

'Never mind what I know or how I know it, just assume I know best and tell me you'll keep away from this thing.'

Darian never wanted to pick a fight with Sholto. He liked

and respected the man too much for that, but there was often fun and sometimes profit to be had in it. There were any number of places Moses Guerra could have been buried, or cremated, and while the graveyard in Heilam, just beyond the end of the urban grey in Whisper Hill, was by far the biggest, that didn't mean you assumed he was there.

Darian said, 'You've been doing some digging of your own, haven't you?'

'Well, I knew you would so I thought I might as well do it properly just to show you how. A pretty girl comes looking for help; I knew what you'd do next. Lack of blood flow to the brain, that's the problem around girls like her. And I'd bet Mrs Douglas's finest jewellery, which isn't up to much, I admit, that you've been round to see the lovely Miss Campbell at her flat, haven't you?'

'You're throwing mud at me when you had your own spade out digging holes.'

Darian was close to laughing and Sholto was close to blowing up. They both paused for ten seconds and drew breath. Sholto said, 'You'll never find out who killed him, you know that, don't you? There are too many gaps that no one can fill without incriminating themselves. If this was to do with his work then it's over because no one he worked with will talk. Sometimes you can't clear the blur of a case and that's the hardest thing for a young cop to learn.'

'I'm not a cop.'

'Neither am I anymore, but we still think like them. This is a job for the police, and it's one they can't finish either. Leave them to it.'

'You looked at it because you thought you might be able to work it out.'

'Doing anything that upsets Corey is a gamble with our own future, and I'm not a gambler, Darian, I never was. Corey, he's... Ach, it makes me mad thinking about him, coming in here and talking down to me like he does every other cop, but I worked hard to get this company started and we do some good work. I don't want that ended by him.'

'If we were careful.'

'We're always bloody careful, and the whole world tiptoes around that man and it doesn't help.'

'If Maeve Campbell hired us because Moses Guerra owed her money, we would be entitled to examine his financial background to try to work out where all his money came from and where it went. We would be identifying cash that our client might be entitled to. If it just happens that his financial work was behind his killing and we stumbled across information that proved it, well, that would be a coincidence within our remit.'

'Maybe.'

'You went looking for information about Guerra, which means it might have been you that Corey found out about.'

'Unlikely.'

'But you do want to find out who killed Guerra. You want to get one over that bastard Corey.'

'Language, and maybe.'

That meant he did.

11

THE FIRST STEP in a joint investigation was to share information. Darian told him everything he had been able to uncover so far, which was a short recap. Moses Guerra must have been attacked outside the building, not inside, and when he ran he picked a route that carefully avoided anyone else seeing him or his attacker.

Darian said, 'Not much, is it?'

Sholto smiled and said, 'Well, you're young; I keep telling you you're young. A big part of policing is hanging round long enough to know who to ask. The police think Moses was attacked outside the flat as well, chased to the alley and he was stabbed there multiple times, enough times that them clever psychologists might start to think there was a personal element involved, although it might just have been that it was dark and rushed and the attacker struggled with it. Suggestion of a personal element doesn't help the pretty piece of work that was in here cooing to us about her innocence.'

'Could be someone he worked with before, knew where he lived but couldn't get in. She would get in, surely, and how would she keep up with him if he decided to sprint? How would she knock him down?'

'Don't you get caught up thinking the little woman couldn't possibly attack the big man, that's foolishness. If she has a blade and an inclination to use it and he has no willingness to fight back then she wins every single time. And if he still loved the girl, daft sod that he might have been, maybe he tried to talk her round.'

'So you think she could have kept up with him and then got him after a chase?'

'Maybe, maybe not. He was stabbed six times, and he covered some ground from the flat to the alley so the person who went after him was fast and determined, willing to stick with the chase in public for minutes instead of seconds. That might well be someone scared of the consequences of failure. We need to work out who he was working with; the people who might have put money into him and not gotten as much back as their imaginations expected, or just people who knew what he was handling, maybe carrying that night, and thought they could carve a slice for themselves with that knife.'

'How do we find out who they were?'

Sholto smiled and said, 'Well, I took a little shortcut and found out all the names the police have on their list of known associates. He was a quiet sort of criminal, which is all too rare, someone who facilitated other people's wrongdoing or tidied up after them. The anti-corruption guys put this shortlist together of all the crimes they believe he was involved in and the people he probably worked with on them. One of them, from the early days, died four or five years ago in a car crash, so unless this is *The X-Files* we can probably stroke him off our list. The rest of them? Murder's not just out of their league, it's playing a different sport, which is probably why he worked with them. That's what the unit think and

I agree with them. Crooks, not killers. Money does make people daft, though.'

'Maeve said there was no family.'

'Maeve, is it? Miss Campbell no longer. Aye, there's no family in this country. Father long disappeared into the ether, no siblings, mother back living in Panama as of last year. It's the work, that's what killed the boy. Someone he worked with or against decided to put a stop to his mathematical gymnastics. There's not much for us to grab a hold of, though. He hung around some bad folk, but so what? There's a lot of people out there to label bad, depending on your definition, and none of us can avoid them all. The police investigation went round in a couple of circles and then fell down dizzy. No pressure from family or media to catch the killer, and they can tell the neighbours it was related to his criminal work and not anything they need to worry about so everyone's happy.'

'Not everyone.'

'Well, no, not everyone. Now we've got Miss Maeve trying to clear her name and muddying the water.'

'She says she thinks she loved him because he was honest.'

'Honest? He might have been honest about being dishonest but that's as honest as he got. You believe that's why she was with him?'

'I don't know, women are strange.'

'And getting stranger all the time. Now, Mrs Douglas, she married me because I had a steady income and no visible scars, and I married her because I had a steady income and she had no visible scars, and we've rolled along just fine for a quarter of a century. These days people think a relationship should be like something out of a movie, or a dirty movie at least. It isn't like that. And that's the other thing I want you to think about. We're taking a risk going up against the devil's wee brother and we're doing it with a job from Maeve Campbell as our paper-thin cover. When Corey tries to punch a hole in our defences it'll only take one swing of his claw, so how dedicated is she? Right now she's angry and she's sad and she wants to know who really did it, partly for Moses and mostly for herself, to clear her name. What happens if she stops caring? We get two weeks into this and she finds herself another boyfriend and doesn't want to rock the boat with the new love so she tells us to stop. It happens. She finds some other lucky sod to bounce around on and we're left with all the aggro and no way of finishing the investigation.'

Darian said nothing. He wanted to argue but he knew it might be true.

Sholto said, 'See if our pal is still singing in the rain out there.'

Darian looked out of the window and saw Gallowglass, who hadn't moved a half-inch. 'He is.'

'Good. You're going to go to the Murdoch warehouses and stare blankly at them for a while and I'm going to stay here. We'll do what we normally do and see which one of us he thinks is more interesting. If we're doing anything at all for Maeve Campbell, we're doing it when wee George Smiley down there goes home for his tea and a sleep.'

Sholto was right, and Darian went to the warehouses to sit and watch nothing happening there, the place going through its boring routines, and no sign of Gallowglass having followed him. It was good to have Sholto on board. The bald man at his desk could seem like he'd dosed up on tranquilisers at breakfast, but when he had his tail up he still showed flashes of the talent he'd started his police career with.

From the Smoke

It was built in a U shape and it was seven storeys tall. The intentions had been better than the budget and the flats had ended up small and the building thrown up quickly with cheap materials. The cobbled courtyard was left bare of the once-planned furniture. The only stairs were in the centre of the U so more space was saved to cram people in. The large storeroom had been placed on the ground floor on the left side of the courtyard inside the U.

The janitor's tools took up the shelves around the door and most of the rest of the space was usually given over to the sacks of coal that were distributed round the building to those who could afford to pay. The coal delivery had been due the following morning so there were no more than a score of sacks stacked against the back wall at the time.

They were fighting the fire on the right side of the building with a chain of men passing wooden buckets back and forth in the early evening. More men were at the stairs trying to get people out, with a few venturing into the burning building to search for anyone who might be trapped. They were risking their own lives to do so. It was chaotic in the courtyard. There was water splashing onto the cobbles and making them slippery as men bellowed deafeningly along the line. Smoke poured out the upper-floor windows where flames had broken the thin glass on the fourth and fifth floors and drifted down in the still night to blanket the courtyard. It was unlikely that anyone still on the upper floors of the building would find an escape.

He was the only one who saw her. He was standing in the middle of the line passing a bucket forward, and as he let it go to the next man something made him turn his head. He saw just a glimpse of her. She wore grey clothes and had grey hair and was moving through the smoke of the courtyard before disappearing in through the door to the storeroom.

He broke from the line and started to walk across the courtyard. Someone called his name but he waved a hand behind him and kept walking. Nobody would follow him on this night when there was so much to fight for. Many had died in the other fires that struck buildings in this area so every man and woman knew the urgency of this one. The others went back to fighting the fire while he moved into the smoke and out of their view.

The door to the storeroom was ajar and he entered knowing what it should look like inside. It was always dark in there as the row of small windows at the top of the wall were filthy with coal dust. It took a few seconds for his eyes to adjust and when they did he saw her.

She was sitting on a wooden chair he didn't remember being there before in the middle of the floor. She was watching him and waiting. Her mouth wasn't smiling but her eyes were. She was trying to seem serious. The woman was trying to pretend that this wasn't a game for her. He took two steps towards her and paused as he was reluctant to be further from the door. The air was already heavy in the storeroom and he knew it wouldn't get better. He was breathing heavily with the mixture of nerves and smoke. He stood looking into her eyes for what seemed only a few seconds and then took a few more steps forward.

'She's here!' he shouted.

He turned and looked at the high windows behind him as though expecting to see some reaction. It was dark still but there were dancing lines of light visible from the fire. As he looked at a window a flicker turned to a burst of flame as a fireball exploded from the other side of the building and into the courtyard. The roar of fire covered the shouts of men to begin with but when the flames settled the men didn't. They were still shouting in the courtyard as they battled fire and fear with volume.

He turned sharply and looked at her. Now she was smiling. Not a joyous smile but a satisfied one. The smile of someone whose effort had just been well rewarded. He couldn't keep the fear out of his face. He moved towards her and was now only three steps away. He opened his mouth to talk and coughed in surprise at the thick smoke that ran into the back of his mouth.

'Stop that,' he tried to shout, but he was coughing and croaking the last word as he felt the soot on his tongue.

He lunged the last couple of steps to her and reached down to try to grab her wrists. She hadn't moved since he'd come in and was still sitting in grey with her hands on her lap almost lost in the folds of her long skirt. He grabbed them with no intention. They seemed at once light and impossible to move. They were frail but powerful. She looked at him in silence. There was no need to say anything.

He started to cough and gasp but the more he did the tighter he grabbed hold of her. If he could stop her the others might have a chance. If he could just hold her in place. He could feel the heat on his hands and could feel the smoke trickling down his throat. He realised as he dropped to his knees that he should have let go. He was still holding her. She watched him drop. She seemed curious but didn't move. He coughed and gasped but only more smoke found its way in. He collapsed on the floor and let go of her wrists.

She sat and looked down at him for a full minute and continued to ignore the sounds of shouting from the courtyard. It took no more than a minute for her to grow bored with the sight of his dead body and to forget why he was lying at her feet. She stood and made her way to the side door beside the tool shelves that led further into the building. She wanted to find more people.

12

IT WAS THE first test of Maeve Campbell, Darian asking her if she had a key for Moses' flat. They sat in her living room, and she nodded her head slowly.

'I do. I didn't tell the police that I did because they had already started to hint I was a suspect by that point. I don't know, I just thought it would be better if they assumed I didn't have one.'

Darian said nothing. She hadn't understood that Moses had been chased from outside his building, so her having access to the flat would have made her less of a suspect.

'I want to get in and have a look around, see if there's anything the police might have missed, or that they might have seen but we don't know about. Have you been in the flat since he was killed?'

'No, God no. I'll get you the key.'

'Thanks.'

She handed it over to him and said, 'Can I get this back when you're finished with it?'

Darian said, 'Sure.'

Sholto picked him up from Glendan Station and asked him about the key.

'She had it, says she hasn't used it since before he died.'

89

'Police didn't take it off her?'

'She didn't tell them she had it.'

'She didn't, did she not?'

'She did not.'

Sholto didn't say anything else, but they both knew what that meant. She had kept the key because she intended to use it; there was no other good reason. At some point she would have made her way back into the flat. Neither Darian nor Sholto needed to say that it was a poor reflection on her, or that it was also understandable. Maeve would know where the money was buried, and there was no one else to claim whatever cash reserves Moses had hidden away and left behind.

As they drove towards Moses' flat Darian said, 'You're going the wrong way.'

'We're not going in the front. People with an unhealthy interest are more likely to be watching the front door because they can sit in the warmth of their car to do it.'

'Who?'

'If Corey has a pet watching the office then he might have another from his kennel watching the flats. We'll go in the back, I know the way. We'll go through the Lady in Grey flats and out across the garden behind them, in through the back of the flats on Seachran Drive.'

They parked and Sholto led the way. He knew the area like a man who had arrested a lot of people round there back in the day, and led Darian across the square of grass where a courtyard had once been and into the front of the U-shaped building. It was one of the few that had been set on fire by someone way back in the 1870s, and the suspect had been a woman seen fleeing the scene of a previous fire. It was always factories she'd targeted, and in this case flats owned by a factory owner and occupied by his staff. She'd killed a few people, if it was a she and if it was even a single person because many think it was a sequence of insurance scams during troubled economic times, but was never caught and may have died in the last fire she'd set. In the end she drifted off into legend and became the Lady in Grey, now shorthand for a fire-starter or just a madly dangerous person in these parts. It is rather typical that a woman with a place in our local cultural history is seen as something wicked, a mysterious killer who was presumably driven mad by something the factory owner had done to her. These days most people don't remember the original story, the factories are long gone and the flats were now just a renovated modern block in an old shell.

Sholto led him in the front door, along the broad corridor, past the stairs and straight out the back. It was dark and it was raining but neither of them could spot a watcher as they walked across the narrow stretch of grass and in through the unlocked back door of Moses' former residence. The stairwell was unlit and Sholto banged his elbow on the bannister as they made their way up. He was still inhaling through his teeth and rubbing it when they got to the door. Darian let them in and they started to search, fast.

Sholto had said, 'Anything that gives us a lead on who he was working with. Paperwork, receipts, anything. Let's just try to get a picture of the man.'

Sholto had told Darian to look at pictures of Moses, as many as he could grab a hold of. It was one of his things, the parcels of wisdom he wanted to pass on to his young apprentice. You see a picture of a person and you can read a lot into it, how they stand, the expression they have, the difference between when they're posing alone and when there are other people there. Sholto had decided from the few he'd seen that Moses put on a false face when others were there, being cheerful to fit in, and that he was quieter and more relaxed when it was just him and whoever took the photo, presumably Maeve. Darian had decided that Sholto's theory was charming quackery. To Darian Moses looked like an awkward but likeable fellow, light brown skin and a round face that made him look fat when he wasn't.

They were in the bedroom of the flat, and they were two men not bound by the limits of great wisdom. Sholto said, 'Just think, Maeve Campbell slept in that bed. Probably did a lot more besides.'

'Hard to picture her here.'

'Oh no it's not, son. You need to get yourself a more potent imagination; it'll see you through the cold nights of a long Challaid winter.'

'I mean it's hard to picture them together, acting like a normal couple. Him seven years older than her and he wasn't much of a looker. Plain and a bit podgy. Even if he was handling a lot of cash, it wasn't his money. He wasn't a rich man.'

'Ah, but she might not have known that when it started. Maybe she thought she was climbing into the bed of a millionaire.'

'No, she's too smart for that; she knew what she was getting into. Girl like her, she would have looked at his life before she leapt into it.'

'Mm. Must have had talents that went beyond his much vaunted honestly, our Moses Guerra.'

They walked back through to the living room. The place was small but tidy, sterile. It was a boring flat, no flair for living on show. Nothing on the walls, a TV but no consoles, no sign of a tablet, no bookcase. If the flat was a reflection of its occupant then it was another mark against Moses.

Sholto said, 'Never trust a man who doesn't need to buy a bookcase. All this stuff is paid for, didn't have a penny of debt so life wasn't a struggle, even if he wasn't drowning in luxury.'

Darian walked into the kitchen and opened a cupboard, looked at a full bottle of whisky and another of Coke. Three glasses stood beside them, and that was all the cupboard held.

Darian said, 'He lived here eight years and you couldn't guess at who he was by looking around. Don't you think that's odd?'

'Odd how?'

'Odd, like a man should leave a shadow behind in the place where he spent his life. You couldn't describe this flat to a stranger, there's nothing distinguishing here, no sense of who he was.'

'Some people don't have a shadow to leave. Maybe Moses Guerra had nothing to distinguish him, no interests or personal touches. Some folk only have their shadow for entertainment, and they take it with them when they go, it's why most people are soon forgotten. Plus, he was a youngish man living on his own, working and living in criminal circles. He had reason to hide the things other people could strip him of.'

'Maybe he was just really boring.'

'Maybe. Is your flat bursting with fun and games?'

Darian said, 'You couldn't fit fun and games into my flat.'

They spent another five minutes searching for signs of life in the dead man's flat. No paperwork that told a person what Moses had done for his money, no personal items that hinted at friends or a girlfriend.

Sholto said, 'So?'

'So I can't get a picture of the guy in my head at all.'

'We've spent long enough looking for it. Let's go before some busybody notices the lights on and knocks on the door. Key or not, we shouldn't be here.'

Sholto drove them both to Sgàil Drive and Darian ran up to Maeve's flat to put the key through the letterbox. It was deep into the night, no need to wake her up for the sake of returning the key. He ran back down and got into the car.

Sholto said, 'She didn't get rich in that relationship.'

Sgàil Drive was not populated by people who had married well. It was the sort of place that someone desperate might reside, and that was Sholto's double-edged hint.

13

THE COLD FINGERS of worry squeezed his heart when he saw the motorcycle parked outside his flat. It was a 1952 Vincent Black Lightning, and it belonged to his older brother Sorley. His one bold extravagance. Darian didn't mention it to Sholto, let him stop the car and say goodnight as he got out. He watched Sholto drive away and then went into the flat.

He loved his brother unconditionally, but there was a wall between them. Clear enough that they could see each other through it, but too firm to knock a hole in. Theirs wasn't a sibling problem akin to The Waiting King and The Gaelic Queen, no violence and hatred, but it was awkward. Darian owed his brother too much, he and his younger sister Catriona both did. Sorley had been seventeen when their father had gone to prison. He had, with minimal help from their aunt Ann-Margaret, raised his curious fourteen-year-old brother and whip-smart twelve-year-old sister. Their aunt was, technically, their legal guardian, but she was a walking screwball comedy and chose not to even live in the same house as them.

The children's hearts had been cracked by their mother's death from cancer three years before, and a hammer was swinging towards them with their father gone, too. Sorley had thrown himself in front of it; let his heart break and prospects crumble to protect his siblings.

He had been an intelligent boy who excelled at camanachd, loved design and had talked about a career in architecture, but instead he dropped out of school and went to work. Odd that Darian, so inquisitive even then, hadn't worked out that his brother was living a life of crime to pay for them. On reflection he could see that he hadn't wanted to know. Sorley brought enough money back to the nice family house in the Cnocaid district to carry on the comfortable life their parents, a teacher and a detective, had given them. Then Darian grew up and moved out when he got a job with Sholto, and Cat went to university. It annoyed Sorley that they both stayed in a city he thought was poison, but he never mentioned it. Instead he sold the family house on Treubh Road and split the money evenly three ways so Cat wouldn't have to worry about student debts and Darian could buy his new flat. Darian and Cat did both wonder if he really split it evenly, or if he gave them both some of his share.

Darian went into the building and up the stairs. He smelled the wisps of a San Jose cigarette before he turned the corner up to his floor. Sorely was sitting on the top step, looking bulky and bored, the cigarette dangling loose between his fingers. Sorley was the only one of the kids who got his looks from their father's side of the family. Where Darian and Cat were both feminine, pretty, Sorley was a solid block with dark hair and eyes, thin lips and a square jaw, a long forehead and nose just slightly too big. He had a moody expression so often it had to be deliberate. He stubbed the cigarette out on the tiled floor beside him when he saw Darian.

'Getting bored waiting for you. I hope your late night was fun.'

Darian smiled sheepishly and said, 'I'm on my own, so…'

He stepped past Sorley, making a note to pick up the crushed cigarette butt when his brother had left so the other residents on his floor wouldn't complain. He unlocked the door and they went inside, through to the living room. Sorley had never been to the flat before so he took a good look around.

'Good job I wasn't planning on swinging any cats.'

Darian got defensive and said, 'It's perfect for me. Good location, near the station, view of the loch. And the value's going up all the time, every place in Bank is.'

'Aye, well, good. Still, about time you got something with an engine in it to get you around instead of using those shitty trains. They're always late and dirty and miles away from everywhere. Only reason the bloody things don't get lost is because they can't. You should get a bike.'

'I'd be pretty easy to spot on some old classic.'

'Aye, well, you can get something a lot more boring than mine that would still let you slice through the traffic.'

The inevitable silence fell, two young men who should have had plenty to say to each other but couldn't hold a conversation down and force it to talk. They were brothers, three years apart, and they cared deeply about each other, which was why Sorley was there. It was him who ended the quiet.

'I hear you're sniffing round after the fragrant Maeve Campbell. That true?'

'Where did you hear that?'

'It true?'

'We have a job on. Her boyfriend was killed and we're

following the money trail, that's all. What's it got to do with you?'

'Doesn't have a damn thing to do with me. I heard about Moses Guerra, and I know Maeve Campbell is worse news than the weather forecast. You should stay away from her, and from any investigation the anti-corruption unit are driving before they run you over with it. You and that fucking amadan Sholto, you'll get splatted if you're not careful.'

'We know what we're doing.'

'No, you don't. You're following a good-looking girl and you got this huge sense of justice right in your face so you can't see much past the end of your nose. She's using you for something, it's all she ever does, and the ACU won't stand for someone like you sticking a finger in their pie. Just leave them all to their bullshit, go back to hassling poor people for rich clients, that's safe ground.'

'They never found out who killed Guerra, but he deserves the truth being known. Don't give me that look, everyone deserves that much.'

'If it was the girl then she wouldn't have hired you, if it was for his work then it was heavier trouble than you can pick up. Either way you're fucked.'

Darian said nothing. He spoke so rarely to his brother and here was Sorley bringing grief to his door in the dark of night.

'If you know something about who killed Moses...'

'I don't. It was probably his work and it was definitely something Corey's unit has a better chance of uncovering than you and Sholto do. Big-time criminals, that's who you're looking for. If you want to see what honour among thieves looks like you can usually find it lying in an alleyway covered in blood. This is out of your league, both of you. I remember Sholto, when he was working with Da; he never had the balls for it then and I don't think he could grow them this late in life.'

Darian frowned and Sorley would have realised, a second too late, that he had offended him. Sholto had been good to Darian, giving him a job after their father went away, keeping an eye on the family. He may never have been the world's most competent detective, but Sholto was a decent man and rarity gave that value. Sorley saw too little of good men in his world to recognise the worth. It went quiet again so the older brother took a different route, aiming for shared interests.

'Did you ever play the game *Brothers: A Tale of Two Sons*?'

'No. It good?'

'Yeah, it is. It's about these two young brothers and their mother's dead and their father's dying and they have to go find the cure for him. I know you're making contacts that can help you prove Da is innocent; get him out of The Ganntair. I'm doing the same, just coming from the opposite direction. You the cops and me the criminals.'

'Meaning?'

'The game, *Brothers*, it doesn't have a happy ending. All the stuff you've been doing, a man like DI Corey can ruin all of that, prevent you from ever getting Da out. Or you could lose more in the journey than you get from the destination. One error of judgement can make it all worthless, that's the point I'm making.'

Darian said nothing to that either. He did try to make contacts with all the cops he could, journalists and business people who might help him uncover the evidence he needed to prove their father was no killer, no thief. He had always known Sorley was doing the same thing using very different methods.

Sorely asked about their little sister before he left. 'How's Cat?'

'Good, I saw her last week. She was saying the three of us should get together a lot more often, Sunday lunch or something like that, make it a regular thing.'

'Yeah, she said something like that last time I saw her, last month. She came down to watch my camanachd team play the university side at Barr Park; she was full of big ideas that'll never happen.'

'You win?'

'Against a bunch of middle-class university nerds? Hammered God's green snot out of them.'

'You wish she'd left the city, don't you?'

'I'm proud she's at university, but I wish it was somewhere else. We should all have gotten out of Challaid first chance we got.'

'Then we couldn't help Da.'

'We might not be able to help him from here, and spending our lives trying might be a bad idea.'

Sorley left and Darian struggled to avoid crying. Sadness ran through him every time he talked to Sorley, his big brother who was so clever, so strong, and reduced to running second-rate scams with bit-part gangsters. He was a talented young man, but he lived a life wasted to give Darian and Cat what they had.

14

THERE WAS A narrow gap in the thick curtains when he woke, a dusty line of daylight filtered through a smudged window. Darian blinked and shut his eyes again. He was beginning to dislike the sun, his best work often done in the darkness and the day reserved for resting. He struggled out of bed twenty minutes later, looking at the clock beside his bed. It was half-eight and he was going to be late for work.

He had a shower and got dressed, jeans and a warm sweater. He had to dress in a way that would allow him to pass unnoticed in the areas he was working and daylight hours meant watching the old warehouses at the marina. He took the time to shave, not bothered that it cost him more minutes and Sholto would whinge about it. No aftershave, because Darian didn't like to drench himself in cheap smells and couldn't afford expensive ones. Then he made himself a cup of tea and sat at the small table by the window in the living room, thinking about a different flat and another man.

Moses Guerra had handled cash for dangerous people, which instantly made the always treacherous money the most likely motive for his murder. There was little chance the dead man would have tried to keep people's share from them because he didn't seem that stupid, but that didn't matter. Moses could have honoured all his fellow thieves and one might still have got it into his numb skull to kill him. People got jealous or paranoid, convinced someone they'd trusted with their secrets knew too many of them. Darian had to find out what Moses had been involved in lately, and if any bad souls had been hunting stolen money. One crook steals from another and hides the money with Moses; when the money gets tracked down the person holding it is punished beyond the last inch of their life.

Darian finished his tea, got up and went to wash his cup in the sink with cold water. He dried it and placed it on the worktop. He had one of everything: cup, spoon, knife, fork. Few people had been in his flat since he'd moved in and none had stayed the night, none had been given a drink or a meal. This is said not to make him sound pathetic but to point out the obsession he had with his work, and the damage it did to him. His relationships were as brief as he could make them, and that wasn't healthy.

He'd wanted to be a detective since he was a small boy watching his father going off to work in the morning. The dream of being a good cop, finding the worst people in a rough society and cleaning them off the streets. The uniform was pulled beyond his reach when his father was accused of murdering a petty crook who had helped him steal precious gems from the criminal gang illegally importing them into Challaid. Darian was fourteen when his father was arrested and charged, fifteen when he was sentenced to life. The son of the disgraced former DS Edmund Ross was never going to find a role within the force, so he had to focus his ambition somewhere else.

The day his father was arrested he didn't come home as usual; instead it was DC Sholto Douglas who came round with their aunt Ann-Margaret to try to explain what had happened. What Sholto said that evening remained true to Darian now; his father was innocent and it would eventually be proven. It was taking too long, but their determination as a family to show he was wrongfully convicted never dimmed.

You might think Darian's desire to be a cop would have died the day he saw the police lead his father into court to convict him of a crime he didn't commit. Accused of working with a known thief to steal illegal items and then killing the thief to cover his tracks and take his share. The diamonds were never recovered and the evidence always seemed flimsy and carefully constructed.

Sorley had needed money to support his siblings, so he went to work for people he should have body-swerved, the sort of monsters the hysterical media like to tell you have a grip on the whole east side of the city, Bakers Moor, Earmam and Whisper Hill. That's a preposterous exaggeration, but those criminals are strong enough for a smart young man to make a living out of, and Sorley did. That gave people who didn't like their father the chance to claim the apple hadn't fallen far from the tree, when in fact it had travelled miles.

Darian left the flat and walked out into a morning as cold as his mood. Challaid has always been a city obsessed with itself, concerned that it needed to upgrade to keep pace with the rest of the world but stay the same to respect its identity. The isolation that was originally one of our greatest defences has evolved into insecurity, a fear of being forgotten in an interconnected world, and the city is always trying to wedge bits of the future into the few gaps the past has left.

Rebuilding, rebranding and waving our oh-so-individual identity in people's faces. But life for Darian was about his work, and, no matter the era, crime in Challaid has always revolved around booze, drugs, money, sex and power.

15

SHOLTO WAS UP on his feet the second Darian came through the door. 'Where have you been? You're late. Never mind, don't distract me. I've got it, I've done it. Cracked the whole thing with a phone call on day one.'

'Cracked it?'

'Smashed the bastard to smithereens. I know who killed Guerra and I know why.'

It came, as many of the best tip-offs do, from a barman, listed as contact #S-39. He worked in a pub called The Gold Saucer, not far from where Moses had lived and died, and Sholto had brought forward the usual monthly update he got from him in case there was something relevant to this investigation. There was, although Sholto didn't tell him it mattered in case the contact decided he wanted to be paid more than his usual pittance.

'My contact overheard a whispered conversation between two very drunk men, which means it wasn't nearly as whispered as it should have been. The man we're looking for is called Randle Cummins; he was the one doing the mouthing off. He was talking about his old pal Moses Guerra, and how he had gone round to Moses's flat to get money from him because he knew Moses was holding a lot. Said things turned nasty but he got into the flat and got the cash.'

Darian didn't know where to go with that. 'He just blurted this out in some pub?'

'He was talking to his pal, lending him cash, didn't know the barman could hear them. Drunk people, if they're stupid to start with, well, they'll let it all out. It works, though, doesn't it? If Cummins knew Moses then he might know when he had money he was supposed to clean. Cummins goes round, there's an argument and a chase, he stabs Moses, takes his key and goes back to the flat for the dosh. They didn't find much cash in the flat of a man who handles money.'

'Is this barman reliable?'

'A hundred per cent, always has been, who can you trust if you can't trust a barman? I'm more concerned that Cummins was just mouthing off, trying to sound like a big man. Wee men with the drink swirling inside them can get imaginative and macho when they want to be.'

'Then we need an address.'

Sholto smiled and said, 'Got one already, that's why I've been so patient waiting for you. Our watcher on the wall, Gallowglass, he's not out there, or he wasn't. Stick your head out the window and make sure he didn't turn up in your wake.'

Darian went over and looked down into Cage Street, saw no sign of the former cop. 'Looks clear.'

'Good, we'll drive round and see if we can wake up Mr Cummins. He doesn't have a job, according to my barman, and he'll know which of his regulars do and don't work. If I had no job and a lot of someone else's money I would be treating myself to a few lie-ins. If we're lucky we'll have him nailed to a jail cell by lunchtime.'

They left the office and walked round the corner at the

bottom of the lane onto Dlùth Street where Sholto always parked his six-year-old Fiat Punto. He drove them at his typical sleepy snail's pace. You couldn't get through a journey of more than ten minutes in the daytime with Sholto behind the wheel without hearing the sound of someone else's horn. One of the benefits of his anti-speed policy was that it gave them the opportunity to talk.

Sholto said, 'You don't think this is our guy, do you?'

'I don't want to talk it down, but this sounds like a drunk who read about the murder in the papers and decided he wanted to put himself in the middle of the scene. He wouldn't be the first infamy whore in this city. And I've never heard of him, have you?'

'Well, no, but I've never heard of everybody at some point. No one starts famous.'

'But to go from some pal of a crook that we'd never heard of to killing that same pal for money? That's a pole vault.'

Sholto went quiet and concentrated on his awful driving. They had to get to Jamieson Drive up on the northern edge of Bakers Moor, the old council houses where Cummins lived. Darian didn't want to piss all over Sholto's new shoes, he really didn't, but the sort of man who whispered loudly in a pub about killing someone wasn't typically the sort of man who avoided detection for over a month after the crime. Any lead was worth pursuing, and anyone who might have known about Moses and his work was worth the effort of chasing down, so Darian said nothing else to put Sholto off. It was rare enough to see the old man with this sort of enthusiasm.

16

CUMMINS LIVED IN a semi-detached house that looked desperate to fall over. The street on both sides was in groups of four houses, all from the forties or fifties, many looking like a giant ruffian had given them a bit of a shake. None was in quite as much disrepair as Cummins'. Beside the front door there was a huge crack up and a small chunk out of the whitewashed wall, about a quarter of the slates seemed to be missing from the roof and the chimney pot had somehow been sheared in half. It wasn't obvious how any of this had happened, but it must have taken a concerted effort. The small front garden was an overgrown obstacle course they traversed before they reached the door. They could hardly see the path for the weeds and the never-cut grass.

Sholto said, 'The state of this place. Wouldn't want to be living next door. Someone should arrest him for this if nothing else.'

He was nervous and sounded it, worried that this shambolic house was a reflection of its owner because when people were this broken down they became unpredictable.

'Maybe he's not in.'

'Only one way to find out.'

Darian knocked on the door and the two of them took a step back, waiting twenty seconds before it was slowly opened by a short and wiry man with a narrow face, blotchy skin pinching at the cheeks, dark hair all over the place, two chipped front teeth chewing on his cut bottom lip. He was wearing a baggy T-shirt that showed a handful of amateurish tattoos and tracksuit bottoms. He looked at them both through sleepy eyes and said, 'Yeah?'

'Mr Cummins? I'm Darian Ross, this is Sholto Douglas, we're here to talk to you about…'

'This about that old bitch next door, uh? The fuck did she call you about this time? She saying I'm the Lady in Grey, or The Taisgealach? Eh? She'll have me trying to bump off King Alex next. What is it this time, you old cow?'

Darian raised a hand to stop him shouting at the house next door. 'We're not the police; nobody called us to come here. We want to talk to you about Moses Guerra.'

The anger slipped from his expression and confusion took its place. He said, 'Well, I don't know anything about that, do I?'

'But you knew Moses.'

'I suppose, sort of, yeah, I did. I knew him but I don't know anything about what happened to him, nothing like that. Nothing I would tell you anyway.'

Cummins sounded cocky now and Darian liked that, it would make him more likely to talk. Darian said, 'We're not cops, but we're looking into what happened to Moses. Can we come in and talk to you about it? We'll make it worth your while.'

Cummins laughed and opened the door a little wider. He said, 'Sure, aye, come in then.'

The outside of the house was an ineffectual prologue for what lay inside. The mess of the exterior was a Herculean effort for an insignificant return, but the real blood, sweat and tears were splattered all over the inside. There were holes in walls, no carpets on the floors, broken furniture and every surface was a canvas of stains in an abstract style. Avoiding the ones that still looked damp was a game that might never end. A few of them looked like blood, a lot were drinks and food, and some were better left unidentified.

Cummins led them into the living room where there was one chair, which he sat in. 'You want to sit on the floor or something?'

Sholto said 'Mm, nah.'

Darian took the first step in the questioning because he was more confident of his footing. 'Moses was killed and there was no money in his flat. You knew him, does that seem strange to you?'

'I dunno. Maybe. I don't know what he did with his money. Didn't spend it anyway, fucking cheapskate.'

'You don't know if he had cash stashed in the flat?'

'I suppose he had some. That was his work, wasn't it, the dough.'

'What about you, what do you do for a living?'

'I'm not working.'

'You making ends meet?'

'Yeah, I'm all right. I pay my debts.'

'You had debts?'

Cummins shrugged.

'And you paid them off?'

Another shrug.

'Did you pay them off recently?'

Cummins looked up at him from the chair, the expression of a man who wished he had a gun in his hand to shut their mouths with. He had let them in because there had been mention of being paid. Now the talk had switched to his money, not theirs.

'How much debt did you pay off?'

'None of your business, that.'

'Who did you owe it to?'

Cummins said nothing, looking down at the floor.

Sholto said, 'Did you owe money to the Creags?'

We'll break away briefly for another detour to tell you who the Creag gang are, because they matter. The name has existed in Challaid, mostly working out of Earmam and Whisper Hill, for at least a century, a multi-generational concern. It started out as a group of low-income tough guys running protection rackets and the like, and with each generation it's evolved, different people using the identity. Sometimes the Creags have been small-scale, a disparate bunch of gangs the police have identified under one badge for simplicity's sake, but sometimes one person, or a small group of people, come along who are strong enough to morph it into a single, functioning unit. That's what it was at the time Moses was killed, a small council running it. If you borrowed money from a lender on the east side of Challaid, whether you realised it or not you were borrowing from the Creags and if you valued the blood running through your veins, you'd better pay them back.

At the mention of the Creags, Cummins looked sharply at Sholto and back at the floor.

Darian said, 'You owed the Creags, and they were leaning on you to pay back?'

'Hey, you want me to answer your questions you arrest me, okay. I got rights.'

'We're not cops, I told you that already. You had the Creag gang leaning on you for money and you knew Moses had cash in his flat. You said you paid your debts, so you must have found money somewhere. Where were you the night Moses was killed?'

Cummins said nothing.

'Can anyone vouch for your whereabouts on the night Moses was killed?'

'I want a lawyer.'

'We know you told someone that you took the money from Moses around the time he died.'

'I want a fucking lawyer.'

Darian and Sholto went out into the corridor and whispered to each other while Cummins stayed sitting on the chair in the living room, looking miserable. He still hadn't grasped that the people questioning him weren't actually cops. If he had he might have tried to find a way to talk himself out of the sewers.

Sholto said, 'It was him. We have to call it in now. It was him.'

Darian nodded, but he didn't say anything.

'You're disappointed, I understand. He's pathetic and someone who took a life should never be that pitiful, but most of them are. This is it, Darian, we got it. A month Corey and his lot spent chasing this and they got nowhere, we've been on it a couple of days and we got it. They should give us a medal for this, or at least a certificate. We call it in.'

Darian nodded. 'We call it in.'

It was ten minutes later when the two cars arrived. There were two uniformed cops in one and two detectives in the other. One detective was a young woman with short, dark hair and a frown that Darian didn't recognise but Sholto said was one of Corey's people, a DC Lovell, and the other was DC MacDuff. The uniformed officers took Cummins away, and MacDuff stood in the corridor with Sholto and Darian.

He said, 'You shouldn't be involved in this.'

It wasn't the threat Corey would have delivered. It was a nervy, miserable warning. Sholto nodded and said, 'We didn't mean to, we just sort of fell arse backwards into the whole thing, working for a client looking for lost money. Led us to this guy. We're done with it now.'

MacDuff said, 'Good, I hope so.'

Sholto drove Darian back to the office. They weren't done yet, but very nearly. Darian would have to tell Maeve about it, and they could expect a huffy visit from the police to find out what else they knew about Cummins, questions that wouldn't take long to answer. Essentially the work was done, and it was an anti-climax. Randle Cummins was a poor excuse for a killer, and paying off a debt he might have the shite kicked out of him for was a lame reason, but Sholto was right, that was how humanity worked. Sholto was buzzing with relief that it had turned out well, that he had proven himself as an investigator again. Darian sat looking out of the window, wondering where Gallowglass had gone.

A SECOND FIFTEEN MINUTES?

FORMER KNICK GORM MACGILLING ON HIS HOPES OF AN NBA COMEBACK

When the car stops outside the Colina Hotel at the top of Stac Voror, the steep hill that overlooks the Scottish city of Challaid, you can see the love of sport down below. Looking across the sprawl that loops round a sea loch you can see multiple stadiums and pitches for soccer and for camanachd. What you won't see, anywhere, is a basketball court. 'I wanted to play camanachd,' Gorm MacGilling tells me, with his deep voice and nervous smile. We're sitting in the café of the five-star hotel, the table and chair too small for him but he doesn't complain. 'It was a teacher of mine in high school that said I should try basketball, so I did.' He did, and for one week in May last year he was the centre of the basketball universe, not that you'd realise it now.

If you follow the NBA, the play that made MacGilling famous hardly needs to be retold; it was the subject of a million vines and gifs, a hashtag and a frenzy of media attention. 'It was pretty mad. We were up in Cleveland for the game and by the time we got back to New York I had gone from 5 thousand followers on twitter to about 30 thousand. Crazy.' It sounds like he's talking about someone else.

So, the play. The Knicks had brought MacGilling to the club in February on a short-term deal, not expecting him to play much. 'I'd been playing in Ukraine but things were bad there so I was out of contract, and my agent got me the chance in New York.' He didn't play a minute in the regular season, and watched without playing as Kristaps Porzingis led the Knicks to the Eastern Conference Finals, and a shot at the no. 1 seed Cleveland Cavaliers.

The series went to a deciding game seven, the game tight going into the last two minutes when Willy Hernangomez fouled out and injuries meant the only big body left on the bench was the Scot. 'I thought we might just go small for the last couple of minutes, but they put me out there.'

Four seconds on the clock, the Knicks down by two. Lee inbounds the ball to Carmelo Anthony, MacGilling sets a screen for him at the top of the key and Melo uses it. The crowd expects a shot but Melo spins to kick out to Porzingis in the corner, but as the ball leaves his fingers it's tipped by Tristan Thompson. 'I saw the ball change direction. I saw it coming towards me and I knew there was no time left. I had to throw up the shot.' With Thompson and Lebron James racing towards him, MacGilling took the shot. Swish, and his world changed.

It hardly seems to matter that the Knicks lost the finals in 6 games and MacGilling got nothing more than garbage time throughout. If you add up all his minutes across the five appearances he made for the Knicks, he was on court for fifteen minutes and twelve seconds. Still, in a world of instant media he hit a shot that mattered and became a sort of legend. 'There was all this attention, but it didn't feel like it, not really. I was right in the middle of it, and the club was preparing for the finals, so I didn't really get the chance to experience it much.'

And after the anti-climax of the defeat by the Golden State Warriors, the Knicks didn't offer MacGilling the chance to come back. 'That was disappointing, I would have loved to stay, I loved New York. They wanted all the cap space they could get for the summer though, I understand that.' There were no concrete NBA offers for him, and as he prepared to try to win a spot on a summer league team, hoping to make a strong impression, he suffered the injury that's kept him out for nearly a year. 'That was tough, the timing of it couldn't have been worse. I came back home, I've been working out every day, getting myself into shape. I've never been fitter than I am now, never.'

He's recognised a couple of times while we chat, both times by members of staff. At seven foot tall and two hundred and ninety pounds he's hard to miss. 'I'm not famous here,' he tells me with a smile. 'I can do normal stuff. I went to New York for a holiday in the summer and got recognised everywhere, but not here. Here I can just be me. Go to camanachd matches, hang out with my mates.' He talks of life here in a way that suggests the NBA is behind him.

'No, no, no way. I'm only twenty-six still, I have loads of time. I need to get a new agent and get onto people's radar again, but I'll be back in the NBA again, I'm sure of that. Might have to go back to Europe first, or the D-League, but I'll make it.' He hasn't given up, and he doesn't want to be forgotten. Gorm MacGilling is a legend for one shot, but he wants to be famous for more.

17

THE JOB WAS done, the case was closed, it was time for life to trudge on somewhere else. The police would charge Cummins with the murder of Moses Guerra and the case, and this story, was done. At the end of the working day Darian should have gone round to Maeve Campbell's flat and told her the goodish news. That was what Sholto told him to do, but once again he chose to defy the orders of his chief. Darian went looking for his brother instead.

There were two places Darian could think of to find Sorley at that time of night. He went round to his flat on Freskin Road up in Earmam but there was no answer. It was a bit of a plod from there to The Continental café on the corner of Kellas Road and Parker Street. Presumably the intention for that café when it first opened was to be a normal, run-of-the-mill place, but it had become a hangout for Sorley and his mates, and they organised a lot of their dubious work from there. It had large windows facing the two sides that looked out to the streets; it was a single-storey, flat-roofed place. The neighbouring buildings were mostly divided into flats, so the dinky little café looked like it was in the wrong place. At night, when the café was lit up and you could see the bar and the tables by the windows, it seemed like stepping into a gruff, cheap plagiarism of *Nighthawks*.

Darian came along Parker Street and could see the lights from the window, the figures moving around inside. The usual suspects, looking ready for their usual night's trouble. There were four motorbikes and three cars parked in front of The Continental, and one of the bikes was Sorley's. If you'd walked past, looked in the window and seen the mob of hardy bastards within, you wouldn't have gone anywhere near them. Darian, being a man of reasonable good sense, wouldn't have either, not if Sorley wasn't one of them.

He pushed open the glass door at the corner of the building and went in. The volume of the music playing in the background was low but he recognised it as local band The Overseen. That would have been Sorley's choice, the man who paid the wages picking the tunes. There were empty and emptying beer bottles all along the counter, but nobody seemed drunk and the talk wasn't boisterous. It was early in their night. They would still have work to do before they started really to enjoy themselves. As he let go of the door, a couple of the people closest stepped towards him. They wouldn't have done it if they thought he was a random guy looking for a drink; they crowded him because they could see he was here on purpose, searching the faces for one that fitted. They were both exceedingly big. One was about six two and built like a professional wrestler, which he had tried to be, and the other was seven feet and built like a professional basketball player, which he had been.

The wrestler said, 'You in the wrong place, pal?'

Darian opened his mouth to speak but someone else beat him to it. A voice from one of the tables at the side said, 'Let him in. He's my brother.'

The two men, Jake Cayden and Gorm MacGilling, stepped aside at their boss's orders. Cayden, head shaved, thick-necked and with small features, had gone down to Glasgow to try to fight for SWF under the name The Last Man, but he lasted two months and came back up the road muttering about contractual issues. Sorely told Darian he'd heard Cayden had gone down there and belly-flopped, just wasn't up to the job. They offered him coaching but he never took well to being told he needed help. That was when he decided the smartest thing to do was start a wrestling company in Challaid instead, fill a gap in the market. It had been a year and a half and he hadn't started yet. The only thing that told you he had tried wrestling was his nickname, TLM. He said he was a born-again Christian, Sorley said he was a psychopath; it's just possible he was both. MacGilling, with his long chin and protruding eye sockets, had actually been a basketball player for some team in America, he had the height but no talent to complement it, and his career looked over as well. He was working a very basic racket for Sorley.

The laundry scam was simple and small and one of many Sorley ran. They went and collected the laundry from the hotels for washing and ironing and took them to the same depot that had been doing the job before, only now they were doing it for 70 per cent of the value while Sorley took the extra 30. The only cost to Sorley was sending Gorm MacGilling in the van to collect the goods instead of the employee the legit depot had sent.

He would go and pick up the laundry in the big van and be recognisable, be every inch the Sorley Ross employee. Darian would later suggest to his brother that the big man didn't seem scary at all, and Sorley agreed.

He said, 'He's not tough, couldn't handle himself in a fight with a toddler, but that's not the point. Guy that size, he doesn't get into fights at all. Nobody who isn't seven foot tall ever picks a fight with someone who is.'

Sorley was sitting by himself in the café, at a table by one of the windows. He had a board and a few stacks of cards beside him. Darian recognised them; Sorley had been playing *Gwent* with someone. Darian sat down opposite him and saw the smile on Sorley's face.

'Didn't think this was your sort of place.'

Darian said, 'I'm not here for the fun of it. I'm here to ask you a favour.'

'So you're going to take the fun out of it for me, too. Go on.'

With his voice lowered Darian said, 'I need to find out if someone paid off a big debt to the Creag gang. I need to know who to talk to about that.'

'What's it about? This isn't still Moses Guerra, is it?'

'That case is closed, the police have arrested a guy me and Sholto led them to. This is about tracking money.'

'Moses Guerra's money?'

'Fine, yes, Moses Guerra's money. This isn't a big deal, though, not to the Creags, it's just to prove whether the person who killed him took his money or not.'

'Every little thing is a big deal to the Creag gang. They don't like people talking about the money they lend. It would be too dangerous a conversation for you to have.'

'I'm not a little kid, Sorley. I've spoken to big, bad people before. I know how to talk to someone without threatening them. I'm not one of your pals.'

Sorley looked round at the others in the café, about twenty people, an even split of male and female, all young and all looking well acquainted with giving and receiving a fist to the mouth. He was growing his gang, and not to help gather evidence for their father's release. This was Sorley being pulled deeper into a world he should have been trying to climb out of.

'I know who it is you need to talk to. You want to know, fine, I'll play you for it.'

Darian said, 'Great, we can play The Organisation. I love that game.'

Sorley frowned at the mention of the card game based on a popular TV show about Glaswegian gangsters, which was a little too close to home. He said, 'We'll stick to *Gwent*.'

Darian picked one of the four *Gwent* decks on the table, Northern Realms he said, selected his hand of twenty-five cards and glanced at his older brother.

He said, 'Not exactly *Casino Royale*, is it?'

Sorely laughed a proper laugh. That raised a few eyebrows along the counter. They all respected their boss, some of them probably liked him and a few feared him, but they all believed he had well earned the nickname Surly. None could remember laughter like this, but the spontaneous joy was the difference between knowing someone as a friend and knowing them as family. What Darian and Sorley had, and the relationship both had with their sister Cat, ran far deeper than anything these co-conspirators could develop with him, and with that depth came greater pain and joy than any of them could bring to Sorley.

The next ten minutes were spent in a tactical battle, a best of three rounds between Darian's Northern Realms deck and Sorley's Monster deck. Sorley loved these sorts of games and this was one of only two he could play with Darian because he knew his little brother would be familiar with it from the PS4 game it came from, *The Witcher 3*. You can be 100 per cent sure Sorley would tell you it was luck, but Darian dominated their match. He won the first round with a lot of spies and doubled siege units, let Sorley win the second and waste some of his better cards in the process and had more than enough in reserve, with the use of medic cards, to overwhelm in the third.

'Huh, I was hoping you wouldn't have as good a grasp of the game as that. Fair enough, I'll tell you what you need to know. You want to speak to Vivienne Armstrong.'

'A woman?'

'Yeah, an actual female woman. You're not getting all misogynistic are you, Darian? Must be hanging around with old Sholto Blowhard that's doing it. What would Cat say if she could hear you?'

'I'm just surprised, that's all. Is this Vivienne Armstrong high up in the Creags?'

'Pretty near the top, one of the few that get to make decisions instead of follow orders. Viv keeps a crushing grip on the moneylending side of it, so she'll know if your suspect has settled his debt or not. Not that she'll want to tell you, won't speak a word to you, but that's a problem you'll have to solve yourself. You can tell her I sent you, but I doubt it'll help.'

'She a friend of yours?'

'Viv? Friend would be the wrong word. She doesn't have anything as useless as friends. Our paths have crossed a few times, that's all. Don't get on the wrong side of her, Darian, she's tough, treats people like shit because she can wipe them all out. If she says it's midnight and the sun says it's midday, you call the sun a liar.'

'So where do I find her?'

'Get out of your bed early, get to Sigurds pub on Caol Lane at eight o'clock.'

'Will it be...?'

'It'll be open. They open early so she can get her morning whisky there, so it'll just be her and the bleary-eyed barman. The drink is part of her mystique, people think she's a mad fucking boozer but she just uses the pub to collect messages. She won't thank you for gate-crashing, but she wouldn't bother thanking you if you donated an organ to keep her alive, so...'

'Thanks for this, Sorley.'

'Uh, huh, just make sure this is the end of you and Moses bloody Guerra, all right? Time for you to go back to being someone I don't have to worry about. Pick something nice and safe to spend your time on and save me the grey hairs.'

Darian smiled and said, 'Sure, and good luck finding someone dumb enough to lose to you at *Gwent*.'

'Get out of here.'

Darian left the café smiling.

18

VIVIENNE ARMSTRONG WAS standing alone at the bar of Sigurds. Darian had walked down the narrow lane in the fading grey of early morning and pushed the door, expecting it to be locked, but it wasn't. The bar was directly ahead, running off to the side, with round tables against the front windows on either side. It was dark in there. What light survived the brave fight through the clouds struggled to then find a route to Caol Lane, four-storey buildings on either side of the cobbles. Darian stepped inside and let the door close, the noise enough to alert Vivienne. She didn't turn round.

She stood straight, wearing dark, tight trousers and a black coat, her black ponytail over the back of the large collar. She was about five feet eight, slender, and when Darian stepped beside her he could see her narrow face and thin lips, small bags under her eyes. She was pale in a way that her dark hair made look unhealthy and her make-up didn't hide it. Darian didn't know how old she was, but he was indiscreet enough to guess at mid-thirties. There was nothing in her general appearance that told you what sort of person she was, but when she glanced back at Darian her look suggested violence was a friend she cherished.

'Morning, Miss Armstrong.'

She looked across again, raised a thin eyebrow and said nothing.

'My name's Darian Ross, I'm Sorley's brother. I wanted to talk to you about a man called Randle Cummins. I heard he owed you a lot of money and I heard he was good enough to pay you back.'

'You're Sorley's brother?'

'Yes, his younger brother.'

'Sorley, Darian and Catriona. Ha, your parents didn't want to give you much of a chance.'

Darian threw her a look that was supposed to be silencing.

Vivienne scoffed. 'Don't get precious about insults towards your parents. You're on the east side. Go take a walk in any direction from here and you'll find a bunch of kids with greater tales of woe than you have. One parent dead and another in jail? They don't hand out awards for that round here; too common.'

'I'm not here to talk about my family; I'm here to talk about my work.'

'Aren't you some sort of cop?'

'No, I work for a research company, but we do investigations into some people's finances. This is nothing to do with you, though, just Cummins.'

'You probably know a lot of cops, don't you, Sorley's brother?'

There was a sneer in her voice and he had to chase it out fast or lose the conversation. 'This will help you. I'm not doing it to help you, that's a side effect, but I'm giving you a warning. DI Corey has arrested Cummins and he's going to charge him with murdering Moses Guerra. Cummins is linked to you through money, through his motive, which means you might find yourself in a courtroom.'

This time her silence was contemplative, not dismissive. This was bad news and it was taking its time to go down. There was a glass of whisky on the bar in front of her, a few drips left. She picked it up and emptied it, put the glass back down.

'Corey's been looking for an angle to take my scalp for months. He has a particular objection to women.'

'His unit doesn't cover what you do.'

She looked at Darian and smiled. This time it was mocking and perhaps rather pitying. 'You might be Sorley's brother, but you don't know the world like he does. Corey's unit covers whatever Corey wants it to cover, and he wants it to cover me so tight I can't breathe.'

'So, Cummins?'

'He paid us back. He owed eighteen and a half thousand, and he had time to pay. We leaned on him a little, not a lot. Not for the whole lot, just a part of it. Suddenly he returns every penny.'

Vivienne stopped because the barman had emerged from the back. He moved towards her, saw the look she gave him and turned like a gale had blown him sideways. He marched back to wherever he had come from.

She went on, 'He paid in cash. As far as we were concerned that was the end of the matter. The debt was on the books, a registered lender. If he's putting the word around that I, or anyone else, forced him to get the money or suggested he steal it or kill for it then he's a lying little shit with a short lifespan.'

Darian said, 'He's not saying that. He's denying he had anything to do with it, but it doesn't look clever for him. The evidence says he killed Moses Guerra to get the money to pay you off.'

'Evidence has a habit of saying what you want other people to hear. Your family should know that.'

'But he paid you the money in cash?'

'He did, and it would have been a day or two after Guerra last breathed out as well.'

'You should expect a visit from DI Corey then.'

'I will. You were right to deliver the warning, but don't think this means I owe you a favour. Say hello to your brother, and tell him to remember what I said to him the last time we parted.'

Darian didn't ask what that was; the tone suggested Sorley should remember and if he didn't he was in trouble. It was enough to make him pause and ask, 'Did you ever work with Moses Guerra?'

'No, and I better not hear you repeating the suggestion that I have.'

Darian turned and walked out of Sigurds. The door banged shut behind him and he was on the uneven cobbles of Caol Lane again, no brighter than when he had gone in but as sunny as it was going to get all day. He walked back to Mormaer Station and took the train to work.

19

DARIAN SAT AT his desk at the window of the office and stared out into the street. Gallowglass was nowhere to be seen. The Cummins case was in the bag, there was no more intimidation for Corey's man to throw around, no more unwelcome investigation to silence. It didn't feel right, but it didn't have to. A man was guilty and that man was going to pay for it, so the job was done.

Sholto was at his desk, writing out an update for Glendan about the activities spotted at the Murdoch warehouses. There was little to report, but he could spool almost nothing out into six or seven pages and make himself look terribly busy. Darian did much of the work on Murdoch, but Sholto wrote the reports. Had it been left to Darian the wording would have been unhelpfully honest, telling Glendan there was no criminality to find there. Sholto kept the possibility alive because that was what the client wanted, and getting what they wanted would persuade them to extend the investigation.

The stairs leading up to the office were bare wood and Sholto's desk being next to the door made it easy for him to hear anyone approach. That was deliberate; he didn't like people sneaking up on him. Occasionally he would hear what he thought were steps and then nothing would happen. That always got the same response, a pause to listen to silence and then, 'Must have been Bodach Gaoith.'

This time, at half past midday, there was a knock at the office door following the footsteps. Sholto got up and answered it because Darian appeared to be dreaming. It was DC Alasdair MacDuff. Sholto recognised him.

'What can we do for you, Detective?'

MacDuff entered the office and stood midway between the two desks looking uncomfortable. He was young, but he didn't have the brashness Darian would have expected from a protégé of Folan Corey.

MacDuff said, 'We've charged Randle Cummins with murdering Moses Guerra and stealing money from him. We thought it would be right to tell you. Chances are you'll be called as witnesses, so you'll have to explain how you got involved in the whole thing. I don't know if that'll be difficult for you.'

Sholto paused while he tried to identify sarcasm. His detector wasn't great but there was none to find. MacDuff wasn't Corey. Sholto said, 'It's good news that you've charged him, good, good news.'

'He hasn't confessed yet, but that might just be a matter of time. The evidence is piling up, especially the money side of it. It all fits, so we'll get a conviction.'

'Well, it's good of you to come round and tell us, we appreciate that.'

'Yeah, well, you were involved so... And you should expect to be called as witnesses. Anyway, I'll let you get on with your work. I'm going to pick up lunch at the takeaway downstairs.'

MacDuff left and Sholto looked across at Darian. He had turned back to the window, looking out at Cage Street and the few shoppers walking by, mostly using it as a shortcut to somewhere better.

Sholto said, 'Go on then, tell me why this isn't good enough for you.'

Darian turned and looked at him. He had to answer Sholto's frustration. 'He seems guilty, but a lot of people aren't what they seem. I don't think Cummins has the wit or the fury to kill, not even with the wolves scratching at his door.'

'You don't know him well enough to know that. And he confessed.'

'Not to anyone that matters, and not sober. He confessed when he was drunk and trying to sound like a big man in a private conversation. We've both heard plenty of people talking crap when they've got the drink splashing around inside them.'

'The money, Darian, the money. How does he pay off that stonking great debt to those thugs without stealing it from the man he killed?'

'I know. The money.'

'You're judging a book by its cover. Cummins is a small man in every way. You want a killer to be big and impressive and striking because murder is all those things, but maybe he did just go round there to mug Moses and things got out of hand, he panicked and pulled the knife. It's nice to think that the man you helped catch was a killer who might strike again and so you've saved someone by stopping him, but getting justice for Moses will have to be enough.'

Sholto was often smarter than he sought or was given credit for. He could be wimpish and old-fashioned and he often seemed motivated by a desire to make as much money as possible by doing as little real work as possible, but the embers of the fire that had pushed him to be a cop in the first place were still warm. Thirty years of chasing after the worst of Challaid had given him instincts worth following.

Darian had to get out of the office, so he went to the south docks again to watch the warehouses. There was nothing to see, but he didn't care. Darian wanted to stare into space.

Summary report: Dockside Police Station, 40 Docklands Street, Whisper Hill, Challaid, CH9 4SS

Summary of reported incidents at 13 Long Walk Lane (Misgearan) for January

Jan 1st – Fight started in bar, spilled out to lane. At least fifteen involved, dispersed when police arrived. Two arrested – James MacPherson (25) William Armstrong (31). Attending officers – PC Vincent Reno, PC Philip Sutherland.

Jan 2nd – Three men entered bar and attacked victim, hospitalising with serious injuries. Victim – Vasco Nunez (40). Possible revenge attack, Nunez identifying witness in previous night's arrest of William Armstrong. No arrests. Note – William Armstrong younger brother of POI Vivienne Armstrong. Attending officers – Sgt Seamus MacRae, PC Carol Lis.

Jan 8th – Knife fight in bar, two men injured. Two arrested and taken to The Machaon Hospital – David Carney (34), William Gow (23). Attending officers – PC Najida Azam, PC Zack Stuart.

Jan 12th – Body of Ruby-Mae Short (20) found on railway tracks behind 13 Long Walk Lane. Miss Short seen drinking in bar with several unidentified people, male and female, earlier in evening. None of fellow drinkers identified. First attending officers – Sgt Seamus MacRae, PC Vincent Reno.

Jan 23rd – Man dragged from building against will, taken away. Victim and perpetrators unidentified, motivation unclear. Probably crime, other witnesses in bar claimed it was a joke. One perpetrator described as 'a giant'. Attending officers – PC Zack Stuart, PC Sam MacDonald.

Jan 25th – Fight culminating in attempt to set fire to neighbouring building. All but one involved party had fled scene before police arrived. One arrest – James MacPherson (25). Attending officers – PC Vincent Reno, PC Philip Sutherland.

20

HE MUST HAVE taken the train to get up to Whisper Hill, although he couldn't remember afterwards. It was destructive instinct that led him there. A young man who didn't know what else to do with his heavy misery so he tried to drown it. If you wanted to kill a few brain cells with a bottle, there was nowhere better than Misgearan.

Sandwiched between Fair Road and the train tracks there's a narrow lane with a collection of shabby-looking buildings on either side. Number 13 is Misgearan, a drinking den with a reputation and a half. Long Walk Lane apparently got its name because so many drinking dens around the north docks were shut down during a crackdown in the fifties and the sailors had to walk or wobble over a mile to the lane for some booze. It's well known for its drunken violence, but most of the crimes are never reported. The few the police hear about are because of the reputation that draws visitors and students to see if it's as grim as the legends suggest, to test themselves against the sort of hard-core alcoholics to whom drinking the city dry is a serious aspiration, not a witticism. Innocent people don't realise that you aren't supposed to call the police. They also don't realise that the police, particularly at Dockside station, use Misgearan as their own private club, and they're not going to let the council shut it down, no matter how much our elected representatives on Sutherland Square would love to try.

Darian had been there a few times before, usually to meet Vinny. He knew he'd be let in when he knocked on the side door. There were people out in the lane, there were always a few shuffling around, waiting for trouble to join them. He could go in the front and sit at the bar, but that wasn't the sort of drinking he wanted. Being among other people and their noise, the inevitable fights breaking out, getting jostled and questioned, someone putting an arm round him and trying to lead him in song or tell him a long-dead joke, that wasn't for him. Darian wanted to sit alone, in silence. That meant a private room and that meant knocking on the side door.

He waited as a train clacked past loudly, invisible behind the corrugated fence. Darian knocked when he knew he would be heard, and the door opened within seconds. The woman looking back at him was short and in her sixties; Caillic Docherty had run the place for nearly twenty years. She had short brown hair that was thin enough to show scalp, deep frown lines and yellow teeth, glasses hanging from string around her neck. She remembered everyone, and who everyone drank with, so she would have known Darian was a friend of the police and wouldn't have considered turning him away. She was a woman in possession of many secrets, and her job depended on her keeping them.

'You wanting in?'

'I am.'

She nodded and held the door open for him. Experience had brought with it both the knowledge of who people were and the understanding of what people wanted. She said, 'You after a room?'

'Aye, and a half-bottle.'

Every private room was tiny, little more than a box you could stand up in. There was a small, round table and two chairs, never more than that. People used them to drink miserably, and they were designed to be too small to allow misery the company it needed to turn violent.

Docherty was back inside two minutes with a half-bottle of Uisge an Tuath, cheap whisky from a local distillery. Nobody went to Misgearan for the quality on offer. A night there tended to deliver an experience akin to being hit on the head with a shovel, and was only marginally more expensive. She put the bottle on the table; Darian passed her a twenty for that and the room and she left.

Darian drank steadily and with commitment until the bottle was empty. He hadn't spent the time thinking about anything because thinking wasn't part of the mission. He got up and shoved past the table, opening the door. He wasn't steady, but he wasn't quite ready to fall over. He got out into the lane and moved through the small crowd without bumping into anyone, which could easily have led to a fight he wouldn't win and injuries he wouldn't quickly recover from. He got out onto Fair Road and started walking, not thinking a damn about where he was going. The streets of Whisper Hill and Earmam were all familiar; he never had a sense that the darkness of the night could trick him into a dangerous wrong turn.

She opened the door and looked at him, at first uncertain of this man standing out in the corridor. Maeve took her time to compose herself before she said, 'Darian. Can I help you?'

'I'd like to talk. We should talk. Can we?'

He sounded drunk, although the walk to her flat had taken some of the weight from his tongue. Maeve held her door open and let him in. Darian had to make an effort to walk straight in a confined space, and the effort of dodging the walls showed. He later convinced himself she was amused by him turning up at her flat in the early hours of the morning pissed out of his skull, although he couldn't actually remember something as subtle as the expression on her face, and drunk people tend to incorrectly assume they're hilarious. Maeve would be an unusual woman to have been thrilled by the evil o'clock arrival of a drunk man she barely knew. She let him in, though, and they went through to the living area.

Maeve said, 'Take a seat.'

Darian sat and looked round the room, taking it all in. He was either too drunk to notice any changes from his last visit or sober enough to recognise that there were none. It might be telling that he didn't remember what she was wearing when he went round to her flat at two in the morning.

He said, 'They got someone. Randle Cummins. He knew Moses. They're going to say he stabbed Moses and then stole money from the flat because he needed to clear a debt.'

'They told me. A cop came round a few hours ago to let me know. He said you and your colleague were the ones who identified Cummins and proved his guilt, even though I don't think he enjoyed giving you the credit. You said you would get the man who killed Moses and you did.'

'Ha. Yeah. I said I would get him and I got someone. Wait, did I say I would get him? Did I not just say I would try?'

'Okay, you tried and you got him.'

'I went and I found him. We both did, me and Sholto. We talked to him and we tripped him up because he's not clever, Cummins, not the sort who can talk his way out of bother. Can talk his way in and you lock the door behind him. He talked, but he never said he did it, not to us, and not to the cops either… I don't think. Never said that.'

'The detective told me he definitely did it.'

'There is no definite, never is. There's a chance, that's all it ever is really. Your man was killed and Cummins had the motive to do it and he knew where Moses lived and he would know how to get at him. It might be that easy. Like dropping all the pieces of a jigsaw on the floor and they all land in the right place for you to see the whole picture. It could happen, but what are the odds?'

'Wait, do you think he didn't do it?'

Just at the point Maeve got interested in his drunken ramble, Darian hit the wall. The more he talked the more his jaw wanted to stiffen into a yawn, but he said, 'I'm saying nothing is definite. If everything's in the first place you look for it then you're either really lucky or you don't know what you're looking at.'

He had leaned back on the couch as he was speaking and tiredness was pushing his eyelids down. It was only when sleep wouldn't take no for an answer that Darian realised how late it was, and that he must have got her out of her bed. He hadn't intended to come here. It was unprofessional. It took a couple of seconds for him to realise his eyes were closed. He opened them sharply, and didn't remember them closing again. He thought he heard Maeve saying goodnight.

21

HE OPENED HIS eyes and found dim sunlight stinging his eyes. Not as much light as he was used to, but any was too much. He blinked heavily, trying to ease the discomfort.

'Morning, sunshine.'

A female voice and that caused him to sit up fast. He wasn't in bed, he wasn't in his flat and he wasn't alone. Darian turned to look through the sleepy blur at the female figure standing a few feet from him. It took a few seconds for his fractured memory to convince him this was Maeve Campbell, but that was as much information as it could compute so quickly. There was no memory of how he had ended up there, not at first.

He said, 'I'm sorry.'

'Don't apologise. You came round here to tell me the truth because you were too drunk to lie. I find most people are braver drunk than sober.'

He nodded but that rattled his brain so he stopped. He had struggled to keep up with her comments. 'I don't know what got into me.'

'Ha, I know exactly what got into you, I could smell it the second I opened the front door.'

'I shouldn't have come.'

'You were right to come, although you won't win any

prizes for your timing. But, then, if you'd waited for daylight and sobriety, you probably wouldn't have made the journey.'

Maeve took a few steps and sat on the other couch opposite him. She was wearing a short skirt, her long hair down. She was amused by his discomfort, smiling her dimpled smile. Darian watched her cross her legs.

He said, 'I should go.'

'You know, my neighbours already think I'm a classic example of the moral decay of this city. A young woman on her own, the man I was sleeping with murdered. Then you come banging on my door in the dark and leave a few hours later. You're not helping me to make a good impression.'

Darian looked across the small room at a woman who had never consciously tried to make a good impression in her life.

'Sorry.'

'You can make it up to me by explaining what you said last night. If Cummins didn't kill Moses then who did?'

'I was havering; I was wrong, ignore me.'

'No, you want me to ignore you now because you were right last night. All the people I've met since Moses was killed, all the people investigating it, there are only two I've seen prove they're intelligent enough to listen to, you and Corey. If Corey told me aliens don't exist I'd start looking out for little green men. You're the only smart one I can trust. You were honest last night and I want you to shame the devil and be honest with me this morning as well.'

There was no threat in her voice, but there was the demand of a woman who had a right to know. Darian had sacrificed his right to keep his opinion to himself at the same moment he had abandoned the policy of keeping his big mouth shut late the previous night.

'I don't know who killed Moses but I'm pretty sure it wasn't Cummins. That guy, he's not capable of much, murder included. He's the sort of guy who runs up a debt, not the sort that pays it off.'

'So it's a hunch?'

'No, not a hunch, it deserves a bigger name than that. You get to understand people when you study them enough, get to know the types. Cummins is a loudmouth but he's weak. If he had done it there's no way he would have gone a month and dodged a large police investigation without it being known.'

'When DC MacDuff came here yesterday he said there was more than enough evidence to confirm and convict.'

'There's evidence. All very neat and just enough of it to be sure Cummins gets a long sentence.'

'What does that mean?'

'It means all that evidence and a man with a brain like DI Corey didn't spot it, but me and Sholto found it within two bloody days of looking. Not to talk our talent down, but I don't find that convincing. They'll put him in a court and they'll get a conviction and that'll be that.'

'That'll be that? If the person who killed Moses is still out there then you don't get to stop looking for him just because Corey and his mob say so. I'm hiring you and I'm telling you to keep looking.'

Darian looked at her, the magnetic fury on her face, and smiled. Someone willing to fight for the dead, long after the final bell had tolled. He said, 'I'll keep looking, but I don't know how much I'll be able to find.'

'You'll keep looking and you won't do it alone because I'm going to help you. I know people that were close to Moses, the sort that might know who he was working with around the time he was murdered. A lot of them wouldn't talk when there was a police investigation going on, didn't want to be tangled up in that unpleasantness. They won't talk to you either because they'll see you as a cop without the credibility.'

'Hold on, no, this is not okay, you would be putting yourself at risk.'

'I'm going to do this, so talking me out of it is a waste of your boozy breath. If I do it without your help I'll be less effective and at greater risk. So you'll help me, won't you?'

When she smiled in triumph she was a woman Darian couldn't say no to.

He said, 'I'll do what I can.'

SCOTTISH DAILY NEWS

A LESS EXPENSIVE FAILURE

Why Government Claims of Banking Success
Hides an Alternative Flaw

It happened again over the weekend, the Scottish government's finance secretary telling a collection of business leaders that sidestepping the worst of the banking crisis that engulfed the world in 2008 was down to their policy and regulation. Its true policy and regulation were a major factor in the shallowness of our recession, but it wasn't their policy and it wasn't their regulation.

No government in the modern history of Scotland has admitted it, but their dirty little secret is that the Sutherland Bank has dictated finance policy, from taxation to regulation, for more than a quarter of a millennium. Every major finance policy that has passed through parliament, from every major party, has been written to fit the austere philosophy of the Challaid-based bank that has dominated the Scottish financial sector since its inception in the seventeenth century.

We don't, in the south, think of Sutherland Bank that way, because we don't think of Challaid that way. It's the remote city, hidden on the north coast, barely accessible and culturally separate. They speak Gaelic, they keep themselves to themselves and the tentacles of their local businesses tend not to reach into our lives. Except for one, the bank that's always been there, that's always presented itself in the way we see the city it sprang from, distant. Talk to people who work in Challaid and they tell you a different story about the power that pulses out of the grand building by the park, not coincidentally next door to the equally grand council headquarters in the city.

Things went bad fast in 2008, but Scotland's recession was shorter and shallower than many.

It was not, contrary to the PR nonsense of the politicians at the time, good planning and rigorous regulation that saved the day, it was a fluke born out of a different kind of corruption. Sutherland gets to decide how every other financial institution in the country operates, because they've been the lender of last resort to the Scottish government since the mid-eighteenth century. They're a company with a long history, a patient and conservative bank that sees gambling as beneath them, so they drew up a set of rules that forced every other bank to operate the same way.

It means that nobody else can ever grow enough to challenge them in their domestic market, and allows their influence to smother Scotland and reach out beyond. That legally enforced financial conservatism meant we didn't get as high a boom as they had in London and elsewhere, and didn't get the crushing bust either. Sure, our economy took a big hit, but not as bad as it could have been. It's often reported that Sutherland actually profited from the wreckage of its rivals. One or

two scallywags have even suggested they played a small part in making the crash happen, so they could look strong and pick over the carcasses of their former challengers.

The real shame of it, though, is not a large bank controlling financial policy, that's simply a more crystallised version of what happens in many countries. The shame is that this distant bank has had undue sway over social policy to boot. They have believed, throughout their history, that progress is made slowly, that risks are for the graceless and that a decent society is always tightly controlled. The progressive agenda in the south has been resisted, and the amount spent fighting poverty has been reduced, because of a banking corporation that won't allow money to be spent on something as frivolous as tackling poverty and social injustice.

At some point in the next few months a politician will address business leaders in Challaid or Edinburgh or Glasgow and they'll call the Sutherland Bank one of the greatest success stories in Scottish history. One or more of the bank's board, all members of the founding family, will be in attendance, and they'll nod politely, trying to look humble. They should. They have more to be humble about than the people they so powerfully influence would ever admit.

22

IT WAS TEMPTING to throw the rest of life overboard and sail wherever Maeve pointed the boat. Darian found himself thinking about her as he walked to the office on Cage Street after going home for a shower and change of clothes. Her strength, her boldness, pushing for difficult truth and willing to take the risks, even enjoying it. He couldn't abandon every other case just to obsess about Maeve; he had to help Sholto pay the bills.

Sholto was in the office ahead of him, the smell of Chinese food from the container on his desk that had held his greasy breakfast.

'Good, you're here.'

Darian said, 'I thought you were on a diet.'

Sholto said, 'Mrs Douglas is trying to get me onto a diet. She's convinced that one day she's going to see me in a news report about obesity. You know the ones where they film fat people on the street and you never see their faces, just wobbles in tight clothing. Got me worrying I'll recognise my wobbles on TV.'

Darian looked at the takeaway and said, 'I applaud your discipline.'

'It's stress release, we've got something and I don't know if I like it or not. Well, I don't like it, I know I don't, when I'm uncertain it always means bad news.'

Darian sat at his desk by the window and said, 'Go on.'

'Some kid, eighteen or nineteen, got the holy smokes beaten out of him last night. He's at the Bob, they kept him in overnight.'

The King Robert VI Hospital is in Cnocaid, which meant he was beaten on the good side of town. It sounded, on the surface, like Sholto's kind of case, easy and uncontroversial. Young man gets leathered on a night out and lands in the hospital, not likely to become a headscratcher. Just find the drunken kid that used the other drunken kid as a punch bag.

'So what's the bad news?'

'Well, he got knocked about last night, he was found alone in the alley behind Himinn nightclub on Malairt Street. They called an ambulance, he told the police he saw nothing, they said they'd investigate. His father's decided that's not enough, that he doesn't trust them to make a job of it, so he called me.'

'So turn it down. It's a police case.'

'I would, I would, but the father, he, eh, he works for Sutherland Bank. He's not a Sutherland, but he's senior.'

Sholto had a policy of not turning down anything that came from the bank. You do good work for those people and they use you a lot. With their wealth you can charge them eye-watering amounts without them complaining, so saying no was bad for business.

'Who are they, the father and son?'

'Father is Durell Kotkell, son is called Uisdean. The father, I Googled him while I was talking to him, he's a senior executive with some control over their operations in Caledonia. Sort of guy with a big office at HQ and the ear of the family in the boardroom. If he recommends us to the company, we're set.'

'And if we stand on police toes we're screwed into the ground.'

'Well, yes, there is that. Come on, I'll drive us to the hospital and we'll talk to the boy while it's fresh in his mashed-up head.'

Sholto drove them to Cnocaid in his Fiat and complained ferociously at the price of parking. As he jabbed the coins into the machine Darian stood beside him.

'I spoke to Maeve Campbell.'

'Oh, right.'

'Yeah, she still wants us to keep looking for the person who killed Moses.'

'She wants us to keep looking for Randle Cummins? He's in the bloody police station, we know where he is, and soon he'll be in The Ganntair. Does she want a photo to prove it? She should be happy with how this worked out. Well, not happy, her man's still dead after all and we're not Jesus enough to bring him back, but she should let it rest. It's finished, and we're finished with it.'

Sholto had stopped at the machine to rant and a woman was standing behind him, waiting to pay for the luxury of switching off her car to visit a sick relative. She cleared her throat and he started, nearly dropping the hard-earned coins in his hand. They didn't speak about the case again as he got the ticket and went back to put it on the dashboard of the car. They went into the large, L-shaped building. Its many facelifts didn't hide its age, and some would suggest the attempts to make it look less nineteenth century only damaged it. There are a lot of buildings like that in Challaid, patched up in the name of modernity because we instinctively don't like rebuilding and they would have been better off left alone.

The boy's family were round his bed in a private room on the second floor. His injuries didn't warrant a room of their own, but his father's status did. His influence had also pulled a bored-looking uniformed officer into its orbit in the room and kept him there for no good reason.

'Hello, I'm Sholto Douglas; this is my colleague Darian Ross.'

The father stood up from his bedside seat. He was short and thin with dark, receding hair and the expression of a man who didn't have to work hard for respect. All the action in his face was around the small eyes, thick eyebrows in a V to show his anger and the deep lines cutting his tan showing that this was his usual expression, a small mole above his right eye. His suit was stylish, and no doubt expensive, but he wore it like an obligation, not a pleasure.

'Finally. I'm Durell Kotkell. It's about time we got some proper investigators here; we've been waiting for hours with just this clueless wonder for company.'

The young officer rolled his eyes but said nothing.

Kotkell said to him, 'You can wait outside, there's nothing for you to add here and I'd like to speak to these gentlemen in private.'

That was an idea the cop liked, and he left quickly. Leala Kotkell was sitting at her son's bedside looked uncomfortable, a darkly tan Caledonian, straight dark hair tied back out of her way, too-thin eyebrows and a button nose. Darian noticed the expensive rings on her fingers. The boy in the bed looked bruised and embarrassed. He was boyishly handsome, a mop of brown hair that needed a brush put through it, small eyes that were the opposite of his father's in their innocence, the beauty spoiled slightly by a line of spots along his poorly defined jawline. The few visible injuries suggested it had been by no means the worst pasting handed out in Challaid that night.

Sholto said, 'So, Uisdean, why don't you take us through what happened.'

Before the boy could open his cut lips his father said, 'My son was brutally attacked is what happened. Unprovoked, followed out of a nightclub and battered senseless for no reason. The police have done nothing of any use; they've made it perfectly clear they don't think it matters much. That's not good enough, so you're going to find out who did it.'

Darian realised that Sholto had already committed to playing the obsequious yes-man so he spoke for the first time. 'We'll need to hear it from your son so we can have as clear a picture to work from as possible.'

Durell Kotkell frowned like a man trying to decide how best to win a fight no one else realised had started. Sholto shuffled, cleared his throat for no reason and said to Uisdean in the bed, 'Can you run us through what happened last night, as much detail as you can remember?'

The boy, and he looked younger than eighteen, spoke like it hurt. His accent was the epitome of posh Challaid, the phlegmy style of a working-class accent designed for Gaelic replaced with silky care, less roll on the r's, a lighter touch on the l's and less spittle all round. 'I honestly don't know what happened. I was having a night out with some friends, we were at Himinn, had a few drinks and we left. I went to use the alley to cut across to Cala Street and get a taxi home from the rank there. I remember going into the alley, I could see the lights from the buildings on Cala Street, and that was it. They must have attacked me from behind because I didn't see anyone waiting there.'

'Uh, huh, and you didn't hear anything or see anyone on Malairt Street when you came out of the club that looked like trouble?'

'No, nothing.'

'There was no bother in the club last night, no arguments or funny looks?'

'Nothing.'

Durell had been silent quite long enough for his tastes and, still standing, said, 'Of course there was no trouble; if there had been then even the clowns masquerading as policemen in this city would have known where to look. You need to find out who did this.'

Sholto said, 'Of course, of course. Was anything taken from you, money or your phone?'

'No, nothing.'

'Do you know if they went through your pockets looking for anything?'

'I don't know.'

'Were you wearing a watch, Uisdean?'

'Uh, yes.'

Sholto leaned towards the bed and said, 'Is that it there, the one on the bedside cabinet?'

'Yes.'

'No scratches on your wrist or anything where they tried to take it off?'

'No.'

'And there was no one you've fallen out with, even ages ago, and you didn't think it was a big deal at the time? There's no one who might have been half-cut, outside the club, saw you come out and thought they'd try to settle a score you forgot they were keeping?'

'No, no one.'

'Right, good. Can you give us the names of the people you were with at the club?'

He looked reluctant but one glance at his father set his tongue running. 'Leandro was there, Leandro Oriol. He's at the university with me, lives in the accommodation there. Others came and went but it was him I went to the club with.'

Darian had stayed silent since his first intervention, letting Sholto show that his years of ducking real work hadn't blunted his talents completely. He'd asked the right questions politely enough to keep the father from raging again. They each shook hands with Durell and Uisdean, nodded to Leala on the other side of the bed, and walked back down to the car.

When he pulled the passenger door shut behind him Darian asked, 'What do you make of it, inquisitor?'

'I wish his father didn't work for that bloody bank so I could have told him to stick his job up his arse and jump out the window with it.'

'Aye. And the boy?'

'Well, it had nothing to do with money. There was good money ticking away in that watch, that really was worth mugging someone for, tempted by it myself. The posh always have fancy watches, it's the only thing they have the imagination to give each other for Christmas. He knows more than he's letting on, and he only gave us the one name because he knows that lad will back him up.'

As the car putted into life and Sholto looked over his shoulder to reverse out of the space, Darian said, 'We'll have to talk to him when he's on his own, when the father isn't there to play stifling defence. I think he'll tell us the story then.'

'Aye, but it might not be the story the father wants to hear, and that doesn't help us much. We're done with Maeve Campbell, by the way. We found the killer and I'll write up a bill for her and stick it in the post. Might even get this one wrapped up as fast as that one. You're bringing me good luck in challenging circumstances these days, Darian, and I'm a big fan of good luck.'

23

IT WAS TEMPTING, when Sholto went home, to make a start on the work Maeve Campbell wanted him to tackle. She needed to know who had killed Moses Guerra and Darian wanted to help her. Of course he wanted to catch the right killer because getting it right mattered to him, but he had been thinking about Maeve all day, the smile and the legs crossing, the fierceness. She was a distraction. If he did some digging on the Moses case then he would have the excuse he wanted to go and see her again.

Darian shook his head as he walked up Cage Street on his way to Glendan Station. He had to prove to himself he could resist the girl. He wasn't in control of the case if he couldn't recognise the need to go home and get a good night's sleep. Maeve had hired him but if he wanted to be professional then he couldn't let her control him. The Moses case mattered far more than Uisdean Kotkell taking a few slaps on a night out, that's why the police had shrugged their collective shoulders in the face of his father's demands, but Darian had no hope of helping either if he was less than half-awake. A night at Misgearan demanded abstinence for the next two.

The train was busy on the short trip west through Bank. His radar was switched on as he walked, not scanning faces but alert to any movements that fell into sync with his own. Darian had lived in that flat on the corner of Havurn Road and Fàrdach Road for over two years and he had made that walk to and from the station at least twice a day every day since. He could see every crack in the pavements and picture every building with his eyes shut. He knew the people that usually hung around outside the doors of the station, the familiar characters he passed on the walk now and again. It took very little for him to notice someone out of place.

The first trick to being followed is to never let your tail know you've spotted them. Darian needed this person to get close, to show themselves, because he didn't recognise him at first glance. He was good at what he was doing and he was well covered, the hood of a puffy jacket pulled over his head; the weather does make tracking a person in Challaid without showing your face easier. Darian walked home, going at the same pace he usually did, making no deviation from his well-worn route. The same footsteps day after day; with paint on the soles of his shoes he would have marked out a very narrow trail. If this person knew he always got the train home and exited through the north door of Bank Station then he probably already knew where Darian lived.

Only when he got into the building could he do something about it without giving his knowledge away. He ran up the stairs to his flat, went into the kitchen and took the bag out of the bin. It was only half-full but that didn't matter. He pulled it shut and bolted back downstairs with it. He was back to being casual, moving at a sedate pace as he opened the front door and stepped out, walking along Havurn Road to the gap between his building and the next where the bins were stashed. He opened one and chucked the bag in, turning quickly and catching a split-second glimpse of his follower, just the side of his face as the man turned away and started walking out of view, but it was definitely Randulf Gallowglass.

Back in the flat Darian sat near the living-room window with the light off, looking down into the street. There was nothing to see there, but he kept up the vigil. Gallowglass wouldn't know for sure he'd been identified, but he had been seen and that would be enough to send him scurrying back under his rock. A good tracker, who doesn't want to be seen, isn't going to risk being picked out on the same street twice, hours apart. Even unidentified, his purpose would be understood. Darian kept looking in the hope that he would spot a car going past with Gallowglass or Corey in it, but that wasn't necessary to confirm his suspicions.

Gallowglass wasn't back on his tail because he'd found a new hobby he liked. It hadn't been a day and already Corey knew Darian was still working the Moses case, and maybe knew Maeve was going to try to help him out. Darian had spent many evenings, when he first moved in, sitting at that window, watching the lights of boats leaving and entering the loch, the view between the buildings down to the water. Now he sat looking down at dark grey tarmac lit yellow by artificial light, contemplating what this meant. Gallowglass hadn't wanted to be seen, so this wasn't a thuggish warning. This was Corey fishing for information before he tried to put a stop to Darian's efforts. This was Darian putting the research company at risk by picking a fight he couldn't win.

The Bust of Acair Duff

It was the story of the year at the university. It was a crime that the police had very little time for. In the bubble we live in it can be hard to appreciate how meaningless some things are. When Michael Watson, the first-year student who was the star of the university camanachd team, and Ben Gauld, the fourth year who was vice captain of the side, were assaulted returning to the halls of residence after a match, it was the only topic of discussion among us students. Michael Watson was in hospital for two days and missed three months of matches; Ben Gauld was only slightly injured and missed no matches. In a city where forty-one murders were reported last year, this was not a priority for the police. That would be why their investigation involved a few easy questions and nothing more. Because it was such a big deal to us all, I dug a little deeper.

To understand why it matters it's worth explaining why the university's camanachd team matters. It's the cheerfully brutal sport of the city, and the university team plays in the national league and cup. It may be the one thing that draws all students together, a flag to rally around. Only current students can play for the team, which has meant success has been, to be polite, occasional. Players may not make a lot of money from the sport, but they can become heroes in the city. The university hasn't won the league since 1988, and only twice in a century, and hasn't won the cup since '96. Even a passionate support can lose its verve in the face of ingrained mediocrity. Then, along came Michael Watson. A first-year student studying mathematics, a likeable black kid from a working-class background, and one of the best camanachd players the university has ever had. With a solid supporting cast already in place he represented our best shot at silverware in a generation. Then he was attacked.

Watson and Gauld had been playing a match that afternoon, beating An Fiadh-Chù, or Earmam Athletic to give them their proper name, 4-2 with two goals from Watson. It had been played up in Earmam, at their Sgleò Park ground, and the Challaid University players had made their own way home after the game. Some had gone for a few drinks, because that's what students are prone to doing in the wake of everything. Watson and Gauld had got the train back to Ciad Station, the largest in Challaid because it's where you get a train south out of the city, and walked down from there. As they made their way up the main approach to the halls of residence they were attacked from behind by three men. Watson suffered a broken ankle as well as facial injuries and two broken fingers, and Gauld suffered facial injuries and a cut hand.

Now, this is where I, Catriona Ross, come in. The police had asked a few questions and then wandered off, leaving speculation in place of answers in their wake. I wasn't satisfied with that, and felt there was more to learn. The place was swirling with rumours about scumbag Earmam Athletic players being behind the attack, and, as my brother Sorley was one of them, it was personal to me.

'They were followed home from the bar they were in,' one student said to me with zero evidence to support the claim. 'Everyone knows it.'

I prefer not to accept what everyone claims to know. They might have got hit in the head with sticks occasionally but they weren't numb to the brain. There was no way Earmam players would have risked being seen leading an attack on campus grounds, where the security was obsessively tight. I know how insane some people are about Camanachd, and I know Sorley can be huffy in defeat, but this seemed like a big stretch.

At times like this it pays to be pushy. I didn't know either of the victims, I was a second-year student at the time so didn't share any classes, but I sought them out. I saw Watson on the east green and made a beeline for him. Even on crutches he seemed energetic, tall and lithe.

'Hi, Michael,' I said with a cheery smile. 'My name's Cat Ross, I just really wanted to say how terrible it was what happened to you.'

'Oh, thanks,' he said, and started to move away. He'd have heard enough expressions of sympathy for mine to mean very little.

'I was wondering if you saw who did it, the three guys? I know some people up in Earmam, a couple who play for their team; they might be able to help identify them.'

'I'm sorry; I didn't see them at all. They jumped us from behind.'

'So Ben saw them? What did he say about them?'

'He didn't really see them either; he got jumped and saw the figures running away after. I'm sorry, but I'm running late... Hopping late.'

'Oh, sure, go on,' I said.

The next step was to visit the security room on the ground floor of the halls of residence. The building is rather grand; a spectacle is how it was sneeringly described when it was built. Most of the university, like many other elements of Challaid life in the last three hundred years, was funded by the Sutherlands. The hall of residence was instead paid for by a donation in the mid-eighteenth security by a shipping magnate called Morogh Duff, who was, in every way, the opposite of the Sutherland family. To say Duff led a full life would be to undersell it criminally. He was wild, gregarious and loved to thumb his nose at the conservative establishment in the city of his birth who called him a pirate, hence the ostentatious building he paid for and the scholarships for the children of his working-class employees.

The security room for the building was on the left side of the main entrance hall, across the colourful tiled mosaic of a ship crashing through waves and in through a small, arched doorway. There were two computers on a long desk and one young man in a shirt with a badge on it saying he was the security officer for the building. That was Nassir El-Amin, and if you were nosy enough to want to know what was happening in the building then Nas was a man you made friends with. It was easily done; he got awfully bored in that office. As resident nosey parker we knew each other well.

'Hey, Cat,' he said when I walked into the office.

'Hi, Nas. Listen, can you help me out, I'm digging around in what happened to Watson and Gauld and I wondered what you'd heard. What did the cameras show?'

'Cameras didn't show anything but blackness. The ones at the front were down on that night because of a software shambles; they'd been down all day. We didn't pick up anything of what happened, or who did it.'

'They'd been down all day?'

'Yep, since the early morning. The police weren't impressed either when they came looking. I think that was the final straw for them. They asked a few questions of a few people, but I think they're done poking around in this already.'

I was about to leave but not before I mentioned something unusual in the office. The bust of Acair Duff, son of the man who paid for the building and himself a significant donor to the university, was on the floor in the corner of the room. It had been outside, atop his pedestal on the approach to the main entrance, but now it was in the security office with a chunk out of the back of its head.

'What happened to your new roommate?' I asked Nas.

'Poor sod was the third victim of the attack, not that he's getting any sympathy. They must have pushed him off the plinth when they attacked; he was all over the pavement. Not the first fellow we've found all over the pavement here after a wild night out, mind you.'

That intrigued me, and I found myself out at the entrance, hood up against the rain, looking at the plinth where the bust had been. There were four, two on each side of the path, of people who had put good money into the university, all men with epic beards. I walked over to Acair's father, Morogh, and gave the bust a gentle push. There was no movement. It was firmly in place, which meant whoever knocked Acair off his perch had hit him with real force. This was no pushover. The bust at head height, held in place with wires firmly enough to stop the Challaid wind blowing it over.

I found Ben Gauld in one of the common rooms, watching his pals playing snooker and looking grumpy. He was sitting alone, so I gave him some company. He gave me an unwelcoming look, and I noticed the plaster on the side of his hand and bruises on his face. He was the sort of leader who could inspire great passion in a very small number of people. No one would build a statue of him, or name a ship after him, but someone might take it upon themselves to engrave his name on a small plaque and screw it to a university bench without permission.

'Terrible business that,' I said, nodding to the hand.

'It was.'

'You can't have expected that to happen.'

'I didn't.'

'You getting hurt, I mean. When you jumped Watson you must have thought it would be clear and easy. You knew the cameras were down, had all day to find that out. You go and play the match and then you go drinking. Watson was probably all over the place on the way back, easy enough for you to drop behind without him noticing. You jump him and go for the ankle and hands because that's what he needs to play, and then you try to run. Turned and sprinted right into poor old Acair Duff, didn't you? It was him that roughed you up from beyond the grave.'

He stared at me, and his friends had stopped playing to listen, standing with snooker cues in their hands, but I must say I wasn't scared. There were other people in the common room that had nothing to do with them, and being a Ross means picking fights with people who deserve it.

'Why did you do it?' I asked him.

'Ben?' one of the snooker players said. That was what did it, me putting the pieces into order for one of his friends who hadn't realised what he had done.

'We've been in that team three years. Three fucking years. Every time we win a bloody game it's him at the bar, the hero, getting the pats on the back and the drinks. Does he do it alone? He's hogging it all for himself and he's only just in the door. He hasn't earned any of it.'

So that was it, one of my first investigations. It never came out publicly that Gauld was behind the attack, but he never played for the university again, claiming a hand injury. Watson made it back, but by then the season was a washout, and Challaid University would have to keep waiting for the drought to end. A month later Watson stopped me in a corridor and took me aside to whisper a thank-you. He was a polite kid, not the sort who wanted trouble, and I think he was struggling to find his place at the university. I believe he knew who attacked him that night, and he was glad someone else had proved it for him.

24

'THIS ISN'T GOING to be worth our valuable time.'

Darian was sitting in the passenger seat of Sholto's Fiat. He said, 'You don't think?'

'Nah, no chance.'

Sholto enjoyed speaking as a master to his apprentice, letting Darian know he'd done this all before. It was an act of basic kindness to let him ramble on about it, even though Darian already knew why the boss was right.

Darian asked, 'Why not? He's Uisdean's friend, he was with him on the night. If anyone saw something it's bound to be the friend.'

'Well, first of all, that beating the boy took, whatever it was for, it was a setup. They knew he was in the club and they tiptoed up behind him when he came out. The friend didn't go with him down the alley, so he wouldn't have seen the attacker because the attacker would have made sure he didn't. Place as busy as that and no one saw him? This person knows how to play the game. Second of all, Uisdean doesn't want us to know what really happened, so there's a good chance this reliable pal he's willing to name will have his lips sewn shut as well. They'll look out for each other.'

'So why bother at all?'

'Passes the time, and Kotkell's paying by the hour.'

It wasn't just their own time they were passing, it was Darian's sister Cat's as well. Leandro Oriol lived in the halls of residence at the university in the south end of Cnocaid, in the same large building she stayed in. They were sticklers for security, so Darian and Sholto needed someone with a pass to get them in. He had called Cat and asked if she could help. She had said yes, but only if she got to sit in on the interview, because seeing them at work promised to be entertaining and maybe even educational.

She was waiting for them at the main doors. The building was old, finished in 1762, and came with a high, arched entrance and doors thick enough to make an invading army pause for thought.

Darian smiled when he saw her, walked over and gave his sister a hug. 'Good to see you, Cat.'

She was always the little sister to him and Sorley, with her thick, red hair, wide smile, pale, freckled skin and slight frame they thought she needed all the protection they could give. That was complete nonsense, of course, and especially so by the time they arrived at the door of the university halls. She was twenty, already planning to be a journalist, and knew her way around the worries of the world without the need of a guiding hand.

Sholto smiled, shook her hand firmly and said, 'Catriona, it's lovely to see you. Goodness me, you have your mother's look if ever I saw it.'

A lot of people who had known their mother said the same, and Cat never quite knew how to react to reminders of her. Death chips a small corner from you, leaves you a different shape than you were before, a less complete person.

Darian knew any mention of their parents would make things awkward so he said, 'Thanks for helping us with this, Cat.'

'I'm just getting you in and watching the show, it's no big deal.'

She led them through the hall and across to the side. The security didn't really kick in until you left the main hall and tried to go down one of the corridors to the rooms. That was where you needed a swipe card to enter, which was where Cat came in handy. She held the door open for them and led them along the wide corridor and round to room seventeen. She had checked the register to find out what room Oriol had.

She said, 'Here we go. These are some of the better rooms; you usually have to be pretty well connected to land one down this end.'

Sholto knocked and the three of them waited. The door opened and a middle-aged woman looked back at them. Cat didn't recognise her so she wasn't a lecturer or member of staff, and it was a fair bet she was a parent. She didn't look surprised. She was tall and blonde, bright red lipstick against pale skin, and she looked at them with the irritated expression Darian and Sholto were used to.

Sholto said, 'Hello, love, my name's Sholto Douglas, this is my colleague Darian Ross, and Catriona Ross. We're from Douglas Independent Research and we're needing to speak with Leandro Oriol. Is he at home?'

'What is this about?'

'Don't worry now; he's not in any bother at all. A friend of his was knocked about like a crisp packet in a tornado and we were hoping young Leandro might be able to tell us one or two things about the stormy night in question.'

She frowned more deeply still and said, 'You'd better come in.'

She stood at the door and the three of them walked past her. It was obvious they were expected, and that, whoever she was, she was there to deal with them. The rooms were bigger and better than Cat's, basically a small flat with large windows and nice views of the side gardens. Cat was two floors up in tiny rooms she shared with two other people and several patches of damp that had lived there a lot longer than them.

The room she led them into was the kind of living room that every student wanted but very few could afford. Gadgets galore, gaming consoles and a bookcase full of games, VR headsets and framed movie posters on the walls. There was a cabinet that had an assortment of bottles in it, many of them still full, which meant it must have been restocked often. They weren't cheap bottles either. On the couch, which had remarkably few stains and no visible rips in it, sat an eighteen- or nineteen-year-old boy. He was darker than the woman, but there was a resemblance there. Where she had the pasty look of a local, the boy's father was presumably Caledonian. Leandro was chubby and he needed a haircut because the long style he was aiming at wasn't working for him. He had a double chin, a fuzzy attempt at facial hair and small glasses, and he was wearing the sort of jeans and hoodie combination that looked like a sarcastic impression of a working-class kid.

Sholto looked at the drinks cabinet and said, 'Hoo, I could get half-drunk on a year's salary on that lot, eh?'

Leandro didn't smile and the woman just frowned again. She said, 'Mm. My name's Kellina Oriol, this is my son Leandro. I'm a lawyer, so if you don't mind I'll be sitting in on this interview.'

Sholto said, 'Oh. Good. We're not police, just so you know.'

'I already do know. You're a private investigator pretending to be something else, I've checked. So go ahead and ask your questions.'

She sat on the couch next to her son and Sholto and Darian sat on the second couch in the room, Sholto slumping back and saying, '*Obh, obh.*'

There was a spare dining chair against the wall by the door, presumably for when their gaming sessions got crowded, so Cat pulled that beside the second couch and sat on it.

Sholto said, 'You don't mind if we take the weight off, do you, Leandro? No point wearing out our feet while our brains are working.'

He half nodded and then looked at his mother to see if he was giving the right answer. It was too late; bums had already hit the seats.

Sholto pushed on. 'Now, Leandro, seeing as Uisdean's already been in touch to tell you we were coming you can crack on and tell us what happened the other night outside Himinn and we can get out of your mother's lovely hair.'

'I don't know what happened; I didn't see any of it. I didn't know it had happened until this morning.'

Leandro had a deep voice that sounded like it was coming from somewhere else, and his tone said he didn't like having to use it in this company.

Sholto said, 'Oh, we know that, but walk me through the things you do know. You weren't so blootered you can't remember, were you?'

Kellina Oriol tutted and Leandro said, 'No, I remember. We went out for a few drinks, stopped in at Himinn and stayed for, I don't know, a couple of hours. We left at the same time, but I went up the street because I was going to stay at my parents' house, so I went up towards Ciad Station. I think he was coming back here so he went down the street to use the alley to get across to the taxi rank on Cala Street.'

All said in the clipped tone of an over-rehearsed performer scared of mistakes. Sholto nodded cheerfully along and said, 'That was it? There was no one at the club trying to turn the dancing into something more physical, or even just keeping an eyeball on you?'

'I don't think so.'

'A nightclub in Challaid and there was no one there looking for a rumble? That seems unlikely.'

'Nobody approached us, or spoke to us. We had no trouble at all.'

'Uh-huh, uh-huh. And what sort of mood was Uisdean in?'

'Mood? He was fine, normal.'

'Good, right. So when you left the club I suppose there would have been some people out on Malairt Street, always busy out there in the festive hours. Did you notice anyone on their own, anyone taking an interest in you?'

'I didn't see anyone I can remember recognising. There were a few folk there, but just ordinary groups of people.'

'So Uisdean, a good enough looking lad, money burning a hole in all his pockets, probably a wee heartbreaker, am I right? Got a tidy wee girl or three on the go, maybe picked one of them up from another lad who didn't want to let go, something like that?'

'No. That's not Uisdean. I don't think he has a girlfriend. I don't know.'

'You don't know? You're his mate.'

'I don't think he does.'

His mother said, 'Really, Mr Douglas, they're young men in college together, they're not Siamese twins.'

'I think they prefer to be called conjoined. So, Leandro, you probably don't know him well enough to know of anyone who might have it in for him.'

'No.'

'No. The big N O. Nothing else springs to mind, nothing that might help us find out who tried to use your not-as-good-a-pal-as-we-thought-he-was as a *piñata*?'

'No.'

Sholto glanced at Darian and they both stood up, so Cat did the same. She had come to see Darian at work but it was Sholto who had made an impression on her. He had always seemed so bumbling, her father's former colleague who had become a byword for sloth. The way he handled that interview, and the lawyer present, was far more impressive than she'd expected. If you wound him up, like Leandro's mother had, he still had some life left in him to spit out. This was the moment Cat realised her brother was in good hands.

Sholto said, 'We won't take up any more of your expensive time, Mrs Oriol. Or yours, Leandro. This card here has my office number on it, just in case a flash of memory hits you and you need to get in touch about it.'

Cat led them back out and through the hall to the cavernous entrance. Darian said, 'Well, that card will be in the bin by now.'

'Aye, and I bet the bin cost more than Mrs Douglas's weekly shop. Imagine a student having all that gear. A student. I could have gone swimming in his carpet. Did you feel it? The kind of people that go on skiing holidays and sail boats around the Mediterranean with no cargo to deliver, they are. Closest I've gotten to a foreign holiday in the last five years was chasing a debt dodger down to Carlisle.'

Cat said, 'I'm sorry it didn't work out.'

Darian said, 'It wasn't worthless. Leandro's obviously holding back, he knows something about what happened to Uisdean. His friend and his mother both told him what to say and he picked the best-sounding answers from their short list of options.'

Sholto said, 'Aye, a couple of well-brought-up liars, that pair. That's the thing about posh people, the rest of us tend to think they stick to the law better, don't duck under it for a quick buck, but they're actually worse because they think they deserve to get away with it.'

Cat said, 'As long as it's keeping you busy.'

'Oh aye. We caught a killer this week, did Darian tell you that?'

'No.'

Darian said, 'It's complicated; I'll tell you in proper detail some time.'

'I look forward to it. Say hello to Sorley if you see him before me.'

They parted, and Darian and Sholto walked back to Sholto's car. Darian said, 'Will we hit Himinn then, see what they have to say there?'

Sholto looked at his watch. It was half-four in the afternoon. 'Nah, better to leave it to tomorrow morning. We've done enough work for one day so I'll drop you back at home if you want. You take my advice, don't become a workaholic, it's one of the worst aholics you can be; it can be the end of you. Nearly happened to me.'

'Did it?'

'Oh yeah, when I was your age I worked all the hours they would pay me for. You get wiser as you get older.'

Darian said nothing to that, but he was thankful for the lift home. It meant he would dodge Bank Station, where Gallowglass would be waiting.

25

WHEN HE LEFT the flat, he did so carefully. Darian had been looking into the street for hours, checking for Gallowglass and not seeing him. He went out the back, onto a large square of grass that served as the shared garden of the four L-shaped buildings that surrounded it. Every time he reached the corner to go onto a street he looked carefully first, worried about Gallowglass seeing him. He didn't take the usual route to Bank Station, or use the usual entrance on Fomorian Road, but instead used the bridge to cross the tracks and onto Sloc Street to enter from the far side of the building. He hadn't seen Gallowglass, and he'd tiptoed through the shadows with enough skill to be sure Gallowglass hadn't spotted him.

Darian took the train up to Mormaer Station and got a taxi from there. It was already after eleven, late enough to be a nuisance, so the long walk to Maeve's flat would have left him too late to be decent. The road was visible in the lamplight as the taxi pulled up, but the flats on either side of the road and the steep Dùil hill behind trapped the light between them, the tops of the buildings and the hill a collection of ominous shadows. On Sgàil Drive you could easily believe these buildings existed in a void, no world visible in the blackness beyond.

He knocked on her front door and it took a while before a response arrived. Maeve pulled the door open, looking sleepy and flustered, wearing just a T-shirt.

Darian said, 'Oh, sorry, I should have called ahead first. Do you want me to go?'

'No, no, come in.'

They went through to the living room and Maeve stood in the doorway. It was cold, and Darian could see her nipples press against the thin T-shirt. She walked across to the record player and picked something up from beside it. When she bent down the T-shirt rode up and, although it was only a split second, Darian had the certainty of hope that the T-shirt really was all she had on. Maeve walked across with a small notepad and passed it to him.

She said, 'You look through that while I put some clothes on. I didn't expect to have to look respectable at this hour.'

'Sorry about that. I don't always keep sociable hours.'

'Well, these hours can be very sociable with a little warning.'

She went to her bedroom to change and he opened the notebook. It was mostly a list of names and numbers, a couple of addresses and a few phone numbers. It was people she knew had worked with Moses and there were educated guesses at the amounts of money he had handled for them. It was mostly small numbers, and there were a few names of committedly mediocre criminals Darian recognised and immediately dismissed.

'You need to keep in mind that he didn't handle big sums of money very often, not the size that a person would kill for.'

Darian looked up at Maeve. She had pulled on a pair of trousers and a raggedy jumper over the T-shirt that had seen many better days.

Darian said, 'People have killed for tiny amounts of money before. Or for no money where they thought some would be. Or a lot of small amounts added together. Could the money he was handling have added up to the eighteen and a half grand Cummins paid his debt with?'

'It could, but he would have had to get his timing just right. Rare for Moses to have that sort of money in the flat, as far as I know. And if he had, Cummins wouldn't have known. I don't think any of his clients would have known and I don't think any of them would have killed him for it.'

'Do you know them well enough to be sure?'

'No, but I knew Moses and I know the only people he handled small accounts for were people he knew and trusted, people he'd known his whole life, and the people with big accounts wouldn't need to kill him for the cash.'

'So what exactly did he do for them?'

Maeve sat and said, 'He would hide the money they shouldn't have had in the first place. It wasn't always in cash; it depended on who it was and how they were receiving it in the first place. If it was cash it would be in the flat, but not for long. If the person who killed him knew he had a lot of money then they must have known that it had either just been delivered or was about to be collected, so they could have found out from the previous or next link in the chain. He would put the money into businesses and they would put it into their books. It was like investing money, that's what he used to say, sometimes more or less would come back than had gone in but what came back was always clean, and it now had a backstory to protect it after travelling through the business world.'

'So he must have had a bunch of businesses helping him?'

'Of course, but I have no idea who they were. Say what you want about Moses but he respected the privacy of the people he was breaking the law with.'

'If we could identify the businesses or the high-value clients then we might find our killer. One of them might have decided Moses was too well informed.'

The lights in the flat flickered and cut out for a few seconds before they came back on. Maeve said, 'Ignore that, it happens a lot. The electricity cuts out a lot under the hill, they say they're going to fix it but...'

'Okay, so, his clients.'

'I think the most likely candidates will be one of the people near the top of that list, the ones I know he handled decent money for.'

Darian looked at the names, some he recognised and some he didn't. A couple of known criminals and a few businessmen of notable standing that Darian hadn't known were dirty but really should have guessed. Neither of the criminals he'd heard of had been identified as working at a level where people died on their orders.

He said, 'Do you know which of them worked with him most recently?'

'No, he didn't give information like that away, I wasn't even supposed to know this much and he didn't realise I did. I overheard whispered conversations, caught a glimpse of receipts he was reading by hovering over his shoulder in passing.'

'We need to be very careful with this. The sort of people we're dealing with won't take kindly to being questioned about the killing of a man they knew, and I don't just mean the criminal types either.'

'Please, just because some of them dress up in nice suits and sit in expensive offices in Bank or Cnocaid doesn't make them less criminal.'

'You're right, I know, and those people will go a long way to protect the image they've built. Lawyers, to start with, and they're dangerous enough, but there could be more after. If one of these people did kill Moses then we have to consider that they might be prepared to silence anyone who shows the inclination to catch them.'

'I know the risk, but I'm going to give chase anyway. I can't just move on from Moses being murdered, not until I'm sure the person who did it is in jail. It would be an insult to him, and I cared too much about him to let that insult pass. And you, Mr not quite a private detective, you wouldn't let an innocent man rot in jail for this, would you?'

'No.'

'So I need to do something. I'll pick the lowest-risk person on that list and have a chat with them, see what falls out when I lean on them.'

'Okay, how about this. You pick someone on that list that didn't give him huge money and knew him well, you see if you can find out from them who else he was working with lately. The bigger a picture we can build the better a chance we have.'

'I can do that, a casual chat with an old pal.'

'Good, because right now we don't want anyone else knowing what we're up to, so don't interrogate anyone. Try to get the little things, details that often seem irrelevant but can provide a small answer to a big question. And keep your eyes open, because Corey isn't going to like either of us working an investigation he's twice decided the book is closed on. He's had one of his pets, a guy called Gallowglass, following me for the last couple of days and I think it's because of this.'

'Well, I didn't tell anyone what I'm doing.'

'I'm not saying you did. I'm just saying, be wary, because if Corey's coming after us he will eventually catch up, and we have to have the truth to defend ourselves with when he does.'

There was a pause for a few seconds before Maeve said, 'Gallowglass, that's not a common name. Is he the one who used to be a detective?'

'He is. Do you know him?'

'Know of him. He used to move in some grubby circles, back when he thought he could get away with it. A girl I knew went out with him just long enough to know she needed to run a mile. When she ran, I picked her up from his house. I can show you where it is, if you'd like. We can take my car.'

He so enjoyed being with her, both because she was beautiful and because they were going to catch a killer together. He couldn't decide which reason thrilled him more. They left the flat together as the lights on the street flickered again.

Light Plays on the Sea

The lighthouse keeper stood outside the door, wrapped up warm in his thick coat, bonnet pulled tight on his head. The wind was loud but he knew its tune and he could hear what lay underneath it. The cracks, the splintering, and the shouts. He was a man of experience, he had heard those sounds before, and he knew what his responsibility was now.

The lighthouse keeper lived alone in the tall building, in his lighthouse north of Heilam. It showed the way for sailors coming into the sea loch, going to the port of Challaid. He was so close to the city, but he couldn't go to it, his job demanding absolute commitment. For months he would sit alone and wonder if any in the world knew his name, if they spoke of him or thought of him. A name unspoken was not a name, a man unmentioned was nobody. His work made it possible for so many to safely arrive at and leave the city, but all of those people thought nothing of the one who helped them. Sometimes he was angry to think of it, but on other days it was to his benefit.

The weather had been poor all day, a fog that was swept away by strong wind and heavy rain. There had been few boats coming into the loch. In the night he sat by the window and looked out to sea, watching the light of a boat rocking back and forth, rising and falling, moving slowly towards the lighthouse. The lighthouse keeper watched for a time as it got closer, able to identify the boat as a large cutter, making a run for shelter. The lighthouse keeper could see what was going to happen, knew the water and the weather, knew the rocks and knew the wrong light that shone.

Now he stood outside the door to the lighthouse and listened to the noises underneath the wind. There was the sound of the wood breaking on rocks, of a mast cracking and falling into the water. The song of a boat breaking apart in the sea was one the lighthouse keeper had orchestrated often enough to know well. The cutter would be mostly underwater, none of its crew on board. They would be in the cold water, the swell pulling them under or pushing them onto the rocks. The sea always claimed its share.

He had the musket tucked under his arm as he walked carefully to the edge of the cliff and picked his path down towards the small shingle beach. The lamp was still shining on the post by the cliff edge where he had placed it, a lying substitute for the lighthouse light. He knew the cliff and the beach; he knew every path and climbing route that could be used in this area. While a stranger would struggle to find their way up in good weather, there was no danger for him going down in the storm.

His boots crunched across the shingle as he made his way to the rough water's edge. The lighthouse keeper hadn't heard a human shout for some minutes, but he heard one now. As the cold water rolled as far as the toe of his boot, the lighthouse keeper made out the figure of a man trying to stand, desperately crawling in the water as he made his way for shore. The man saw the lighthouse keeper, struggled forward until the water reached only his knees. He stumbled the last few feet and landed heavily beside the lighthouse keeper, looking up at him. 'I am the only one,' he said in shaking gasps. 'The sea took the rest. It is only me.' The lighthouse keeper smiled, aimed the musket and shot the man in the head.

Over the following two hours the lighthouse keeper carefully moved all valuables that washed ashore to the small basement of the lighthouse. It was a good haul, interesting items he would examine carefully over the rest of the week. He took two hours and stopped, even knowing there were some boxes left on the beach. He switched off the lamp and put the lighthouse light back on. Enough time had passed for people to miss the cutter, so he began the long walk down to the north of Challaid to raise the alarm. The little-known lighthouse keeper, doing his sad duty.

26

IT WAS AN excuse to spend time with Maeve, nothing more than that. There was no benefit to Darian in seeing what hole Gallowglass slithered into of an evening; it was something he could have uncovered for himself if he'd cared. Doing it alone would have meant doing it without Maeve. The two of them together in a small, battered old car, trundling north through Whisper Hill. The heater was on but it seemed to be blowing cold air, and Maeve kept looking at the needle to check how much petrol she had.

She said 'We won't run out... I don't think.'

They drove in the shadows of the hills until they reached Drummond Street at the north tip of the city and turned onto Heilam Road going north out of Challaid. They were leaving the bright lights of what could generously be called civilisation behind and going off into the moors towards the mouth of the loch. The day will come when the city sprawl will reach up there, too, you can be sure of that, but so far the landscape has held it back. There's only a narrow passage between the steep hills and the loch at the very top of Whisper Hill, and the road north out of the city almost filled it. That stopped anyone developing up there, because everything had the ominous, or comforting if you like that sort of thing, sense of being cut off.

There was a dark gap through the moor before you saw the few lights of Heilam. It wasn't much to look at, a council estate in the open that was supposed to be the first step in developing the area and turning Heilam into the seventh region of Challaid. Another of the council's grand plans that went awry, started by one party with big dreams and a big budget and ended by the next. The houses, all white roughcast, had gone up in the early seventies when Labour led the council, the expansion stopped when the Democratic Party took over and talked about without effect now the Liberal Party was in power. It was probably only because they were out of sight and out of mind that these houses hadn't been pulled down.

Late at night was the best time to visit Heilam. With the moon on the loch lighting the view out to sea, and with the hills rising darkly on the other side, the brooding graveyard behind you, you could almost believe it was beautiful. It was the sort of scene in which a songwriter would set their folk tale of heartbreak. It was the smudge of old council houses in the middle of it all that spoiled the picture. Remember that we're talking about a village whose biggest selling point was the large number of bodies buried on its outskirts. You could make a sturdy argument that the dead had better accommodation than the living. The only building of any age was the old lighthouse at the north end of Heilam and no one lived there anymore.

Maeve said, 'It was along here somewhere.'

She turned onto a short street with houses in blocks of two on either side of the road. They all had small front gardens and they all looked cold, huddled together against the weather on the moor like lost sheep. Maeve stopped the car across the street.

She nodded across at two houses and said, 'It was either one of those two. My friend texted and told me to come and get her from here, she was standing outside that gate when I arrived. From what she told me, Gallowglass is hooked on madness. He was always looking for trouble and creating some if there was none around. Maybe he's calmed down now he doesn't have the police shield to hide behind, but he doesn't seem like the sort who would. He'll keep pushing his luck until life pushes back.'

'If the protection of the force let him run wild then he still has Corey looking after him now.'

They sat and watched in darkness. After half an hour a car pulled up and stopped, a little too close for comfort. Gallowglass got out of the driver's seat and went into his house, not bothering to look around as he went. From where they sat he looked very ordinary. Mediocrity, when wrapped in the right kind of skin, can travel a long way before anyone thinks to challenge it. He slammed his front door shut with a bang that would wake the neighbours.

Maeve said, 'Looks like someone didn't find what they were looking for in the great city tonight.'

'It's nice to be missed. Come on; let's get out of here, bad enough he's following me without him thinking to get on your tail as well.'

Maeve started the car and drove Darian back south. They chatted as she drove, a journey shorter than Darian would have liked. He hadn't had a girlfriend for a while, too wrapped up in being a pretend private detective to have a relationship, and Maeve was reminding him how pleasant the sensation could be. Not because she was beautiful or sexy, although she was both, but because she was someone to talk and laugh with, to share time with away from work. She dropped him outside Three O'clock Station and he took the train home.

27

MALAIRT STREET EARLY in the morning is not the same as Malairt Street late at night. At night it's filled with middle-class students and an array of careful fun-seekers. The main party area in the city used to be over on the edge of Bakers Moor, a little closer to the working-class east side. Over the last twenty years or so party central has drifted west towards Cnocaid, where a safe night out can be had amid gentrified surroundings. During the day it was populated by quiet shoppers, and, on this morning, Darian and Sholto.

They were outside Himinn, Darian leading the way because Sholto was old enough to call a nightclub a discotheque and would rather have spent his morning in the McDonald's next door. The doors to the club were open, but the interior was silent. They walked along the hall, ignoring the doors that led to the balcony stairs, and went into a small bar area tucked away from the main floor.

It was a gloomy little nook in which a heavily bearded man was kneeling beside the bar, cleaning the rail that ran along the front of it. The place seemed to be a slapdash approximation of the sort of pubs your grandfather might have drunk in. Darian could smell the brass polish and there was a box of rags and bottles of cleaning products on top of the bar. The whole place had a genteel air about it, which none of the Challaid pubs of your grandfather's generation suffered from.

The man with the beard looked up at them and said, 'You cops?'

Darian said, 'No, we're not.'

'Huh. So what do you want?'

'You in charge round here?'

'Maurice Gomez, bar manager for the time being. What do you want?'

'We want to ask you about an assault that happened in the alley at the side of the building a few nights ago. Uisdean Kotkell, was drinking here, went out, got taken apart. You hear about that?'

'Yeah, I heard about it.'

'And?'

'And nothing. I heard about it when it happened, but it was peaceful in here that night, like it is every other night. We don't have trouble here.'

'Well, that's super to hear but what do you know about the young man who was attacked?'

Gomez looked at them both and said, 'You two ain't cops?'

'No.'

'So I don't have to talk to you at all?'

'No.'

'Good.'

Gomez went back to his cleaning, ignoring Darian and Sholto. Darian glanced at his colleague, sensing he had lost his chance to make a connection so now it was Sholto's time to shine in the last-chance saloon.

Sholto said, 'We're working for the victim's family, so you'd be doing them a favour. We can make it worth your while.'

'No, you can't.'

Sholto looked at Darian and shrugged. They had tried to find what they could here, but it was a poor use of time to chip away at a brick wall. Darian hated to walk, especially when there was nowhere else to go. They left the nook and walked past the arches that led into the club proper, that place in darkness. On their way through the entrance hall they saw a young man coming down the stairs.

Darian said, 'Ally, you working here now?'

Alfonso Bosco saw who was talking to him and his expression collapsed into that of a man who can hear a favour being called in. Nearly a year before, Darian had helped Ally out of a little jam when a former friend scammed a lot of angry people out of their money, laid a misleading trail to Ally's door and skipped town. Ally wasn't a man you crossed and stuck around. He was a bouncer of formidable renown, partly due to the eyepatch he wore. He had lost his right eye in a knife fight when he was nineteen and could have worn a glass eye with no discomfort, but he liked to be looked at. He was six-three and had a long goatee beard he tied in a ponytail with colourful bands, so he was tough to miss.

Ally said, 'Aye, I do.'

'So you'll know what was going on with Uisdean Kotkell when he was whomped round the back the other night.'

Ally puffed out his cheeks and said, 'Come on next door and you can buy me breakfast. I talk better with a burger in each hand.'

The three of them sat in a booth away from the front windows of the McDonald's next to the club and Ally did his talking in a full-mouthed near-whisper between bites.

'That kid was at the club quite a lot, him and his posh

mates. There's a bunch of them, little rich kids, I dunno. They drink somewhere else before they get to the club, I think they go on to their own little parties afterward. Richer stuff than I've ever been to. It wasn't anything that happened in our club, I know that, we'd have spotted something. I told the cop that came to ask about it. MacDuff.'

'What was he asking about?'

'Nothing specific. Pissed off Gomez with a couple of questions, that's all it ever takes with that grumpy sod. Then he asked me and a couple of other staff who were working that night about it, general stuff, did we see him that night, did we see anyone looking for him? We had nothing to tell. The thing I didn't tell him, and I'll tell you because it's you, is about that boy's ex.'

'Oh.'

'Yeah. There was a while there when the Kotkell boy was coming in here with Dillan Howard. Now, Howard, he's got a short fuse and likes playing with matches. The story I heard was that they had a big falling out, went their separate ways. Howard ain't the sort to shrug it off if he thinks he's been badly treated.'

As Sholto had the expression of a man watching an alien invasion unfold, it was Darian who said, 'You know where we could find Howard?'

'Pretty sure he lives up in Earmam somewhere, but I don't know where exactly.'

'That's a good start, cheers, Ally.'

If Sholto hadn't been there Darian would have slipped Ally some cash and added it to the client's bill, but Sholto objected to that sort of thing. Keep the bills as low as possible or the client goes elsewhere, like Raven Investigators with their detailed expenses and special offers. It was a shame, because the bouncer at a club where young rich kids partied was a worthy contact. Darian would catch Ally up later and slip him a twenty, seal him as an ongoing contact. Darian and Sholto walked out of the burger joint and down the street to where Sholto had parked the Fiat.

He said, 'Bloody hell.'

Darian said, 'What?'

'The father didn't mention the boy was gay.'

'So?'

'So what if the father doesn't know? He's not going to want to find out from one of my skilfully written reports, is he? I knew this case was bad news. Any case with young people is awkward because young people are terrible at life, keeping open secrets.'

'We can find Howard, talk to him.'

'Aye, and hope the whole bloody thing doesn't blow up in our faces.'

The city of Challaid still has corners where Presbyterianism and Old Testament morals are extolled by influential people, like the Sutherland family who employed Kotkell, which made Sholto nervous. Any complication stood like a mountain before him, while the map in front of Darian showed a path to a possible solution.

28

THERE ARE A few streets in Earmam shabbier than Mòine Road, but the list is short. The whole area had once been dominated by factories, built in the nineteenth century and spewing out dirt nonstop until the post-war period. Then they became useless and unnecessary and were mostly pulled down to make way for cheap housing, like the flats Dillan Howard lived in. A few streets away, closer to the loch side, there were old factory buildings that had been converted and actually looked rather good, classic buildings allowed to age. These post-war shortcuts were ugly, and even the reasonable effort the occupants made to keep the area neat made no dent in the unsightliness.

It had taken them two hours to find Dillan Howard's address. Sholto parked the car across the road from the entrance to the flats, set back from the road. The council had laid some grass down where the floors of the sprawling factories would once have been. All sorts of stuff had been handled there back in the day: tobacco, whale oil, textiles and anything else the city could lay its grasping hands on.

Darian looked at Sholto and said, 'You want me to handle this one?'

'No, no, I can do it. Better I do, try to make sure none of this gets back to Kotkell. A Sutherland executive getting upset with us. Can you imagine what that'll do for business?'

They got out of the car and went across the road to Howard's flat. It was on the ground floor, and Sholto knocked. The door was opened by a young man, tall and handsome, dark brown hair, and not nearly as unhinged looking as Ally had led them to expect. He had light stubble over the sort of face you could tell would age well, only early twenties now.

The man nodded and said, 'Yes?'

Sholto said 'Dillan Howard?'

'That's me unless you're trouble or wanting money.'

'My name's Sholto Douglas, this is my colleague Darian Ross, we work for an investigations company and we're looking into an assault in the city three nights ago. Could we chat?'

Sholto asked as though he hoped to be refused, but Howard was happy to disappoint him and held the door open. He led them through to a sparse kitchen where they sat at a small, round table. There wasn't much of anything to look at in the kitchen. It was small, with a window looking out at the side of the building next door, and a gap where a washing machine would go.

Dillan said, 'Would you like a cup of tea or something?'

They both said, 'No thanks.'

'What's this about? Private investigation, so you're not cops?'

Sholto said, 'No, we're not, so you don't have to answer anything if you don't want to. We're here about Uisdean Kotkell. You'll have heard he was beaten up outside Himinn the other night?'

'I heard.'

'And what do you think about that?'

'What do I...? I think it's very sad, that's what I think. I was going to go and see him in the hospital today but I heard he's out, back home with his parents. It was a shame what happened to him, he's a good guy.'

'And do you happen to know anything about why this great shame happened to this good guy?'

Dillan leaned back in his chair, his face getting harder and taking on the look of a man hanging onto the end of his short fuse. He said, 'How would I know anything about it?'

'Well, what do you think happened to him?'

'I suppose he must have got jumped, someone got pissed and wanted to be a hardman, or thought they could mug him and make a bit of money. No shortage of young men getting pissed and violent in this city. Surely your investigations have taught you that?'

'So you and him didn't have a big falling out, he didn't dump you? You weren't the one who got pissed and violent, waiting for him outside the club so you could give him a little bit of relationship counselling?'

Howard was smiling dismissively. He looked almost childish when he did. He said, 'Do you think I got in a fight with him, or do you just wish I did so you could pin it on me, get an easy bad guy to point the finger at? That would make it nice and easy for you, go back to Uisdean's father with my head on a pike, because that's who you're working for, isn't it? Private investigation. The police would never be good enough for him; he would always want special treatment for his family and he could pay any price for it. He's a dangerous man, Uisdean's father. All that power. I hope you realise what his reaction would be if you tell him something he doesn't like.'

'I can't tell you who we're working for.'

Dillan laughed at the stiff delivery. 'Oh, you are playing with fire if you're playing with that man.'

This was going round in a circle so Darian interrupted and said, 'Were you and Uisdean in a relationship?'

'A relationship? No. I've known him about a year, we partied together a bit, had some fun, but there was nothing more than that. Neither of us could have dumped the other. If you want a scapegoat you'll have to go look in another field.'

'Do you know anyone who might have had it in for Uisdean?'

'He isn't the sort of guy that goes round making enemies. He's not flash, not a troublemaker, so don't try to blame what happened on him. Some drunk, I don't know, a random attack. I'm sure you'll find a way of wrapping it up without catching anyone and without embarrassing his father.'

Sholto, with surprising force, said, 'We will not wrap it up, we will not. A crime has been committed and we will investigate it fully.'

There was a slightly stunned silence for a few seconds before Darian hurdled over it, saying, 'You hadn't heard anything about someone threatening him, maybe trying to get money off him?'

'No, the only person Uisdean ever complained about was his father and by the time he was done whinging about him there was no time left for anyone else.'

'All right, we'll leave it there.'

They left the building and went back to the car. Sholto looked annoyed by a spiked dead end, no solution but a reminder of the danger that upsetting Durell Kotkell posed. He slammed the car door shut behind him. Darian gave him a look.

'Waste of bloody time, and he didn't need to get that chippy either, as if we're the bad guys.'

He was flushed, looked unsure of himself. For Darian it brought back the memory of Corey in their office, telling them they were hiding there, that Sholto didn't have the guts for real police work and its dangers. He'd lost one verbal battle that didn't matter a damn and he was losing the rag about it. Maybe Corey had a point.

Darian said, 'So what now?'

'We'll try to get the boy on his own, without the father or mother there. He's the last person left who knows more than he's told us.'

They drove back to the office.

DOUGLAS INDEPENDENT RESEARCH

Douglas Independent Research
21 Cage Street
Challaid CH3 4QA

Tel: (01847) 041981
Email: Sholto.Douglas@DouglasIR.sco

Dear Miss Campbell,

I'm writing to inform you of the conclusion of the investigation regarding the financial affairs of Moses Guerra. You will by now be aware that a suspect, Randle Cummins, has been arrested and charged with murder, and that my colleague and I played an active part in uncovering the suspect and securing the charge against him. Overleaf you will find a sheet detailing the work carried out by us on your behalf that led to this conclusion.

Overleaf you will also find a separate sheet detailing the expenses incurred in pursuance of this investigation. I am pleased to say that as the investigation was relatively short the cost to you is much less than previously expected. All expenses are in line with standard practice, as presented to you at the beginning of the investigation, and if you have any questions regarding them then please don't hesitate to contact the office.

While the suspect charged has not yet been convicted, and a trial is yet to occur, I wish to express my relief that we have been able to aid you in this matter. If, as expected, Mr Cummins is convicted then it will take a very dangerous man off the street, and your determination to not let the matter rest was the cause of that. I wish you well for the future.

Yours Sincerely,

Sholto Douglas

Douglas Independent Research

INVESTIGATION INTO FINANCIAL AFFAIRS
OF MOSES GUERRA

By Sholto Douglas, Douglas Independent Research
– For Miss Maeve Campbell

My colleague, Darian Ross, began the investigation at your request, starting with information provided by yourself and another contact. No contacts will be named in this report as all receive strict anonymity as a condition of their assistance.

- Darian began by questioning the waiter, Benigno Holguin, who had been in the alleyway where the victim's body was found, on the night. No new information was gained.

It was at this point that Darian and I began to work together on this case, believing it required as much manpower as we could provide.

- I learned from a separate contact that Randle Cummins had stated that he had previously been a friend of Moses Guerra and had taken a significant sum of money from his flat, with the suggestion that violence may have occurred in the process.
- We carried out research to identify the address of the suspect and made our way there to speak with him.
- We gained access to the house of the suspect and spoke with him at some length about his friendship with Moses and whether he had taken money from the flat. While he denied that he had killed Moses, he did let slip that he had owed a significant sum of money which he had been able to pay off.

At this point it was clear to us that Randle Cummins was a suspect in the murder of Moses Guerra and that the police needed to be informed. They subsequently arrested the suspect.

• As a further part of our investigation my colleague, Darian Ross, was able to confirm that Randle Cummins paid a debt in the region of £18,500, within forty-eight hours of the murder of Moses Guerra.

The suspect has now been charged with murdering Mr Guerra, and we believe the evidence against him is convincing and our work on your behalf concluded.

DOUGLAS INDEPENDENT RESEARCH

Douglas Independent Research   TO   Maeve Campbell
21 Cage Street   44-2 Sgàil Drive
Challaid   Challaid
CH3 4QA   CH8 6DG
Tel (01847) 041981

	JOB	PAYMENT TERMS	DUE DATE
	Researching finances of Moses Guerra	Due on receipt	

QTY	DESCRIPTION	UNIT PRICE	LINE TOTAL
	Travel expense – petrol		£26.52
	Travel expense – rail card		£12.00
	Telephone		£4.60
	Office expenses		£8.00
	Labour		£205.05
		TOTAL	£256.17

Quotation prepared by: Sholto Douglas

To accept this quotation, sign here and return: _____

Thank you for your business.

29

THERE'S NO PARKING on Cage Street, it's pedestrianised after all, so Sholto always parked on the road at the bottom, Dlùth Street. From there it was a short walk for him and Darian to the office. They came round the corner at the bottom of Cage Street and Darian stopped. Sholto kept walking, oblivious, but Darian grabbed his sleeve.

He said, 'You see that guy outside The Song? That's MacDuff.'

Sholto very obviously stared at the young man who was taking the opportunity to have more of Mr Yang's spring rolls. He looked casual, like he wasn't watching for anyone and wasn't in a hurry.

Sholto said, 'Maybe he's just back for the food.'

'He came a long way out of his way to get it.'

They walked up the street to the building, nodding to MacDuff in passing. He looked a little sheepish, Darian thought. They went in and upstairs, Sholto putting the key in the door and finding it already unlocked. That spooked him, and he went paler. He pushed open the door and stepped in to find DI Folan Corey sitting patiently on the chair in front of Sholto's desk, playing the role of the happy visitor. He'd probably been in that office a while and he'd have had a good look round before they turned up. Darian wanted to ask where he'd got a key but Sholto didn't and it was his conversation.

He said, 'Folan, good to see you, how are you, what can we do to help you, would you like a cup of tea?'

Corey ignored the barrage and looked past Sholto to Darian. He glared at him for a few seconds, and then turned back to his former colleague. Sholto had taken his usual seat behind his desk, facing Corey over a stack of folders. The DI ignored Darian completely now, focusing on the cage he knew he could rattle.

'I'm hoping you can help me out, Sholto.'

'I'll try.'

'You see, I have a problem with people harassing me at my work. It started out when they targeted a vital contact of mine.'

'Oh, right.'

'And then they tried to get involved in a large murder inquiry, and are still hampering that inquiry despite the fact a man has been charged with the murder in question.'

'Gee whiz.'

'And now they're getting involved in an assault inquiry handled by my station that has nothing to do with them.'

'Blimey pink.'

'I'm starting to think they're trying to provoke me, maybe hoping I'll do something that gets me into a lot of trouble.'

'*Muirt mhòr.*'

'Are you taking the piss out of me, Sholto?'

'What? No, Folan, no. You know me, I wouldn't do that.'

Corey stared at him a while, watching the nerves twitch on the jowls of the former detective. He said, 'You may not be doing it knowingly, but that doesn't mean it doesn't sit on your shoulders. You have to take responsibility for the things your staff do, Sholto. The buck stops right there.'

Sholto looked down at the spot on his desk Corey was pointing at, and then said, 'Okay.'

Corey turned slightly in the chair to look at Darian, now sitting at his own desk. Corey said, 'Oh yes, I can see a lot of your father in you. Perhaps not as much as is bubbling away in your crooked big brother, but still enough to be obvious. You know, I have a theory that ninety-nine per cent of people under the age of twenty-five are insufferably boring. The thing about most smart young people is not how deluded they are, because most smart people get deluded by their cleverness, but how pretentious and worthy they think they have to be to prove it, always trying to be superior. They haven't been beaten down enough by the world to respect its power. You may actually be a one-per-center.'

It was a sort of compliment, the kind you weren't sure you had received, and Corey was skilled at giving.

Darian didn't bother pointing out that they had been hired by Durell Kotkell, because Corey would have known that already. He also didn't bother pointing out that he considered Cummins innocent, because Corey would know that, too. Instead he said nothing as Corey got up from the chair and strolled over to the door he'd already made his own uninvited way in through.

Corey looked at Sholto and said, 'I'm sure a skilled investigator like you will find out who's been harassing me and put a stop to it, won't you, Sholto?'

'Yes, Folan.'

'It's DI Corey.'

He left the office. Sholto stared back at the spot on the desk where the imaginary buck was still sitting. It was obvious he was furious with Corey, but the cop was gone and, even if he wasn't, Sholto wasn't going to aim his guns in that direction.

'You're still working with Maeve Campbell? I told you not to, we're finished with her. I posted her report and bill this morning, so that's it, we're officially done with her. Tell me you're finished with her, Darian.'

Darian looked at Sholto and then looked away without saying anything.

Sholto threw up his hands and said, 'Ach, I don't know why I bother trying to teach you anything, all my years of experience and you won't listen. You're like a dog staring at a seagull on a chimney pot, convinced you can jump and catch it the second it takes off, and I can't make you understand.'

There were a few hours of awkward silence in that office until the security officer at Glendan called and told Sholto they would pay for two more weeks of watching the Murdoch Shipping warehouses. The promise of more easy money cheered Sholto up no end, and two weeks sounded like long enough to spot something that could be dressed up in the clothes of criminality. He remained convinced that it was impossible for any of those old shipping companies to be entirely clean; if Murdoch were, then they'd be the first in a thousand years.

'You go and sit and watch those warehouses. Don't get seduced by them if they show you a bit of leg, don't get led astray by their whispers, and don't go sticking your nose into Corey's business because they tell you to. Just watch them.

Can you do that?'

'I'm going.'

'Aye, good, and you can call up Maeve Campbell and tell her the party's over as well.'

As Darian got up from his desk he said, 'I'm going round to see her tonight. I'll talk to her about it then.'

'Going round to... That's the problem, once you see her you're under her spell like that old witch with the snakes on her head. Just use the bloody phone so you don't have to get beguiled by her, it's what they were invented for. There's no helping you, there really isn't.'

Darian left the office and headed for his usual spot in The Knarr café, watching the warehouses. He was thinking about Maeve, about Corey, and about how Sholto's attempts to educate Darian were really efforts at helping himself.

30

IT WAS DARK by the time he got to Sgàil Drive, but it always seemed to be dark on Sgàil Drive. This time Maeve was ready for him, fully dressed and armed with information.

She opened the door, smiled, and said, 'Come in.'

He walked through to the living area and sat on the same couch he'd been on last time. He watched her walk out of the room and come back thirty seconds later with her notebook and a bottle of cheap wine clutched in one hand and two glasses in the other. She filled the glasses quickly and passed one to him. He took a sip and was careful not to wince.

'I got my bill from your boss today. You're not cheap for a day's work, you two.'

'He said he sent it. He might round up the expenses now and then, but he's not a cheat, that's the going rate. I take it the report told you nothing you didn't already know.'

'Not a damn thing. He wrote about it being an investigation into financial affairs and then talked about the murder without saying anything much.'

'He's always careful with that. Doesn't like the client knowing too much, especially when the client is you. He told me to call you and tell you I'm finished helping you. We had Corey in the office today, warning us about this, and other things.'

'Shit. Corey. So are you finished helping me?'

'I didn't call, did I?'

Maeve smiled and said, 'Have you found out anything?'

'No.'

'Right, so here's what I've got. The first thing I did was go and find out who the best friend of Moses from the list was. None of the big-money people, but I thought about which one he talked about most and I went to see him. I don't think now that he was that big a mate of Moses, but he was willing to speak to me. His name's Nick Palazzo. Have you heard of him?'

'Doesn't ring a bell, apart from being on the list.'

'If you'd ever met him you would remember. He dresses to be seen from space and I'm pretty sure he's crazy enough to be locked up as a precaution. He'll burn the world down one day. So far his criminal life is just working for other people, so he's probably under the radar and he was just using Moses to clean up the small amounts of cash he got occasionally paid. There's no way Nick was involved, he knew nothing about it and he rabbited on for ages about Moses and how good a guy he was. Sometimes, the way he bangs on like that, I think it was sarcastic, but he was surprised by what happened, that much was true. I wrote down all the little things he said, like you suggested, but I can't see much to help us.'

Maeve held up the notebook for him to see the scribbled writing across two pages. She was excited and her movements were jerky, caught up in the thrill of the chase. It made Darian smile, remembering that he had been the same way when he started out, not that long ago, Sholto always telling him to damp down the fire.

'So we can scratch Captain Crazy off the list?'

'Yeah, we can. But I had time to go to someone else on the list, Frang Hunter. Now, I know he's a proper criminal type, so you've probably heard of him.'

'Yeah, I have, and he's exactly the sort of person that you shouldn't be talking to on your own. He's a violent criminal and he's sent people to Heilam for less than digging around in his financial affairs.'

'Oh please, Frang was fine. You need to stop thinking that every criminal is a terrible threat to every decent person they meet, that's naïve. And you need to stop thinking that a woman on her own can't go and have a conversation with someone without being in terrible peril. I didn't need rescuing and I didn't need you there to hold my hand. If I'd turned up with a private detective in tow then I might have needed rescuing, but so would you.'

'I'm not a private detective, I'm an investigative researcher, but point taken.'

Maeve smiled at his sulking tone and said, 'So I went round and met him and his wife, Brenda, who was there as well, and they both told me how sad they were about what had happened to Moses. I asked Frang what he thought about the killing and he sort of clammed up, used the whole "they've got someone for it so that must be who did it" argument. I said I wasn't sure and, Brenda, she gave him a nudge and then he admitted he wasn't sure either. The way he saw it, Cummins couldn't have killed Moses even if he'd wanted to because he didn't have the guts or the muscle. Moses wasn't big, but he could handle someone like that. And there were much better candidates that might have used Cummins and his debt as a shield. When he started talking he was going on about the kind of people who did business with Moses, how he didn't know who many of them were but some of them had to be serious. Then he said the people with the money to use Cummins as a shield, pay off his debt in exchange for him taking the spotlight for a while, weren't just the people that used Moses, they were the people that Moses used.'

'Meaning?'

'The businesses that Moses cleaned the money through and the people who ran them. According to Frang, a lot of those people weren't just small-business owners looking for a quick buck on the side; some of them were major companies who want a slice of the dirty market. He thinks some might have been major companies working with criminals who use the legitimate to cover their criminal earnings, especially when it goes offshore to Caledonia and back.'

'I thought of them, but, I don't know, the way it happened didn't seem professional.'

'Maybe the person they sent botched it, or deliberately made it look amateurish. It makes some sense, doesn't it, that we've been pointing in the wrong direction with this? We've been looking at the people who used Moses instead the people Moses used.'

'It does make sense, yeah.'

Darian took another sip of wine, which reminded him how appalling it was. He looked across at Maeve and saw how excited she was by the progress they had made, her face flushed. She was looking down at her notebook with an intense expression, and then looked up at Darian.

She said, 'What?'

He shook his head a little and said, 'It's good to make some progress, but we have to remember that the chances of us getting where we want to go are slim. We have to find proof, real proof, that we can put in front of a judge.'

'I know that, it needs to be something that can stand on its own two feet without us propping it up, but I think you and me can do it. I think you and me make a hell of an us.'

'Yeah, I think we do, too.'

He finished the glass of wine out of iron-stomached politeness and refused a top-up. Darian was tired; he needed some rest, so he got up to go. At the door Maeve gave him a brief hug of thanks. Her body pressed against his felt good.

31

LETTING MAEVE DO all the work and take all the risks felt like a failure to Darian. That was why he was up early the following morning, taking a detour up to Earmam before he went to work. Down Caol Lane and into Sigurds to interrupt the morning of a woman he should have been sensible enough to avoid. If Maeve was meeting with dangerous people then the least he could do was match her daring commitment.

Viv was standing at the bar, in her usual spot, with no drink in front of her, which meant she must have just arrived. She was wearing tight trousers and a coat, looking tremendously respectable and refined to Darian. She looked like she was taking a drinks break halfway through the school run. He stepped up beside her and got an annoyed glance.

'I'll pay for your next one.'

Viv said, 'I don't pay for drinks here.'

'Free drinks? Any tips on how you swing an arrangement like that?'

'What do you want?'

Darian took a look around at the pub. There wasn't another soul in there, not even the barman, although he could hear crates rattling in a backroom behind the bar. Seemed like the barman always found something to do in any other part of the building when Viv was there. Despite that, Darian kept his voice down when he spoke.

'I need to ask you a couple more questions, nothing that'll cause you any trouble.'

She looked hard at him when she said, 'You're nothing but trouble.'

'Don't be dramatic. I gave you fair warning of bad weather heading your way last time, and all I have this time are a couple of very minor questions. I want to ask you about the money Randle Cummins paid you. You said he paid it all off soon after Moses was killed.'

'I remember what I said; it's a brain inside my skull, not a cabbage.'

'You said he paid it in full, in a oner, this guy who didn't have a penny to his name beforehand, and he didn't tell you anything about it? He wasn't reading from a script when he handed it over?'

'I wouldn't know.'

'What sort of state was he in when he delivered the cash?'

'You think I was there waiting for him, my heart aflutter?'

'Someone must have seen him.'

'No, he dropped it at the unit.'

'The unit?'

She sighed through her nose and said, 'We have an industrial unit off Tobacco Road; we use it as a drop-off point.'

At that moment the barman emerged from the door behind the bar, wiping his hands on a dirty blue towel, finished with his crates and ready to serve the woman he dared not leave dry. As he moved towards the more expensive whisky bottles he nodded and said, 'Morning, Viv.'

'*Thalla is cac.*'

Without any hint that he'd been offended, the barman turned quickly on his heel and disappeared back through the door.

Viv turned to Darian and said, 'With a lot of people we pick the money up from them. If they're hard to get to, or they suddenly find themselves with cash they want to be relieved of, there's a drop point. The unit is open, there are lock boxes inside. You put the money and a message in the open box, close the box and it locks automatically. They're welded to the floor, not that anyone's stupid enough to steal from us.'

'So there was no one at the unit to see him deliver, and I guess no camera.'

'Ha, good guess, Rebus. Of course there's no bloody camera at our drop-off point. We're trying to encourage people to use it, not chase them away. He left a note in the box with the money.'

'Do you have the note?'

'Do I have the note? You think I keep notes from people like Randle Cummins? They're not love letters, scented and kept in a little shoebox, tied with a ribbon.'

'What did the note say?'

Viv gave him a look and said, 'You started this saying you were only going to ask me a couple of questions, we're past a couple now, in case you're innumerate. I don't remember what the note said, the same nonsense they always say. Here's your money, it's all there, the debt is repaid. They always put that last line in about the debt being cleared, as though we might not realise.'

'All right, I'll leave you to your breakfast.'

'If you think I'll ever repeat a word of what I've said here in front of a cop or a judge you'll be crying yourself to sleep.'

'I expect nothing more of you.'

Darian was halfway to the door when Viv said, 'Say hello to Sorley for me, and remind him to remember what I told him.'

It was the same instruction she'd left him with last time, so it meant something to her. Darian said nothing, and walked out of the bar.

THE CHALLAID GAZETTE AND ADVERTISER

07 Mar 2018

LETTERS TO THE EDITOR

THE GANNTAIR REPORT

Dear Sir,

I'm writing after reading in your paper the article *New Report Condemns Conditions in The Ganntair* (01/03/18) and being angry with the reaction to it. In your report council leader Morag Blake (Liberal Party) said that she supported the new leadership of the prison and would work with them to improve standards. Hasn't she said this before? Hasn't she said this every year for the last three?

I have experience of the prison through my family, and I know that what was in the Inspectorate Report was only the tip of the iceberg, everyone with family at the prison knows. No one wants to talk about it because no prisoner wants to become a target for the staff or for the gangs that really control the place.

The report said that use of force was high and records of it poor. That's because use of force by staff is routine and the prison leadership doesn't want it properly reported because it would show how little control they have over prisoners and how violence is the only answer they have to that lack of control. That's not so much the staff's fault, it's because there are far too few of them to begin with.

I know, and everyone who visits the prison more than once a year like the inspectors knows, that prisoners aren't safe in The Ganntair. The culture of violence is rife and the only way most prisoners can have any safety at all is to join a gang they previously had nothing to do with. Young men are going in there for offences that had nothing to do with gang violence and they're coming out tied to gangs because it's the only way to survive. Again, the prison and its leadership know this and have done nothing to stop it.

Drugs are common in the prison, and criminal business is

conducted in the open. There are men in there who would like to change their lives for the better, get rehabilitated, but they can't because the conditions make it impossible.

Convener Blake needs to stop supporting failing leadership in the prison and start taking action. How many years will we keep seeing the same report and the same reaction from our political leaders? How bad does the situation have to get? The understaffing and completely outdated facilities mean that we will be talking about this as a tragedy before long.

I know there isn't much sympathy for families like mine, with members in The Ganntair. People are there because they broke the law and people want them to be punished, but how will anyone ever be rehabilitated when the environment they're going into is far more dangerous and criminal than the one they're being taken out of? That's the question the convener and the prison leadership have to answer.

(Name and address supplied)

THE NAME GAME

Dear Sir,
I read with some amusement your editorial (03/03/18) re the campaign underway to change the name of Bank district. Your argument appeared to be that as it has been called Bank for three centuries, and we don't know the origins of the previous Ciùin Brae name, it would be pointless to change now, but isn't that an argument to the contrary?

We know that it was called some variation of Ciùin Brae for far longer than three hundred years, and we know too why it was changed. The shift to Bank has nothing to do with the location on the south bank, every district in the city is on one or other bank of the loch, but an attempt to satisfy the industry (cont.)

32

'THROUGH HERE.'

The man leading Darian wasn't in uniform, just a plain middle-aged man in a suit. He was involved in administration at the prison at a high enough level to get Darian an unrecorded meeting with a prisoner. He was a contact Darian and Sorley had worked together to cultivate, one of several in the prison they used to keep updated about their father.

He knew the prison in Earmam well, went to visit his father every month. The three kids all went on separate weeks, their attempt to make sure their father always had someone to speak to and a visit to look forward to. He was an isolated man in there, with very few people it was safe for an ex-detective to be around. He always told them he was doing fine, but they didn't expect him to tell them the truth when he was trying to protect his children from it.

The man, who we won't name because he shouldn't have been helping Darian, said, 'Your father's still doing well, far as I can tell.'

'Good.'

'Wait here.'

He had led Darian into a small office on the second floor, sparsely furnished and obviously never used. There was an empty desk with a chair on either side and a metal filing cabinet by the door with the top drawer missing and nothing in the others. There were no bars on the large window, but you'd have needed to learn to fly before you tried to jump.

Darian looked out of the window at the wing jutting out opposite the one he was in, and then down at the yard between them. His father was in that wing somewhere, that sprawling place populated by some of the worst examples of humanity Challaid had produced in the last half-century. The female prisoners were sent down to the central belt, Cornton Vale. The minor offenders went to softer prisons, Huntly usually. The paedophiles were sent to Peterhead because they had a rehabilitation programme there and any sent to The Ganntair would have had slim chance of leaving with the same number of body parts they'd possessed upon arrival. They protected the paedophiles, but they sent his father here, among men he had locked up. They had insisted, the prosecution arguing it was necessary to show that Edmund Ross wouldn't get preferential treatment because he was a former police officer. The family all saw it as an act of malice.

The door opened and a prison officer shoved Randle Cummins into the room with gleeful force. The prisoner looked over his shoulder and tutted as the door was closed, the officer on the outside, and then looked round at Darian.

'Oh, it's you.'

'Yeah, it's all me. Sit down, Randle.'

He did as he was told, a dirty look the extent of his protest. He was still as sallow and blotchy as before and now he was picking at a small cut high in his forehead with dirty fingernails. As he sat at the table he said, 'What do you want? Come to try and throw more shite at me, have you?'

'Actually, no, I'm trying to wipe off some of the shite you're already covered in. They've charged you with murder because they know they can get a conviction. You don't have to be guilty, Randle, you just have to do a good job of looking like it, and so far it's uncanny.'

'It won't get to court, I know that.'

'If there wasn't enough to get you to court you would be sitting in your grim little house right now, instead of this relative luxury.'

Cummins blinked heavily and said, 'I know what your game is; you're here to try and get me to say something stupid, try and trick me to make me look guilty. I'm not daft. You say you're here to help me but I got to help you first, and then you get me to say something that gets me in even worse fucking trouble.'

'You've been charged with murder. How much worse do you think I can make it?'

'It won't get to court.'

'I'm trying to help you here, Randle, but you have to be willing to help yourself.'

'Uh-huh, here it comes, here it comes.'

'I'm going to talk and you're not going to interrupt me, Randle, got that? They have charged you with murdering Moses Guerra and stealing money from his flat. Within hours of Moses being killed, someone went to the Creags' unit and paid off your debt in full, leaving a note claiming to be from you. I don't believe for one second that it was you who delivered that cash.'

Cummins looked like a man whose brain was falling over its own feet trying to find an answer. There was nothing behind his eyes to help him, so he just scoffed and looked towards the window.

'Who paid your debt off for you?'

No answer.

'Someone came to you and told you to take the fall, didn't they? They'd handle your debts and make sure you were looked after in here, maybe get you out nice and early. Was that it?'

'What the hell are you talking about? You've lost it, pal.'

'Someone is making a mug out of you, Randle, and they haven't had to work hard. What was it, huh? They pay off your debts and you spend a few months in here before they make sure you get released? Is that what they told you?'

'Oh, *dùin do chlab.*'

'You're in here and they're out there and you still think they're going to come back for you. You've been left behind, Randle. The only way the case against you falls down is if someone knocks it over and right now I'm the only one trying. You can scream and bawl for their help all you want but they've abandoned you. That was always part of the setup you fell for.'

'You're more full of a shite than a farmer's field. I'll be out of here soon enough, it won't go before a judge.'

Darian leaned back in his chair and shook his head. Sitting in a prison office, looking at an innocent man making a bad job of trying to look guilty. Whoever he had done the deal with, Cummins trusted them more than he was ever going to trust Darian. They had paid eighteen and a half grand for that privilege, and they were obviously still providing for their patsy. Cummins hadn't run up that debt on the outside paying for home improvement, and whichever addiction it had fed was probably being maintained in The Ganntair.

'I'm going to keep trying to get you out of here, because no one else will.'

'Ha, you're priceless. It's your bloody fault that I'm in here at all.'

Darian stood and led Cummins to the door. The man in the suit had been waiting with a prison officer out in the corridor, the latter leading Cummins back to a life at least as comfortable as it had been outside. The man in the suit led Darian back down towards the rear entrance the staff used and a long walk out towards a back gate that needed two members of staff to unlock. They'd gone to more trouble to help Darian than he thought his payments to them warranted, which made him wonder how much Sorley was doing to keep them loyal.

On the walk to the exit and the taxi ride up to Mormaer Station, Darian was trying to glue together the broken pieces of information he'd gathered. Cummins had wanted to be arrested. The drunken talk about Moses Guerra and taking money from him, the debt being paid within hours of the killing, that was choreographed to imitate guilt. And Cummins was so sure of his position. Darian got the train down to Glendan Station and went into the office for a long, slow day of boringly honest work.

33

MAEVE WAS WAITING for him at her flat, looking more excited than he did when she opened the door. They went through to the living area in what was becoming routine.

As he sat Darian said, 'I've had a couple of useful chats, although whatever direction they move us in, it isn't forward. I do know for sure now that Cummins didn't pay his own debt, someone paid it for him. That's more evidence that he probably didn't do it. I talked to him.'

'In prison?'

'Yeah, but it was off the record. I spoke to him and he didn't speak back other than to point out that he doesn't trust me. He was very confident that he's going to get out, and quite soon. I don't know if he was in on it from the start, but he's in on something now. Someone killed Moses and then paid off the debt, maybe then they went to Cummins and told him he had no choice but to play guilty for a while.'

'He's going to get life for someone else?'

'He doesn't think it'll be life, he's certain it won't even get to court. A few months and he'll be back on the street, debt-free and able to return to the crumbling wreck of a life he had before.'

Maeve frowned and said, 'If someone else clears his name, isn't there a chance they implicate themselves in the process?'

'I don't think that's occurred to Cummins. Someone used him, got him to take a fall, and by the time he realises they're not going to bother getting him back out, no one will believe his accusations. He won't know who was behind it all; Cummins will only have met a third or fourth or fifth party.'

Maeve nodded and said, 'Well, while you were digging those bones up, I was doing some handy work of my own. I've been writing down way more notes, the stuff that everyone has said to me about this, going right back to when the police were questioning me about it. I think it was MacDuff who mentioned Moses' paperwork, about how they hadn't found any. I shrugged it off because of course he wouldn't keep any when it was all incriminating to him and the people he was working with. But when I spoke to Frang he mentioned documents. It was just a passing comment, laughing about how complicated they were, but Moses always knew how to work it out. When the police went through the flat they didn't find anything, neither did you and your boss.'

'No, we didn't, but we checked thoroughly.'

'Maybe you did, but I think I know where his hiding place in the flat was. I thought it was just cash he kept in there. I was going to go check it when I knew the coast was clear.'

Darian gave her a look.

'Oh, come off it, you think Moses would have preferred I left it for DI Corey to find and slip into his pocket, or for the next people who live in the flat to stumble across it and take a holiday on his efforts?'

He said, 'Fine.'

'No, not fine. Don't give me that look and say that as if you're judging me. That money would come to no good, but

I could use it properly, the way it should be used. I can put it towards finding the person who did this. Isn't that a better use?'

Darian raised his hands to calm her. 'Okay, I get that, the money would be taken away and used for no good, but you should have been honest with me. If I'd known he was hiding things in the flat me and Sholto could have found it earlier.'

'I am being as honest with you as I can be. It's not that long since DI Corey was accusing me of being some deranged killer. It could have been me instead of Cummins playing the scapegoat, only it would have been because the police round here can't be bothered looking past the first target they bump into.'

She was close to tears. Darian got up and went across to the other couch and sat next to her. 'That's not going to happen, not now. We're going to do all we can to find out who did this, and if the money can be used to help then I'm sure that's what Moses would have wanted.'

He was speaking of a man he had never met, but Maeve didn't point that out. She looked him in the eye and put a cold hand on his cheek. 'I need your help, Darian. I would do it on my own, but with your help I feel like we can do this. We're a good fit together, you and me. It works.'

'It does.'

There was a moment when they were half an inch apart. Maeve leaned in and their lips touched, but she moved to the side and turned it into a hug that lasted for thirty seconds. She was right, they were a good fit.

When she pulled back Darian said, 'You still have your key?'

'I do.'

34

MAEVE DROVE THEM south to Seachran Drive. They parked along from Moses' flat and sat in the car for a few minutes, watching for any sign of the charming Challaid Police Force. They had to hurry, up the stairs and Maeve fishing the key out of her pocket to get them into the flat. She closed the door quietly behind them.

Maeve led the way through to the kitchen and opened the door to a shallow cupboard. There were shelves on the back wall and just enough room for a skinny person to step inside. Sholto had opened the door and glanced around when they were in the flat, but hadn't seen anything that surprised him.

Maeve said, 'Hold on.'

She stepped across the kitchen and pulled open a drawer, fished about among some utensils and came up with a curiously small screwdriver. She walked back over and said, 'I know it was in here, and I know he used this, but I don't know exactly where or how.'

It doesn't take long to find something odd when you know what odd thing you're looking for. When they moved a dustpan and brush and a small bag of tools out of the corner they saw the screws on the floorboards. The tops of them were painted with the same varnish as the wood, but you could see the scratches the screwdriver had made and could feel the dents they made in the wood with your fingers.

Darian unscrewed them and lifted the board, pulling out three envelopes from the small space underneath.

He said, 'Here we go.'

Maeve took them over to the kitchen table and they went through the three of them. All the envelopes were open, some of the papers pushed in sideways or badly folded.

Maeve said, 'He wouldn't have done that, no way. He was tidy with his work.'

All of the papers were either letters or invoices, and the only name mentioned on any of them was Moses Guerra. The only sums of money mentioned were small and references to money he could easily have acquired legitimately. It implicated no one.

Maeve said, 'This can't be right, it can't be. There's no reason why he would have this screwed down under a floorboard, there's nothing here worth hiding. There must have been something else.'

She was upset and Darian knew why. She had convinced herself this was going to be a breakthrough and instead they'd found a raised middle finger.

Darian said, 'Maybe he kept other things somewhere else.'

'No, I don't think he had anywhere else. The person who killed him must have known about it, they must have cleared out everything that could implicate them when they killed him.'

'Would he have told them about that place?'

Maeve shook her head. 'I don't know... No, probably not, not unless it was forced out of him somehow, maybe when they were attacking him. Or if it was someone that was really close to him, but I can't think who that would have been. I don't know.'

Darian said nothing. He took the envelopes and slipped the useless letters back into them. He wiped them with his sleeve before he put them back in their needless hiding place and screwed the single board back down and covered it again. Maeve was still sitting at the kitchen table.

Darian said, 'Come on, let's go.'

She drove him up towards Bakers Station so he could make his way home from there. It was busy outside the station, hard to find a parking space, and there was a lot of noise and light. Darian sensed the change in her mood. The excitement of catching a killer was waning as they stumbled closer to ugly truths and awareness of their own limitations. The dirtier the case became, the less of a noble cause it seemed, the less of a giddy thrill.

When she stopped on a single yellow line he turned to her and said, 'Will you be okay?'

'I'll be fine. I don't need the heroic private detective to hold me through the night, if that's what you're suggesting.'

She was looking at him mockingly, a hint of a smile as she got her composure back. Darian said, 'I just thought you seemed rattled, that was all.'

'I was, but I've stopped rattling now. I just assumed it would be someone, I don't know, distant. Now I think it might have been someone close to him and it upsets me that I don't know who that could be. Maybe I didn't know him as well as I thought. And I'm worried it's going to be someone I know, and that's a weird feeling, that I might be hunting down a friend. It doesn't change anything, though, I'm just as determined to catch whoever did it.'

'So am I.'

Maeve touched his hand and then let go. It felt strange being so close while they talked about her murdered ex-boyfriend. It felt insulting.

'You noticed there was no cash in those envelopes either, so my chances of paying you Sholto's going rate for this are pretty slim now.'

Darian smiled. 'I'll be generous when I put my bill together.'

He stepped out of the car and watched her drive away. Darian took the convoluted route home again, getting the train down to Bank Station and leaving by the south exit. It lengthened the walk home as a means of avoiding Gallowglass, who might not even have been there. It gave him time to walk in the cold air, trying to think about the case and the little more he had learned. His mind wasn't playing ball. All he could think about was Maeve, the touch of her hand, the smell of her. It was unprofessional, but it made him feel happy, and sometimes that matters more.

THE CHALLAID GAZETTE AND ADVERTISER

17 Feb 2018

CONCERNS RAISED AGAIN OVER HOUSING CRISIS

In an endless echo of worries highlighted repeatedly over the last ten years, a housing charity has brought up the issue of affordable accommodation in Challaid. A recent survey has shown that rates of homelessness are continuing to rise, with the average house price in the city now exceeding £210,000, with the increase being driven by rocketing prices on the west side of the loch where average prices are now approaching £400,000.

The survey of house prices has again raised the issue of availability on the east side, with particularly acute problems in Earmam and Whisper Hill. Rates of homelessness there continue to be high, with the city council under increasing fire regarding its housing policy. With so few new properties being developed in those areas, landlords have been able to raise prices unchallenged, knowing demand vastly outstrips supply.

When we reached out to the council for a response to the survey they released a statement saying, 'Challaid City Council takes seriously its obligation to improve housing availability and conditions for all residents in the city. We have already instigated a policy encouraging owners of brownfield sites to develop them for housing and this will begin to show results in the coming year. We have also made clear our determination to ensure that landlords charge fair rent for their properties, but do not accept that a rent cap will help solve a complex problem. Finally, we will soon put forward new plans to expand developments in Heilam as part of a long-term strategy for increasing housing stock and improving housing conditions in the city.'

It has already been pointed out that this statement bears a striking resemblance to one released in the wake of a similar survey carried out two years ago. The problem of housing on the east side is one that has rumbled within Challaid for generations, too many people living in cramped conditions with the only people benefiting being the landlords. Solutions have repeatedly been sought but not delivered, and Fair Housing Challaid, the charity who carried out the latest survey, has stated that it expects nothing to change. There is no will among large developers to build on land they own on the east side while there are sites on the south bank and west side that can provide far greater returns, with the marina development on the south bank a notable example.

There is another, less often mentioned, problem exacerbating the issue. With house prices going ever upward on the west side, the Barton district has become something of a super-rich ghetto, and the mere rich have been pushed further south. This has the knock-on effect of pushing up prices around the south bank, making it impossible for anyone on average incomes to think about moving off the east side. As prices continue to rise the inevitable consequence will be a creeping unaffordability, with Bakers Moor the next area to rise out of reach for most, and the crisis in Earmam and Whisper Hill will become even more acute.

35

THEY'D PARKED FURTHER down Parnassus Drive because Sholto didn't feel the Fiat was worthy of a spot on the Kotkell family driveway. From the street they could see a large garage on the opposite side of the driveway to the house, the sort of building that could hold at least three cars, and it was a fair guess the Fiat didn't belong among the company it would keep there. Not that it belonged out on the street either, mind you. Parnassus Drive is about the richest of the rich streets up in the north of Barton.

Sholto tried to comb what was left of his hair in the rear-view mirror with his fingers, wanting to look presentable. He said to Darian, 'I hope they don't have a dog. I get nervous around dogs and rich people.'

They walked up the long drive, admiring the manicured front garden. Sholto took a guess at the gardening bill and puffed out his cheeks. He couldn't wrap his head around the money on casual display. He said, 'Imagine having the money to stay here and then choosing to stay here. Give me enough dosh to buy a house round here and I'd be off somewhere sunny.'

Darian pressed the doorbell and a dog started barking and a rich person opened the door. Leala Kotkell looked down on the two men her husband had hired and sighed, her small features crumpling into a frown. She said, 'What do you want?'

Darian took the lead, saying, 'We'd like to speak with your son, please, Mrs Kotkell.'

'My husband's not home.'

'That's quite all right; it's just your son we need a chat with. He's in, I take it.'

She didn't like being spoken to that way, and there was a moment when it looked like she was going to turn them away. Instead she opened the door for them. She led them through to what was presumably a study, a desk and two leather couches, no TV, bookcases against three walls and a large bay window looking out across the front garden. Leala Kotkell went to fetch her son, but not without a backward glance to show how reluctant she was to leave these two chancers alone with the valuables.

When she was gone Sholto, standing at the window, said, 'A cop's salary was probably the best I could do with my life, but you're smart enough to have stuff like this if you'd picked a better career than working with me.'

'Aye, well, I think I'd rather have the one-bedroom flat and a proper job.'

'Mm, maybe you aren't as smart as I thought.'

Uisdean Kotkell walked into the room by himself, still sporting a few fetching cuts and bruises that added a dash of purple to his boyish face. Darian and Sholto had both seen much worse injuries plenty of times before on people who insisted they were no big deal.

Darian said, 'Uisdean, how are you?'

'I'm okay, fine. I'll be fine.'

He sat on the couch opposite them and Darian and Sholto shared a quick look. Darian said, 'Have you thought of any other details about what happened to you? Is there anything else you can tell us about the attack?'

'Uh, no, nothing. I told you everything I can remember at the hospital.'

He seemed nervous, a young man trying to be polite but worried his good manners would invite more questions and prolong the ordeal.

Darian nodded and said, 'So you haven't thought of a reason why someone might want to attack you?'

'No.'

'One of the people we talked to in the course of our investigation was Dillan Howard. We suspected him for a while, but I don't think he did it, but I did wonder if maybe someone attacked you because of your relationship with him.'

'I don't have a relationship with him.'

'Friendship, then.'

'We just hung around a bit, went to the same clubs, that's all. I don't see what that has to do with this.'

'He's a bit of a lad, Dillan, from what we've heard. Maybe someone thought they could rattle him a little by rattling the hell out of you.'

'That's nuts, he has loads of people closer to him than me.'

'Someone was waiting for you, Uisdean, watching out for you. I don't think this was random and I think you know why it wasn't.'

'No.'

The door to the study opened and Leala Kotkell walked in and sat next to her son. Darian looked at Sholto and gave him the nod to take over. He was fresh out of questions and figured it was probably time to say a polite goodbye and leave this waste of time behind.

Sholto said, 'What we'll probably try to do next is go public, get the word out about what happened and see if someone who was outside the club that night will come forward. It'll mean a lot of people finding out about it all, but that's what it takes sometimes.'

Sholto looked at Uisdean and Uisdean looked back, silent. Sholto's expression suggested he didn't like trying to lean this hard on the kid, but it was one of the few remaining ways of tempting the truth out of him. It had no effect.

Uisdean said, 'Good luck. If you'll excuse me, I have a headache.'

Uisdean got up and walked out of the room. His mother stood and looked at the two of them with hatred and said, 'Now that you've made my son ill perhaps you'll consider your work here done and leave.'

Sholto said as he got up, 'Sorry, Mrs Kotkell, we certainly didn't want to make the boy sick, we just want to try to resolve this as quickly as possible, for his own sake. I don't blame him for having headaches, though, it can be very traumatising, getting beaten up and then having to go over it again afterwards so carefully, so many times.'

If her mood softened at the sound of an apology it was imperceptible. She led them out of the study and to the front door.

36

LEALA KOTKELL OPENED the front door for them and
Sholto went out first. He stopped in his tracks on the top
step, blocking Darian's exit. Looking over Sholto's shoulder,
Darian caught a glimpse of what had caused the breakdown
ahead of him. A large, sleek car was in the driveway now, its
engine still running and the driver behind the wheel. The man
who had been in the back was out and walking fast across to
the front door, a furious look on his face, and Durell Kotkell
did fury like a pro. If Leala had phoned her husband as soon
as Darian and Sholto arrived, then that driver must have put
Jim Clark to shame getting up from Bank in that time. Kotkell
could afford the speeding fines, although how his driver
found roads clear enough to speed on is an otherworldly sort
of mystery.

'Why exactly are you here without informing me first?'

He stood with his hands on his hips, a hard expression that
was supposed to convey rising anger and provoke the subject
into trying to placate him. It probably worked on his many
staff.

Before either of them could answer, Leala said, 'They upset
Uisdean, upset him terribly. He's had to go back to bed with
another headache because of these men you hired.'

There was venom in those last few words and it was directed at all three people in front of her, although the sneer in the word 'men' was just for Sholto and Darian. Sholto turned and looked at Leala with a hurt expression, as though she had betrayed a confidence. He said, 'We were just asking a few questions relating to our investigations, trying to do the right thing, that's all.'

Durell said, 'That's all? The man who assaulted my son is still out there and the most you've achieved on my money is to upset my son further.'

His tone was mocking and Darian had heard enough of it. 'We had a few questions for him to help us rule out things that related to what we've uncovered so far. We were hired to do all we could to catch the attacker, and that means asking questions, even if they're sometimes uncomfortable.'

'Uncomfortable? What uncomfortable questions do you think you have the right to ask my son?'

Sholto said, 'Well, I'm sure you don't want to talk about this out on the doorstep.'

'I asked the question on the doorstep and you can provide me with the answer here as well.'

Given the gaps between houses on the street they would have needed a loudspeaker for the neighbours to overhear them, so Darian said, 'We asked him about his relationships, whether he was still in touch with someone we had thought might have been involved in the incident, and we can now rule that out.'

'Relationships? You think if this was some strop over a boy my son wouldn't have said? I can assure you both he is a very responsible young man; he would not be keeping it to himself if it was something as mundane as that. Bloody hell, I would expect even the halfwits in uniform at Challaid Police could have solved that little puzzle.'

Sholto breathed out a sigh of relief that Darian had to cover by talking over it. 'As it happens, we agree with you. It has nothing to do with his private life. But our investigation led us in that direction and it's right and proper that we gather all the information before we ruled it out. We need to be thorough.'

'Thorough enough to upset both my son and my wife, both of whom have been through enough of an ordeal without you piling in on top of it. I'm beginning to think I may have hired the wrong people.'

He looked at them with an expression that was designed to be a challenge. Darian could feel his temperature rising, ready to snap back, when Sholto said, 'Of course we're very sorry if you feel that way, Mr Kotkell. We were hired to get a result, to make sure we found the person responsible, and we weren't going to hold back in doing that. I'm sorry it's arrived here.'

Kotkell scoffed and said, 'I should sack the pair of you, go and find someone with more good sense, which wouldn't require much of a manhunt, but I won't. You two need to buck up your ideas, start putting some proper effort into this instead of chasing easy options. I'll give you a week, and if you haven't made progress by then my reaction will be very bloody notable.'

His tone made it clear it was time to get the hell off his front step and into the city to look for his son's attacker. They scuttled down the drive and along the street to where the Fiat was parked. There was another car along the road that actually looked like it was in the same price range, and presumably belonged to someone's cleaner. They got in and Sholto started driving, eager to clear out of Barton.

Darian said, 'The man's an arsehole.'

'Aye, but the thing about arseholes is that they can cause a terrible stink. We need to work out what the attack was all about and if it wasn't his bedroom business than we don't have a single lead.'

'Why didn't he sack us? A guy like that, upset with us, thinking we've done a bad job, why didn't he sack us?'

'Bloody hell, Darian. Don't talk us out of work. You've brought us enough bad luck this week already.'

Sholto kept driving, and Darian kept thinking about Kotkell and his surprising reprieve. A man who probably sacked people every day of his working life and could afford to replace them with any investigator of his choosing and yet he had kept them on. Darian thought back to the coincidence of Kotkell hiring them to investigate a case Corey's station had shrugged off.

37

DARIAN NEEDED A bit of help. For day-to-day work it was fine to take the train; he was rarely in a terrible rush and spent more time sitting stationary outside places like the Murdoch warehouses than was conducive to a healthy lifestyle. To do the job he wanted to do that night he needed a car, and that meant going to Tuit Road in Bakers Moor to visit JJ's car hire. It was a place you went when you had a sad lack of funds and didn't care what state the car was in, as long as it was basically mobile. It was a small building and patch of dirt tucked away in the gloom under the hills, and that might have been why standards authorities hadn't swooped in and shut it down yet. JJ made most of his money selling death-traps masquerading as automobiles, but he hired out to customers he knew wouldn't complain, and they included Darian. JJ was another useful contact to have.

In the yard behind the office, JJ and Darian sauntered among the cars. If you took a photo of the parking lot and said it was a wrecking yard all the evidence would suggest you were telling the truth. JJ's face was almost perfectly round and yellow, with a damp-looking, thin beard, like someone had cleared out a drain and slapped their findings on a turnip. He dressed in filthy blue overalls and he plainly didn't give a crap what his yard looked like. When he spoke it was with a heavy slur that suggested he was halfway into a long line of mini-strokes and was determined to bluster his way through them.

'This one will stay underneath you.'

Darian looked at the dark blue Skoda Octavia, nearly a decade old. 'How many miles has that got?'

'Eesh, round the world and back, hundred and fifty thousand. It goes, though, Darian boy, got a few thousand more left to run before I turn her into parts.'

It was what he was looking for, an ordinary-looking car that could trundle round the city without drawing the eye. It was also remarkably cheap, which put it right in his price range. JJ went back to the office to get him the keys. The car, when he opened the door, smelled overwhelmingly of sweat, and even JJ, used to ignoring the hellish stenches that floated around him, grimaced.

'Hold on, I'll get you a wee doofer to put over the blowers.'

He got an air freshener from the office to clip over the heaters, but when Darian tried to switch them on, no air come out.

'Hold on, I'll get you a forest of magic trees.'

So Darian left with four colourful trees hanging from the rear-view mirror, a mixture of sweet smells that was only slightly better than the sweat. He drove north, through Earmam and Whisper Hill and out to Heilam with the windows open. He parked round the corner from Gallowglass's house and waited for the former cop to make an appearance.

At twenty to eleven Gallowglass came out of his house and got into his car. He drove south into the city and Darian hung back, putting his tailing talents to the test. He wasn't going to the station to watch for Darian, which meant that the spying mission had been terminated. Tracking suspects was one of the things Sholto was markedly better at than him, because practice made perfect and Darian didn't have as much experience as he'd expected because following people didn't happen too often in the world of pretend private detectives. He had decided at the start that he would rather lose him than risk getting too close. Turning the tables was fine so long as you didn't smack into one of them.

It was a long drive, back down to the end of the loch and round into Cnocaid. They went through neighbourhoods that were familiar to Darian, near where he'd grown up. All the streets look the same round there, detached houses with small front gardens, close together so few have driveways and there are rarely available parking spaces out front. Some roads have trees lined beside the pavement; Treubh Road where Darian had grown up had cherry blossoms. There were none on Pagall Street, where Gallowglass's journey ended.

He stopped when Darian was too close to do the same without being spotted, so he drove past and caught a glimpse of the ex-cop, sitting in the car and watching a house across the street. Darian drove to the end of the road, circled round the block and came back to the top of Pagall Street, finding somewhere out of view to park. He took out his phone and zoomed in the camera function, just able to make out the back of Gallowglass's head, still in the car.

This was more the sort of work he was used to. Sitting in a smelly car watching nothing at all happen nearby. For all the skills that investigations require, patience is the most important. Darian recognised what Gallowglass was doing; it was the same tactic he had used on Cage Street when he stood outside the office, unpleasant and unmoving. He was watching the house that was directly opposite his parking space, which guaranteed that anyone inside would have a perfect view of him when they looked out of the window. This wasn't a man trying to spy on someone; he was trying to intimidate them.

Shortly after three in the morning another car drove past Darian's and stopped further up the street, just in front of Gallowglass. A man got out and leaned down to the window of Gallowglass's car, talking to him. It was DC Alasdair MacDuff. They shared a short conversation in which the man in the car did most of the talking and the man leaning down to the window looked somewhere between angry and embarrassed. MacDuff went back to his car and sat in the driver's seat while Gallowglass pulled away.

MacDuff did as Gallowglass had done before him, sat there and watched the house directly opposite, making no effort to look like anything other than a thinly veiled threat. At about twenty past seven there was movement, and Darian was just able to see a man appearing at the front gate. He hadn't seen the door open – the angle he was parked at didn't give him a great view of the house – but MacDuff had. When the middle-aged man reached the gate, the young detective started his car and drove away. No need to stick around in daylight, with neighbours seeing him, now the message had been delivered.

Darian waited for a few minutes, until he was sure the householder had gone back inside. MacDuff had wanted to be seen but Darian didn't, not until he knew who the person he was stalking had been stalking. He drove the Skoda back to his flat and parked outside. He left a message on Sholto's work phone saying he would be late in because of some extra work he had done, not specifying exactly what because Sholto was still detective enough to guess, and he went to bed.

THE CHALLAID GAZETTE AND ADVERTISER

EAR UNITED 2 - 2 CHALLAID FC

SPFL Premier League Union Park – Att: 34,988

It began as expected, and for eighty minutes it looked like Challaid were heading for a typical derby tale in this lunchtime fixture. A comfortable lead, holding on until the end, leaving the home of their bitter rivals with three more points. But the last seven minutes of football turned a mediocre match into a classic, and reminded everyone of the power of the Union Park crowd.

The match began in an atmosphere of noise and hate, the small away crowd drowned out, but not for long. The warning signs for Ear were flashing as early as the eighth minute, when Casper Foster flapped madly at a corner and was fortunate to see the ball fall to Challaid centre-half Havard Prek at the back post only for the Norwegian to blaze it high over. The young keeper, yet another product of the club's academy, has been in fine form this season, but this was not a game he'll remember fondly. The crowd got nervous

and that translated to the pitch, where mistakes became abundant and good football was substituted for blood and thunder effort.

The breakthrough, when it came, was predictable. A run to the by-line from in-form winger Florent Albert who fizzed a cross in to the front post where Arthur Samba met it with a diving header to open the scoring. Questions can and will be asked about the defending, and a young keeper beaten at his near post, but none are being asked about Samba. The £2.8 million fee paid for the Englishman, top of the scoring charts with 27 in 31 league games, continues to look like the bargain of the season.

With the crowd quietening and Challaid dominating possession the second goal was no surprise when it came. This one was all about Samba, taking possession, beating two men and driving the ball low into the corner of the net from twenty yards. Two minutes before half-time and a team known for their stifling defence was two goals in front.

As the second half wore on the game became a classic example of the two teams' styles. Ear playing at a high tempo, crunching into tackles and picking up five bookings, without creating a single meaningful chance. For all the buzz about the derby game, this was heading for typical disappointment for Ear, who have won only two of the last ten derbies against their richer rivals. Now the Challaid fans were making themselves heard, revelling in what looked like three more points in their championship charge.

In the eighty-third minute the game changed. Ear created their first clear chance of the game when Pataki Bozsik won the ball in the centre circle and played a perfectly weighted ball through for the onrunning Feliks Brozek to slip it under the keeper and into the net. 2-1 and the crowd were back in the game, the momentum behind their side. Their screaming encouragement, wordless and loud, pushed the side forward in wave after wave of attack, the Challaid defence holding firm until the ninety-first minute. A long ball from keeper Foster, allowed to bounce by the defence, and a half-volley from much-maligned Costa Rican international striker Joel Cayasso had Ear level.

In truth, a point in an away derby is not a bad result for Challaid, and although it was the home fans that left the happier, staying to the end to a man, Ear needed the three points more. The draw moves them up to third in the table, a point ahead of Rangers, but Challaid move four points clear of Celtic at the top as they aim for back-to-back title wins.

38

IN THE AFTERNOON he drove past the house on Pagall Street just in time to see a couple walk out and get into a car. They had scarves on, Challaid FC colours of red and white, and they were heading for the football. A big derby, big crowd. If anyone was going to follow them it would be across to the game at Union Park in Earmam, clearing the scene for Darian. He spent an hour or so at the office with Sholto, before leaving again in the afternoon.

As he was going Sholto said, 'I get the impression you're working hard at things that aren't your work.'

Darian tried to think of something to say that would defend him. 'I'm working hard.'

It was no defence at all, and he felt bad about letting Sholto down the way he was. He was abandoning the man who had given him a job for no reason other than he was his father's son to work alone while Darian chased a case with Maeve. He deserved better, and Darian's belief he was doing the right thing was zero consolation.

He parked the Skoda on the next street and walked round the corner. There was no cop or ex-cop watching the house on Pagall Street now, so he took the opportunity to jog along the side of the house and wait in the back garden, out of sight of the road.

It only took thirty minutes of standing around like a burglar with Alzheimer's before he heard a car pulling up in the driveway, two doors thudding shut as the couple got out. He heard the front door close as they went inside and counted to ten before he knocked on the back door. It might alarm them, someone knocking on the back door when they knew their house was being watched, but he was working on the assumption they wouldn't be so scared that they wouldn't answer.

The same man who had been at the front gate hours before stood in front of Darian when the door was opened. He had a pale and featureless face, eyes and mouth barely noticeable, like someone had poked some holes in a lump of mashed potatoes with their finger. He looked concerned and a little angry.

'Yes? What do you want, hm?'

'My name's Darian Ross. I wanted to talk to you about the people who've been sitting outside your house recently.'

The man's first reaction was one of shock, then a look of horror, as though he had been caught doing something he shouldn't. Then a different look, something that might have been a rush of relief. He said, 'Come in, please, you need to speak to my wife.'

The man led Darian through the house to the living room where a wary woman in her late forties was standing with her phone in her hand, the expression of a woman who'd pressed two nines and wanted to know if she needed to press a third. The man said, 'This is my wife, Moira, it's about her.'

She looked puzzled and annoyed with her husband, so Darian jumped in and said, 'My name's Darian Ross, I'm working on a private investigation into Moses Guerra and it's led me here.'

She was a short woman, short brown hair neatly styled, and she looked older than she probably was. Her large glasses showed the lines around her eyes, her veiny hand around the phone showed a cluster of diamonds on a gold band. If you saw her selling cakes at a church bake sale you wouldn't be the least bit surprised. Her face crumpled into resigned disappointment, a woman who had been expecting an unwelcome visit for some time but didn't quite know what shape it would take. There were two possible approaches for Darian to take with her. He could try to find out exactly what this woman knew with careful questioning or he could accept the scale of his ignorance and try to fix that fast.

Darian said, 'I need to know why Gallowglass and MacDuff were outside your house last night, and that means I need to know your name, what connection you have to DI Corey, and why his people have been out there trying to scare you.'

With a casual laugh she said, 'Trying?'

Her husband said, 'Moira.'

She looked at Darian with the smile of a woman in charge, throwing the phone onto the couch and sitting next to it, crossing her legs. 'All right, okay. You want every little detail, Mr Ross, you can have them. My name is Moira Slight, born on 16 July 1965 in the King Robert VI Hospital...'

Her sarcasm grated and he said, 'I don't think we have time for your whole life story.'

'A dig at my age, how very ungallant. Fine, the bits you do care about then. I trained as an accountant and, not blowing my own horn here, I was rather good at it. My speciality was tax, which was every bit as thrilling as it sounds, but there's good money in it because a lot of people are intimidated by Mr Taxman. He even scares the criminal class, but I don't suppose I need to tell you that. I've worked for a bunch of them over the years, helping them tidy up the jumble of numbers their work created. I knew who they were and what they were doing but I was careful and, as I told you, I was bloody good at my job, so there's no evidence to prove I did anything wrong and I'll never admit it in front of anyone that actually matters, no offence intended. Am I going too fast for you, dear, would you like to sit down?'

'Carry on.'

A smug smile and she said, 'One day DI Corey came to me, a cop who knew a lot and was able to pile plenty of pressure onto my shoulders. He came to me with money, told me it was clean and that he wanted me to handle the tax side of it, filter it offshore. Of course I knew what dirty money looked like, even if it was in the hands of a cop, but I didn't say a word. I made sure his money took a plane to Panama and snuck past the taxman in such a way that Corey would never be associated with it and when it came back across the Atlantic I tucked some of it safely away, nice and tight, for him to collect when needed. Now he wants his money, but he wants a lot more than that, he wants a lot of the money from other criminals that he knows I can get my hands on. I don't know how he found out so much about the money I have in circulation right now, but he did and it's why he has his pet thugs outside. I know you're not here for me, Mr Ross, because you mentioned Moses Guerra and that means you're here for Corey.'

Darian had frowned through the monologue, hating every ounce of the confidence the swindler before him possessed. She had hidden any fear behind a wall dripping with sarcasm. He said, 'Those men will only be outside your house for so long. If Corey wants something from you then it's only a matter of time before they make their way in.'

'Don't I just know it. I had a phone call from Corey this very morning, telling me his men would be in the house tonight if I don't come up with the money he craves by five o'clock. I'm trying to work out whether to give him his own money and hope it'll stall him or take his dirty money and run like hell with it. One thing I will not do is steal other people's money for him because he's not the only scary bastard in Challaid that I can call a customer, I can assure you. I told him I wouldn't be able to get him more than what he'd given me, and that I was going to the derby today with my husband. He did at least tell me to enjoy the match, so he's not totally without manners.'

'He said tonight?'

'And he meant it. Corey isn't mucking around. Not like him to grasp at cash like this. He has the terrors in him; a patient man turned desperate, whatever's gotten into him all of a sudden.'

'I'll be here to find out. Someone will come here tonight and I think I know which of his men it'll be. Your husband can go, stay with a friend or family or in a hotel tonight, no need for any more people to be here flailing their arms at fight time than necessary. You and I are going to stay and provide the welcoming party for your visitor.'

'Oh, wonderful, you're really selling it, young man. I'd rather a night in a hotel, if one's on offer.'

'I think we're past the point where you get to do the things you'd like.'

'Ha, been that way for a long time now. Don't worry, I'm quite used to life's disappointments.'

Mr Slight left, albeit reluctantly, to go and stay in a nearby hotel. Darian and Moira settled in to wait.

'You can tell me a few stories about your criminally minded pals to pass the time.'

Moira Slight smiled easily and said, 'I'd need to be very drunk for my loose tongue to invite that sort of danger.'

'No drink.'

'Well, you are a lot of fun, aren't you?'

39

THEY SAT AND they talked for a few hours. Moira liked to rattle through her sentences without ever giving away a word more than she wanted to; she was a woman with long experience of evasion. The only time she delved into any meaningful detail was when she was talking about Corey, having decided that on that subject some honesty would go a long way.

Darian asked, 'You seem relaxed. Do you fear Corey?'

'Well, of course I do, I'm terrified of him. You're either very brave, very stupid or both if you're not afraid of him, Mr Ross. I suppose we'll very soon find out which it is. I'll tell you, I may be more afraid of DI Corey than I am of any other criminal I've ever met, and I've had the pleasure of the company of many. You want to know why he scares me?'

'Go on.'

'Because every other criminal in this city has to at least pretend to fear the law.'

'So does Corey.'

'Oh, come on now, if Corey had to fear his colleagues he wouldn't have earned a tenth of the money he has in the time I've known him. He really should be in a cell in The Ganntair along the corridor from a lot of the people he's locked up. Not that he'd last a fortnight inside, by the way, and if I know it then so will he. I've heard people in the criminal world talk about him; they all hate the man to his bones. Just because he's bent doesn't mean his fellow crooks like him. They know he can't be trusted and he's locked some of them away for doing no more than mildly upsetting him in the past. People who thought they had his protection only for him to pull the rug away and send them falling into a cell because it suited him. I assume the fact he's still a more effective cop than the honest ones is the reason he keeps dodging responsibility for the mountain of slime he sits on.'

'Shouldn't matter how good he is if he's crooked.'

'Ah, but it does, in this city it really does. I don't know a lot about heady things like justice, but I know about gold. In business a person can be the biggest shit you ever met, a liar and a bully, corrupt to their blackened core, and all anyone will judge is whether that person makes a profit. That's the attitude this city was built on.'

'Then maybe it's time this city changed, and that happens by taking action against people like Corey.'

'Ha, that's good, oh, I needed that laugh. Good grief, you are young, aren't you? Let me tell you, as a woman with considerable experience of what a corrupt culture cultivated over a millennium looks like, it isn't ready to change. Challaid ten years from now isn't going to be radically different from Challaid ten years ago, or a hundred years ago. The cosmetics change, the faces are different and the buildings keep getting taller and shinier, but the spirit of the place has been unbendingly the same since day one. All the stuff that's deep down in the black heart of this place, that won't change because most people don't really want it to. They much prefer a profit maker to an honest man.'

Darian didn't argue because he didn't want to go further down that badly lit road when only Moira had a map. She would have gone on for hours about the wicked ideals the city had been built on, but Darian didn't want to hear it. Talk of a conspiracy of corruption being ingrained in a city was defeatist.

Nerves were rising and Moira had sent a couple of reassuring texts to her husband. It was coming up to eleven o'clock when she said, 'Of course I might be the biggest fool of the lot of us for believing your charmingly naive talk about being an honest young man. You could be one of Corey's boys for all I know, sitting there pretending you're David looking for Goliath when really you're the chains that keep me in place, stop me running with the money. I'm sure a man like Corey could tempt an idealistic little squirt like you to his side, flash a few glimpses of his dirty power your way.'

'You have nothing to be concerned about there.'

'Well, I do hope not. You'd have to be a very sadistic young man to be stringing me along like this, but you don't have the shifty eye of the sadist.'

Every so often Moira would get up and take a look out of the window to see if anyone was outside, but the inconvenient bushes in her front garden didn't give her much of a view of the road. They had the light on and the curtains open. At one point Darian sent Moira to the front step to make sure she would be seen.

'They could shoot me on the doorstep.'

'I think, having talked up his evil genius for the last few hours, you can credit Corey with more subtlety than that.'

Moira went out for a minute and came back in complaining of the cold and its effects on the joints of a woman her age. She hadn't seen anyone, and seemed relaxed. Darian could see that somewhere in the back of her mind was the faint hope she had wriggled off Corey's inescapable hook.

He said, 'You can go upstairs, put on the bedroom light, make a show of looking out of the curtains, and then put the light off like you've gone to bed. Then come back down here.'

Moira did as she was told without complaint, taking a few minutes to replicate her usual bedtime routine before jogging back downstairs, nervous about being alone up there. They sat together in the now dark living room as the clock passed midnight. They weren't waiting long.

40

MOIRA SAID, 'What was that?'

There was a sound at the back door, like someone trying to force it open. Darian said, 'Is it locked?'

'And bolted.'

Darian smiled. Corey's man, or men, had thought that beating the lock would be enough to get them in and now they were forcing the door, not willing to waste any more time announcing what was supposed to be a low-key arrival. There was a loud thud from the back of the house as a large man shoulder-slammed the door. Darian left the living room and went into the corridor. He whispered to Moira, 'Stay there, don't get involved.'

'Don't you worry.'

Darian moved along to the kitchen door and stopped without going in. He pressed himself back against the wall and waited. Someone was already inside the house, walking slowly in a belated attempt at stealth. It wasn't one of Challaid's intellectual giants in the kitchen then, tiptoeing around after battering down a door. Listening carefully, Darian worked out, to his relief, that it was a single stupid person.

The large figure stepped out of the kitchen and into the unlit corridor, a foot away from Darian and not knowing it.

Darian recognised him even in the dark, they were so close. Gallowglass, on the prowl again.

Darian said, 'You can stop there.'

Gallowglass paused, stood where he was, the cogs turning slowly.

Darian said, 'This doesn't have to be trouble, but breaking and entering is a very serious offence for a man who isn't a cop anymore and you're going to have to talk your way out of it very carefully. You can tell me what you're up to, that would be a start.'

Gallowglass turned slowly and looked at the silhouette talking to him. Seeing it was a single person, and smaller than him, was all the analysis he needed. Gallowglass bolted for the kitchen, trying to leave the way he had come in, only quicker. Darian leapt on the bigger man, locking him in a bear hug and pulling him backwards. Gallowglass threw his head back, catching Darian on the cheek and sending a snap of pain through him. He let Gallowglass go and the former cop tried to run again, back into the kitchen. He was close to escape, but Darian was never a quitter. He lunged into the darkness, through the doorway and onto the floor, managing to reach out a hand and trip Gallowglass up. They were both on the kitchen floor now, a graceless tangle, Darian diving on top of the bigger man. They grunted and rolled around a bit, both throwing punches with no force because they had no room to pull their arms back and a fear of punching the floor. The former detective was bigger and stronger and he was getting the upper hand until a shadow moved behind them and swung something solid into the back of Gallowglass's head and he collapsed forward onto the floor beside Darian.

The light was switched on and Moira stood there, looking down at Darian and Gallowglass with shock, and said, 'Well, thank God I hit the right one of you.'

Darian got unsteadily to his feet and looked down at Gallowglass and the broken lamp that was now on the floor beside him. He said to Moira, 'I told you to stay out of it.'

'And miss a chance to clobber that bastard? Shame, though, I liked that lamp.'

Gallowglass was conscious, but it was a thin thread supporting the weight of his awareness. Darian and Moira had to half drag him through to the living room and get him into one of the chairs there. Moira put the light on and they both stood over him, waiting for him to regain whatever wits he'd had at the beginning of the evening.

When Gallowglass looked up at him with a frown Darian said, 'I already asked you to tell me what you're up to.'

'She assaulted me.'

'You broke into her house and assaulted me. Last time, what are you here for?'

'Ask her.'

'I already asked her. I want to see if your stories match.'

'She's a criminal.'

'I already know that, and it's not an answer to my question. Tell me what you and Corey are doing leaning on her, trying to rob money. You just hoovering up easy cash like a common crook now, that it?'

Gallowglass scoffed and looked sideways. He had no fear of Darian, no fear of the situation, and there was nothing Darian could say to change that, although he tried.

'You think Corey's going to protect you from this? You think he's all-powerful, capable of twisting every situation to fit his needs? You're very wrong. Things have changed, Gallowglass, Corey's on his way out, that's why he's chasing dirty money that doesn't belong to him. Surely you can see that he's finished and he's planning to leave you a long way behind when he goes. All that money will buy a lot of miles between him and Challaid, but I'll bet a finger it only buys a ticket for one. You'll be sitting in your house in Heilam wondering where he is, and if I'm on a roll with my gambling I'll say that your fingerprints will be on Corey's crimes, not his. You have very little chance of getting out of this mess, and I'm the little chance you have.'

Gallowglass laughed at him. 'You think a guy like you can lay a glove on a man like Folan Corey? Get your head out of your arse, kid, Corey's running rings around you and you don't even know it.'

'You're living in the past and you don't have a future without my help.'

Gallowglass looked past him to Moira and said, 'You've blundered again, up to your armpits in shite. You should go call Corey right now, tell him you're sorry and that you'll do what he tells you.'

Darian said, 'Shut up, she's not calling Corey. You've broken in and committed an assault on me. Do you really want to have to sit in a police station and explain that? Even if Corey gets you out, it still neuters you, makes you useless to him. He can't have one of his little dancing monkeys on the police radar, he knows that. The only thing you'll be able to do for him then is be his patsy.'

He ignored Darian again and said, 'Go call Corey.'

Darian turned to Moira and said, 'Can you wait in the kitchen? I'll come and get you when we're done here.'

Moira looked at Gallowglass and at Darian before she walked out of the room and left them to it. With that distraction removed, Darian felt he could make some progress. 'You need to tell me everything. Tell me what Corey's had you doing for him.'

'You don't need to lean over me, kid, I'll talk to you.'

'Talk the truth, and all of it. I bet there are a bunch of cops who would love to charge you with something if I called them up right now.'

'Oh please, you think I haven't heard every half-arsed threat under the sun? I'm the one who's usually delivering them, so don't try to scare me with that crap. You're just some wee kid who thinks he can be a superhero without the cape. Let me tell you, junior, you can only save people who want to be saved and that isn't me and it isn't most people in this shithole city. People won't take you seriously either, not with your father worse than Corey. You can't throw a punch at him.'

'I can get other people to throw the punches for me, just like he does. He's got his little failed projects, the cops he took under his wing and didn't train properly, didn't protect.'

'Ha, aye, very good. That your clever wee attempt to turn me against him, is it? Pretend that everything I did wrong was actually his fault, that you sympathise with me? Very good.'

'So you're happy working as muscle for Corey?'

'It isn't like that, I don't just go round intimidating third-rate crooks like your new best pal Armstrong. I do all sorts of important things, for Corey, for Challaid.'

'For Challaid? You don't really think this is your civic duty?'

'Take the piss all you want but you said to tell the truth and I'm telling it. I've stopped more crime since I left the police than I ever did when I was a cop, and that's not a word of a lie. Not all justice comes from authority. Not all good is done by the decent.'

'Stopping more crime than you did as a cop is not a high bar given that you've always committed more than you prevented.'

'Not true, son of a killer, not true. You said the truth so you got to stick to it, too. I did my fair share of heavy lifting when I was a copper; my record was worth pinning to the wall. But, see, since I've left, that's when I've been able to go after some really bad eggs, exercising crime prevention that's done more for this city than you'll do in your self-absorbed little life.'

'So Corey has you operating as part of his own private police force. Does he pay you for your work, or is it all out of the goodness of your bloated heart?'

'I'm not doing charity work. I'm good, but I still got to eat.'

'So he pays you by stealing large sums of money from people like Moira Slight because he thinks a crook like her can't complain.'

'Nah, nah, that's not what this is. Corey isn't Robin Hood. The little I get paid he doesn't need to rob the rich for. This is something totally different.'

'So tell me all the gory details.'

'Well, if anyone's going to be telling gory details it'll be me.'

A new voice from the doorway behind Darian. He spun round to see Corey standing there looking amused, MacDuff behind him looking like he'd rather be anywhere else in this world or the next. Darian looked down at Gallowglass again, at the smile that told him it was three against one and the circle Corey was running round him had just formed a noose.

THE CHALLAID GAZETTE
AND ADVERTISER

23 July 1950

HERO WITH HIS OWN STREET

World heavyweight champion boxer Cliamain Craig was in Cnocaid on Friday morning for his final public appearance before his title fight against German challenger Lothar Eisenberg on Saturday night at Challaid Park stadium. He attended the unveiling of a new street name for a development near the waterfront in Cnocaid that will now be called Cliamain Craig Square. Mr Craig was full of smiles and seemed relaxed as he pulled the curtain aside to reveal the street sign in his honour. Mr Craig said, 'I'm thrilled to receive such an honour from my home city. It means the world to me to be recognised in this way.'

There had been speculation about the city council recognising its most famous son since Mr Craig won the world title in London almost eighteen months ago, although it had been expected that any honour would be in Whisper Hill, the area of the city Mr Craig hails from. Nonetheless he was in fine mood ahead of what many are saying will be the biggest fight of his life, and the undefeated champion, with a record of forty-eight wins (thirty-eight by knockout), no draws and no defeats, was buoyant.

When asked about the sell-out crowd of over 60,000 for his fight on Saturday evening Mr Craig was quick to praise the fans, saying, 'I can't wait to fight in front of so many people, and in my home city. I want to thank all of the fans who have bought tickets and who plan to come along and cheer me on.' Indeed, the fight will provide the largest crowd Mr Craig has ever fought in front of, and the largest ever for a sporting event in the city that isn't football or camanachd. It's thought many of the fans will be travelling from the east of the city and people are reminded that trains will be extremely busy in the hours before and following the fight, which is scheduled to start at 8 p.m.

Mr Craig's trainer, Mr George Lyall, was in confident mood ahead of the fight, declaring that his fighter has never been in better shape. 'We respect the German, he's a fine fighter, but Cliamain has been working hard to ensure that he's in the best possible shape to defend his title in front of his home crowd. We're confident about the fight ahead.' There was much cheer in the gathered crowd and among the dignitaries present as the towering figure of the world champion told the crowd he would knock out his opponent during the fight.

The street named in his honour is currently being developed by Glendan, and is a picturesque cul-de-sac with family housing and a small square at the end of it. It's expected that families will begin moving into the houses by September and all of the houses on Cliamain Craig Square will be occupied by the end of the year.

DISPUTE OVER DOCKING COSTS

Fears have been raised that an increase in the cost of docking ships at the south docks in Bank will lead to all docking in the future being carried out in Whisper Hill, and the end of centuries of tradition in Challaid. A spokesman for Murdoch Shipping, who own several warehouses on the Bank docks, said, 'Docking charges have been rising steeply every year, but only at Bank. Ten per cent increases every year are pushing companies north to the new docks, where prices have been frozen in each of the last four years.' Fears have been rising since Duff Shipping began to dock all its ships in Whisper Hill two years ago.

It's thought there has been shipping of some sort using Bank for almost a thousand years, with some arguing the culture of the city is being irrevocably changed by the move – P12.

41

DARIAN STOOD AND looked at the two detectives, but he didn't say a word, not until he had some idea of how hot a fire he had stepped into. Three to one were odds he couldn't beat, but he didn't yet know the price of losing. He needed to find out what had brought Corey there so damn quickly.

Gallowglass, sitting comfortably back in the chair now, said, 'I told her to phone, and I bloody well knew she would.'

Darian's face fell and Corey chuckled. The detective said, 'Well, you're half-right, which is still half more than young Mr Ross here. My dear friend Moira texted me much earlier and told me Darian was waiting for you with open arms. She called me again as we were heading here to tell me Mr Ross was in the corridor and about to bop you on the head. I told her that, if she got the chance, she should intervene on your behalf.'

Gallowglass rubbed his head and said, 'Yeah, well, I don't think much of her aim.'

'Ah, never mind, you were taking one for the team. You see, Moira was sitting here all evening in the company of the noble Mr Ross and decided she didn't want him here anymore, but he wouldn't leave. That was when she asked me to send a friend round to remove him but when that friend entered the house, with her permission, he was attacked by Mr Ross. A terrible set of events.'

Gallowglass said, 'Don't see why she had to clobber me in the process.'

'A temptation too great to resist, I'm sure.'

Darian said, 'How you don't choke on the shit you're so full of I don't know.'

Corey laughed. 'Oh, Darian, Darian, no need for insults, we're all friends here. This isn't about me beating you, it's never about that, never. It's about the job, doing it properly, making sure the people of Challaid are protected from corruption in all its many forms, and making sure the bad guys are hobbled. You're young; you don't understand that the best way to do my job is not always the way it's portrayed on television by heroic but quirky detectives. I mean, you're not going to learn much working alongside Sholto Douglas, God love the man. I want tonight to be a valuable lesson for you, but here isn't the place to teach it, in another person's house. Come on, the four of us will go for a drive.'

Corey stood in the doorway with an arm extended out into the corridor where Darian had thought he'd won this fight. Gallowglass got up from the chair and stood in place, making sure Darian was thoroughly surrounded. MacDuff, who hadn't spoken a word yet, led him out through the front door and down the path.

As they went through the gate Corey said, 'We'll all go in my car, just for this wee trip.'

Corey was enjoying himself, and the casual tone of his voice suggested he was well used to the pleasure of such victories. As MacDuff held the back door of the car open for him and he dropped in, Darian cursed both Corey and himself. It was humiliating to think of how that old crook viewed him, the daft kid grasping out for heroism he never had a chance of catching, sickening to realise that Corey didn't fear him at all.

Gallowglass sat on the back seat beside him and MacDuff drove, the city rushing past. Corey was in the passenger seat, looking back over his shoulder at Darian. He said, 'So what part of my fair city are you from, Darian?'

'Cnocaid.'

'Cnocaid, of course. You'll have grown up in a good neighbourhood, not far from here, not far from the station where your old man worked. I remember him, you know, I worked with him. A nice, middle-class family, comfortable. Your parents probably hoped you'd become a doctor or a lawyer, something like that. Mind you, I didn't know your mother. Maybe she was the artsy-fartsy type, hoped you'd be a playwright or a poet. Was that her type?'

Darian sat in silence, knowing there was no answer that mattered when Corey just wanted to hear the sound of his own voice.

'Oh, come on now, don't be like that, sitting there in a big huff and blanking me. You had a grand plan to bring me crashing down and I went and spoiled it for you so now you're pouting. Well, Mr Ross, I'm afraid your plan was doomed to failure from the start, and it was doomed because of the simple fact that I am a far more honest cop than you have ever given me credit for.'

They were driving north, still in Cnocaid, taking a route direct enough to suggest the driver was aiming for somewhere in particular.

Darian said, 'You can lean on me all you like, it won't change anything. You can get your gullible gorilla here to knock me about, but you know you can't overreach. If you killed me there would be hell to pay.'

'Kill you? Bloody hell, lad, you need to cut back on that sort of talk; it's making you sound awfully stupid, and you didn't sound blindingly bright to begin with. Nobody respects that sort of melodrama outside of a Greek play. I can put my hand on the holy bible and say that I have never killed another man, have never tried to kill another man and have never asked anyone else to kill another man. I know you want to think the very worst of me and the best of yourself, but you need to get it out of your head that I'm the devil in a Debenhams suit and that all the world's morality emanates from your good self.'

Darian decided to revert back to silence. They were driving along Cliamain Craig Square, the square itself gone now, the area redeveloped and turned into a cul-de-sac of half-empty business units. No one much remembers the life of the man it was named after, just his death and the aftermath. At this time of night there were no lights and no people. MacDuff pulled the car over to the side of the road and Corey got out. He opened Darian's door and nodded for him to follow.

Corey said, 'We'll go for a wee walk.'

He led Darian down between two buildings, along the damp grass, Gallowglass a short distance behind and MacDuff staying at the car. It wasn't quite a long walk in the woods, but it was designed to feel that way.

As they moved up a slope Corey said, 'You think I was there to try to extort money out of Moira Slight, don't you? I bet that's what she told you, the old she-devil, and because you're so desperate to believe I'm the big bad wolf you accepted every word without question, even though questioning should be your instinct. I'm disappointed in you, very disappointed, but I suppose I shouldn't expect anything better when you're learning from your father the killer, your brother the thug and Sholto the coward. The reason I was there tonight is a reason you actually agree with me on.'

'Is that right?'

They reached the top of the rise at the back of the buildings and stopped. The view looked down on the loch, the lights of the city around it and of the boats on it.

Corey said, 'I love this area. It's worth reminding yourself now and again that there's beauty in this city, even if you have to go looking to find it. Now, I'm about to agree with you so you should savour the moment in picturesque surroundings. I don't believe that Randle Cummins killed Moses Guerra, I don't think the half of a wit he has left is strong enough for the job, so I continue to look for the person who did the deed, a person that will be easier to find when they think I've stopped the search. My investigations in that direction led me to the doorstep of my long-time acquaintance, Moira Slight.'

'You thought Moira was involved?'

'I thought, indeed still think, that Moira may have a good idea of who was involved, even if she wasn't in the middle of it herself. I've known she was handling dodgy accounts for a while, it's why I always kept close to her, a hell of a potential informant for the anti-corruption unit, and she has proven useful several times. Now, Moira's been chatty enough in the past, throwing others overboard to protect her place on the gravy boat, but she wouldn't tell me a thing about her work with Guerra and she got downright evasive after a while. So I've been leaning on her to loosen her lips, give me a few details about Guerra's recent business activities, and then you came stumbling into the picture like a frightened rhino, armed with nothing but your righteous hatred of my good self. You've probably done me a favour, mind you, turning up and rattling her the way you did. She thinks she can handle me because she knows me, but you're new and new is dangerous. I have a better chance of getting the truth out of her now.'

'Happy to have helped.'

'Ah, degenerated to sarcasm now, Darian, a new low. My point is that you and I are chasing the same shadows on the Guerra killing but the difference is that I actually have a net in which to catch the person responsible. You, on the other hand, would be doing yourself a considerable favour if you stopped getting under my feet every day of the bloody week.'

'A threat? What sort of low is that?'

'There you go with your exaggerating again. That was hardly a threat and pretending it was is the sort of childishness that gets a young man a reputation as unreliable. This is me generously trying to teach you, seeing as you've only been learning at the feet of failures so far in your life. You're very lucky I've taken an interest in your future, so I'm willing to impart all this wisdom.'

'I feel lucky.'

Corey chuckled and shook his head. He turned on the spot and said, 'You can take a walk back to your car; I'm sure a young lad like yourself will enjoy the exercise on a fine night like tonight.'

Corey walked away from him, Gallowglass ten yards behind, falling in beside his former boss, and they made their way back to MacDuff at the car. Darian gave them a few minutes before he started his walk. Letting them get clear, taking in the view and calming down.

42

AS HE WENT into the office the following morning, Sholto said to him, 'I hope she was worth it.'

'Eh?'

'Whoever left you looking as knackered as you do. If it wasn't some buxom beauty then you had a waste of a night.'

Darian decided not to ask who the hell used the word buxom anymore and just said, 'Good one.'

'All my jokes are good ones, you just don't listen close enough to realise. I'll assume it was Maeve Campbell and I'll delay my lecture on the subject of that woman if you tell me you've made progress with the Murdoch case.'

'The warehouses? Not unless you consider ongoing confirmation of their legality progress. There's nothing to see there, Sholto, and I'm not going to make stuff up.'

'I don't expect you to make stuff up; I just don't accept that any shipping company that's ever worked out of this city hasn't been up to something. I've seen that industry and its ways before; I know they're all playing tricks to bring down their costs, thinking they can pull the wool over the eyes of the goofy landlubbers. You get down there and poke about some more, maybe see if you can get a low-paid and loose-lipped member of staff talking. Be proactive.'

Darian did as he was told, heading back to the warehouses at the marina. He didn't try to make contact with a member of staff, just drank coffee and watched the old brick buildings to pass the time. In the late afternoon he went back to the office and wrote another report that turned doing nothing into three hundred words before he took the Skoda round to Sgàil Drive.

Maeve opened the door and quickly said, 'I'm glad you're here, I've...'

She stopped when she saw the look on his face. She held the door open and they went through to the living area. They sat opposite each other and Maeve looked hard at him, waiting for Darian to explain the angry and miserable expression.

He said, 'I had a long night last night. I thought I was making progress, found someone that was connected to Moses and might have had knowledge about his killing, but it all fell apart in my hands. Corey showed up, took me for a drive, made a bundle of threats that he dressed up as valuable life lessons.'

Maeve was silent for a few seconds. 'You found someone who might know what happened to Moses?'

'I thought I did. An accountant that was involved in handling a lot of dirty money and might have been a link in the chain tied round Moses's money. I found her through Gallowglass, he was hassling this woman. I thought the connection might just have been to Corey, a chance to take a swing at the corrupt bastard, but it grew legs. Then it ran off a cliff. The accountant, she was working with Corey all along, I think. Made me look stupid, and I suppose that was the point. Gave Corey the chance to laugh in my face and warn me about sticking my nose into his business, lean on her at the same time. She said Corey's trying to force her to hand over all the dirty money she has, he said that was bullshit, but I don't know. He did say that he agrees Cummins didn't kill Moses, and that he's going to keep working the case to try to find the person he should have found long ago. That should be good news, I suppose, if I believed a word of it or trusted him to conduct an honest investigation. At this stage he's just looking for ways to shut down everyone else's questions and escape with the cash.'

'You must have rattled him into action.'

'Nah, if he is going to keep looking for the killer it's not because of anything I did.'

'No, I mean, you're not the only one that had an unwelcome warning. I was going to tell you when you came in; I had a visit early this morning. It was before eight o'clock, I stumbled out of bed and answered the door and there was DC MacDuff, looking a whole flock of sheepish.'

Darian remembered when he had turned up unexpectedly and Maeve had opened the door, wearing nothing but a T-shirt. He could understand the sheepishness. 'What did he want?'

'He said he knew I had been asking questions about the police investigation and that it was hampering their ongoing efforts. Tried to make it sound like official police speak rather than a weak thug's threat. I told him I thought there were no ongoing efforts, that's why I was still asking questions. He didn't know how to answer that. I could tell he'd been sent here to speak someone else's words that his tongue isn't forked enough to handle and once he had to think for himself he was stumped. He said I should stop what I was doing because I was putting both myself and the investigation in danger, which I think was supposed to be his hardman act, but he sounded like he didn't believe it himself. Then he asked me to tell him everything I had found out about Moses' killing so far.'

'Did you?'

'Of course not. I told him the reason I was asking questions myself was because I couldn't trust him with the answers in the first place. Then I told him to leave and he did, faster than a confident man should. He was just following orders, although you can still prosecute a man for that. He didn't scare me, but the phone call I got not long after he left was more effective. A man, local accent, telling me it was time to stop asking questions and hanging out with people that were going to get me into trouble. By which I think he meant you, incidentally.'

'How long after MacDuff left?'

'Just long enough for him to tell this person I hadn't been as cooperative as they would have liked so needed to be leaned on by someone with a little more grunt.'

'It must have been Gallowglass, must have been.'

'I've never heard him before, I don't know. He sounded like he was a lot more comfortable playing the part of grand thug than MacDuff.'

Darian looked at her and sighed. He was complicit in dragging this woman into something dangerous, even if her tendency was to walk towards the threat.

He said, 'I'm worried about how aggressive they're getting. I think they know who killed Moses and I think they're involved in protecting that person. Corey is dangerous. If he's going to run with the money then he's desperate, and that makes him more dangerous than usual.'

She got up and walked across to sit next to him. 'Well, I knew that from the first conversation I had with the bastard. He carries his nastiness in the open with him. I'm not scared of him, but I'm scared you might stop helping me with this.'

'I won't.'

They were face to face, an inch apart. They kissed, Maeve put her hand up to his face, and they pulled apart. She hugged him tightly again and said, 'I know I can trust you. Will you stay here tonight?'

They kissed again and Maeve led him through to the bedroom.

43

DARIAN WAS IN no hurry to leave in the morning and Maeve was in no hurry to let him. They spent a couple of hours together that we don't need to describe in excruciating detail. Let's leave it at the fact that they were a young couple who had just kicked down the thin fence that had been holding them apart since they'd first met and they were, understandably, full of imaginative and exhausting ideas about what to do with each other.

Eventually he left because he was contractually obliged to get to work. Had to stop at a petrol station on the way to fill up the Skoda, which was more expensive than he had been hoping for and more than the car was worth. He drove home to change and shower and then went round to Cage Street. Sholto was there long before him, and didn't try to hide his annoyance.

'You know this job isn't optional.'

Darian said, 'I'm here, and I've been working long hours, late into the night.'

'Is that what you were doing last night, working?'

'Sort of.'

'Maeve Campbell?'

'Maybe.'

'Well, if you're not sure either it wasn't much of a night or it was a hell of a night. We need to talk about that girl, I told you that already. We need to have a good, long, detailed, angry conversation about her, but before we do that we need to have an even longer one about Uisdean Kotkell.'

'Go on.'

'I was actually hoping you'd be able to start it because I have nothing. We need to make some sort of progress instead of running down more dead ends. It won't be long before Durell Kotkell is phoning in a huff wanting an update and I don't have half a sentence to say to the man.'

'You could tell him to ask his son. We know Uisdean is holding something back, holding a lot back maybe, so point the finger in that direction.'

'That's not what he wants to hear so it's not what I want to tell him.'

They sat at their desks and they talked through everything they'd learned so far, a tactic Sholto swore by. In his mind it got them thinking of all the little details, got them talking to each other about things they'd noticed that they might not have mentioned before, the subtle hints they thought they'd picked up along the way. Darian was happy to talk about the Kotkell family rather than Maeve, so he kept the conversation going.

He said, 'What I find strangest of all is the fact that he didn't sack us when we upset him. You saw how annoyed he was, didn't you?'

'I saw. I remember everyone who's ever complained about me. I need a good memory.'

'It would have been easy enough for him to cancel the contract and go and hire Raven instead, but he didn't.'

'Maybe he knows what a shower of piss that lot are.'

'I hardly think that would bother him. He works with worse people than them every day of his life, not least himself. Maybe he didn't sack us because he thought we were doing the right thing, even if he didn't like it. Us questioning his son like that, upsetting him, it showed we were willing to do the dirty work. He liked that. But we weren't on the right track and he knew that, too. He's convinced it wasn't random otherwise he wouldn't be pushing us this hard, and he already knew it had nothing to do with Uisdean's private life.'

'Are you implying that the father shares the son's habit of holding back information that would tell us what happened?'

'Why did he hire us, rather than Raven, in the first place? Raven handle contracts for Sutherland, don't they?'

Sholto tutted at the gaudy sums of money his rivals were making from that and said, 'Yeah.'

'So it would be the easiest thing in the world for him to go and hire them. He's probably met all their senior investigators before. Instead he came out of his way to get us.'

'It might just be that he heard we're good at our work.'

Darian didn't look at all convinced. 'Might be, might not. Did he say who had recommended us?'

'I think he might have said it was a cop the first time he called, I don't really remember. He wasn't what you would call keen to give me details, just orders.'

Darian got up and went out of the office, fishing his phone from his pocket. He stood on the stairs, sure that no one could hear him, and phoned DC Cathy Draper. Took a little while for her to answer, but she did. They hadn't spoken since they'd met at the record store to talk about Corey and the Moses investigation.

'Cathy, do you remember if you spoke to Durell Kotkell, his son got beaten up outside Himinn a wee while back?'

'Yeah, I spoke to him. I think it was the morning after it happened. He was looking to hire someone in and I suggested you and your boss instead of his usual people.'

'Why?'

'He didn't want anyone that was connected to the bank, I don't think. When I mentioned you two he asked if you had any connections to Corey, and I said not good ones, you had stood up to him already and he didn't like you for it. I figured he wouldn't hire you because of that.'

'Oh. Well, he did.'

'Good, that's another favour you owe me.'

'I'm really not sure it is, you've dropped a nightmare on our heads and we're struggling to wake up. Anyway, thanks, Cathy.'

Darian went back into the office. 'Kotkell hired us after hearing we'd stood up to Corey. You know I've been digging around in the Corey stuff, right?'

Sholto nodded and grimaced at the same time, making him look like he'd swallowed a spider that was trying to crawl back out.

'Well, I know that Corey was connected to an accountant called Moira Slight and I know she was connected to Moses Guerra. What I don't know is what companies those two were using to filter money through. I think I might just have worked out the answer. We need to go round and see Kotkell.'

44

DARIAN KNOCKED ON the door of the posh house in Barton and the unseen dog started barking again. Sholto took a step back and then straightened his tie, wanting to look presentable for when the posh dog bit him. He said, 'This is a bad idea.'

Darian said, 'This is the only idea we've got.'

'I wish we were smarter.'

The door opened and Leala Kotkell looked back at them, her face falling into an expression designed to let them know there would be zero effort on her part to play the polite host, the bridge to her good books had already been burned. She said, 'What do you two want now?'

Darian said, 'We'd like to speak to your husband or your son or both.'

'They're not in.'

'That so? Uisdean must be feeling a lot better if he's gone from stifling headaches after one conversation to out and about already. What we'll do then is we'll wait while you call one or both of them and tell them we're here. We can wait out on the street if you'd like.'

If looks were weapons she could have held the world to ransom with the one she gave Darian, but he just smiled back in response. She didn't want them out on the street where the neighbours might see them so she reluctantly let them in, Sholto nodding apologetically as they went through to the same study they'd been in before.

Leala Kotkell stood in the doorway and said, 'Stay there and don't touch anything.'

Darian sat heavily but Sholto stayed standing, already sweating and looking around the room, glancing often at the doorway as if he was afraid the now silent dog might be planning to creep up on him. He said, 'I bet she's giving the dog our scent right now, telling it to chew us to pieces.'

'She might be telling her husband that, but I doubt she's telling the dog. If she knew you were as scared of the dog as you are of the husband she might.'

'I'm not terrified of the whole dog, just its teeth.'

Darian thought, when they were quiet, that he could hear her voice from another room, trying to talk quietly but her volume rising in anger every few seconds and betraying her. He said, 'She's on the phone.'

'We shouldn't have forced our way in like this, it's just antagonising them more.'

'It's now or never.'

'And what if we're wrong about this?'

'Then it's never again.'

'Aye, well, the way my wee heart's pumping away right now it might be never again for me anyway. When I started this business it was supposed to be police work without the pressure. No murderers or madmen to catch, just good old pilferers and runaways, simple follow the breadcrumbs stuff. I could always do those. Maybe Corey was right about me, hiding from the serious stuff.'

'If he was right you wouldn't be here.'

'Maybe he was right and I'm just too lazy to prove it.'

Leala had been silent for a couple of minutes and Sholto was still pacing when a figure emerged in the doorway. Uisdean Kotkell stood looking at them, not saying anything at first. Sholto sat down on the couch just as Darian stood up and said, 'Come in, Uisdean, sit down. There's just one question I want to ask you.'

Uisdean looked like he was considering the offer when they heard Leala's voice from the other end of the long corridor, shouting to her son. 'Uisdean, what are you doing?'

She appeared beside him in the doorway and Darian said, 'Look who showed up. I really just need to ask him one question.'

'He's not fit for it; he needs to be resting in his bed.'

'That's a remarkable deterioration; a minute ago you said he was out and about.'

Leala glared at Darian, but Uisdean said, 'If it's just one question.'

He walked across to the opposite couch and sat on it, his mother sitting beside him. Darian sat back down beside Sholto and said, 'Uisdean, when Randulf Gallowglass beat you up, what message did he give you for your father?'

Leala turned her head to the side and Uisdean stared straight at Darian for a second before he said, 'He told me to tell my father that it was time to do what he was told, and that if he didn't he'd come after me again.'

'And you told your father this?'

Leala put up a hand. 'My husband is on his way, he won't be more than another five minutes. You can ask him.'

Sholto said, 'Five minutes? Bloody hell, what road is he driving on?'

His attempt to inject a little humour was met by steely looks from the Kotkell family opposite and his smile crumpled. Leala bundled Uisdean out of the room, wanting to protect him from any more outbursts of honesty. He already knew more than he should about his father's work. It was four minutes later that a car stopped with a small squeak of tyres outside and Durell Kotkell burst in.

'What's going on now?'

Darian stood up and said, 'Why did you hire us when you don't have any desire to see the man who attacked your son being brought to justice? You don't want Gallowglass put away; you don't want Corey in the dock because you'd end up next to him.'

Kotkell straightened and held eye contact with Darian. Huffily, he said, 'Well, shit, you've got the wrong end of the right stick. Took you long enough to get this far. I hired you because I knew it was Corey and I knew the police would never get off their backsides and do something about that man, no matter how much pressure I put on them. They close ranks. I do want Corey in the dock, but it'll never happen, not with that one, but I want him to know he doesn't get away scot-free. Attacking my son. My son. I wasn't letting that go unchecked, so I brought you in to put some pressure on him.'

'Because he's been using you to clean dirty money.'

Kotkell shook his head. 'It's a hell of a lot more complicated than that. He hasn't been using me, but I run the department at the bank that handles Caledonian accounts, business accounts mostly, the majority in Panama. That bastard's dirty money goes into a clean company that then runs it through us, it looks like Panamanian money so those are the tax rules we apply. An accountant called Moira Slight was the link, she took money that had been picked up here and banked it through us under the names of clean companies. We put the last sheen of respectability on it, but we were just at the end, I don't know who was involved earlier in the chain. Hiding money is a lot harder than it used to be and a lot of the young banks run scared from it these days. When I found out it had been going through my department, well, shit, heads rolled, I'll tell you that.'

Darian said, 'But you don't want the police involved.'

'Ha, that's a good one. You know what department handles this sort of crime? The anti-corruption unit.'

Sholto looked at Darian and said, 'So Moses was the first link, collecting it from the criminals. Him and Moira worked it through companies and banked it with Sutherland because they had people at the bank who wouldn't ask any questions about it.'

'Which reinforces the link with Moses.'

They stood looking unusually thoughtful for a few seconds before Kotkell broke the silence. 'Corey has money tied up in accounts with our Caledonian branches, most of them controlled exclusively by Moira Slight. I've dug around and found them. He wants control of the accounts from Slight and he's been causing trouble to try to get it. A good system when things were going well, he was too distant from them to ever be caught, but now he wants them and she doesn't want to let go. There's about half a million there, hardly enough for this sort of mayhem.'

Darian and Sholto looked at him like he'd grown a second head and Darian said, 'Your son's beating may tie in with other crimes, and I can't guarantee that we can keep your involvement out of the story.'

Kotkell was fighting to keep the bank's reputation clean. Links to money laundering would blacken the name and cost him his job, and that was worth a good deal more than half a million pounds. 'If you do, you will have a very valuable friend within the bank. We do a lot of investigations, and I could make sure some of that starts coming your way.'

Sholto perked up but Darian didn't look impressed by the offer of money for silence.

Kotkell said, 'He attacked my son. All I wanted was to force him to back off, leave my family alone. Picking a fight with me is business, but my family are not a part of that. The money my department handled for Slight, I knew nothing about it and when I found out I sacked everyone connected. It can never be proven that we knew where it had come from so it would be no good pointing the finger at us. We can make sure the bright lights of any investigations burn others instead of us. If you help me a little, I can help you a lot.'

Darian said, 'We'd better go; we have a lot still to do. We'll be in touch.'

Sholto wasn't so enthusiastic about departing on these terms, but they left without committing to anything Kotkell wanted of them. They had what Darian needed – the truth about what had happened to Uisdean.

As they got into the car Sholto said, 'Moses got killed and that sent Corey running to get his dirty money from Slight and Kotkell. That's what the Moses killing provoked, but it still doesn't tell us who killed Moses. It's a good spot to take our next step from, though.'

Darian was thinking about it as they went back to the office. Corey was the fraying thread that ran through all of this, him and his hired thug Gallowglass. There was a man capable of violence, perhaps murder. If Corey had decided he wanted his money before Moses was killed, then the link could be stronger than Sholto realised.

45

THE REST OF that working day was spent putting together two separate reports on the Kotkell case. Sholto was writing one for Durell Kotkell to have, Darian was writing the other for their files. This wasn't rare. There had been plenty of cases where Douglas Independent Research sent a different message into the world than the one they kept back for their own records. Kotkell's report would be full of the things he wanted to read, it would reassure him. The one they kept in the office would be splattered with every unfortunate speck of truth.

Sholto went home and told Darian to do the same. He said, 'You're having too many late nights. Don't care how entertaining they are, if you want to be able to do the job then you need to be at least half-interested and two-thirds awake. Off you go home.'

Darian nodded, almost a commitment to do what he was told but no words to implicate him should Sholto find out he had done differently. He was planning on going to Sgàil Drive to see Maeve again. He walked down the stairs and out onto Cage Street, pausing as he realised he was hungry. He walked into The Northern Song to grab some food he could take round to Maeve's with him.

It was busy, and he had to wait twenty minutes for his order. Chatted with Mr Yang for a while, then Mrs Yang emerged from the back with his food and passed it to him. She had a rather sly smile on her face, like a woman who knew the food for two wasn't for Darian and Sholto because she'd seen Sholto go home already. She didn't, thank goodness, say anything about it, because Darian wasn't ready to have a running conversation about a relationship that was still learning to walk.

She looked almost proud when she passed him the bag and his change and said, 'Have a nice evening.'

He was blushing when he left the restaurant. He walked down to the bottom of Cage Street and onto Dlùth Street where he'd parked the Skoda. The war between the air fresheners and the car's natural smell was being lost, but the food helped to paper over the cracks of defeat for a little longer. Darian had just started the engine when his phone rang.

No name, which made it a number that hadn't called him before. He answered and said, 'Hello?'

'It's Vivienne Armstrong. You and I need to meet, right now. I have something to tell you.'

She sounded harassed, like she wasn't keen to share what she had to say. Darian said, 'You can tell me now.'

'No, no phones, I don't know how safe yours is and I bet you don't either. You need to come to me, I'm not going to you because I don't trust anywhere you choose. You know the old multi-storey in Whisper Hill?'

'I know it.'

'Go in the old main entrance and there's a blue door on the left that leads down steps to the underground level. Meet me there in half an hour or forget about it.'

'I don't know what I'll have to forget about.'

'Don't be stupid, of course you do. There's only one thing you've been pestering me about in the last week. It's starting to cause me a problem and you're going to help me solve it.'

Vivienne hung up. Darian sat in the Skoda and thought about the call, the danger of it. Meeting Vivienne Armstrong anywhere came with risk; meeting her in the basement level of an abandoned multi-storey car park was something few with a brain would consider wise. Darian considered it, started the car and drove quickly north.

The building, if we can still call it that, is on Letta Road in Whisper Hill, not too far from the Machaon Hospital. It had been four storeys tall, with another parking level in the basement, and had been useful in an area with too few parking spaces. Then one of the floors had collapsed. About a year before Darian met Viv, the second-storey floor had descended onto the first, injuring several people and wrecking a lot of cars. There had been fears the whole building was going to come down but it didn't. Engineers had managed to make it safe for the time being. It should have been pulled down, but there had been a long delay because of the investigation into what had caused it, and the suspicion that it wasn't as much of an accident as it had looked. That was why the owners hadn't received the insurance pay-out they thought they were entitled to, why everything was in limbo and why Darian could meet Vivienne in the basement without fear of being seen.

He parked across the road and watched the entrance. Viv had told him to go in through the main door at the front, which was flimsily boarded up and easily entered through. The building had no defences worthy of the name and had become a haunt of bored children, inquisitive dogs and desperate drug addicts. He didn't want anyone but him and Viv to be there, and it wasn't the kids, the dogs or the addicts showing up he was worried about.

Darian sat in the darkness and watched for fifteen minutes. Nobody came out and only one person went in. Vivienne walked across the street and down towards the car park from the opposite direction to Darian. She wouldn't have been able to see him on a street whose lampposts were cheating a living. He gave it another couple of minutes, knowing he would be late but wanting to see if she was followed. Nobody showed. She wouldn't leave if she was anything like as desperate as she had sounded on the phone. Whatever problem she had with the Cummins money, she wasn't going to walk away from a potential solution because it showed up two minutes later than requested.

He got out of the car and locked it, for all the good that would do if someone in Whisper Hill decided they wanted to break in. He walked slowly up Letta Road, on the other side from the car park, and took in the scene. There are high buildings on either side of the road and only a few windows on the upper floors had lights visible that night. The concrete car park was squeezed unnaturally into what had been a gap between old, red-brick buildings. In the middle of a densely packed part of the city, and with occupied flats and offices all around it, the car park seemed remarkably isolated. He crossed the road and went in behind the boarding, enough of a gap for a person to squeeze through. The place was dark, silent and cold, and the blue door stood to his left, exactly where Viv had said it would be.

The Sea My Brother
Drowned In

Sorley opened his eyes slowly. He could feel her, asleep on his chest. He raised a hand and slowly tucked her hair back. He wanted to see her face. Asleep she looked peaceful, awake she never did. She frowned at the touch and the moment was gone. Vivienne scowled and opened her eyes, looked up at the man she was lying naked on top of.

Sorley smiled and said, 'Good morning.'

Viv said nothing. She lay where she was, looking down at his chest. There was no happiness in her expression, instead a look of regret. She seemed almost guilty.

'We've done nothing wrong,' Sorley said quietly.

'That doesn't matter,' she told him, and rolled to lie beside him.

They hadn't planned to be there. They were, technically, competitors. Sorley and his group worked at a much lower level than Viv and hers, but even small scavengers are considered an enemy of the big predators. The Creag gang had long been the biggest in Challaid, and they maintained that position by crushing anyone who tried to make money from criminality in their city. It could be argued that the Creags did more to stop crime in the city than the local police because they stomped on even the smallest possible rivals. It could also be argued the reason the government plans to have a national police force fell through was because the Challaid force refused to be a part of it to protect their own criminality, but that's not the story I'm telling here.

They had met a couple of years ago, Sorley a rising star in the criminal world. An awkward man, not filled with the same enthusiasm as his contemporaries. He was the son of a cop. He was smart and tough, but they said he had only got into the business to make money for his siblings. Once they were old enough to live for themselves, he was stuck in an industry that traps any it likes. He built his own little group around him, a tough lot, and they worked small scams. Viv was going to destroy them like all the rest.

The Creag gang doesn't have any one leader. There's a group at the top and Viv was a part of it. She handled moneylending, which meant she was in control of a lot of cash. Not the biggest earner of the senior group, but it was a good number. Others were jealous, and she knew it. Other people wanted what she had. People in that senior group. People who worked for her. Viv was always on the lookout for trouble, from inside the Creags as well as outside. Sorley Ross was the challenge on the outside, and she wasn't aware of any trouble inside.

Not until she met Sorley. Viv didn't believe in going to war unless you had to. War is expensive. First she would try to scare the opposition off the battlefield. She sat in Sigurds pub and watched the young man sit opposite her. He had come alone, as instructed. Sorley smiled across the table at her.

'Nice to finally meet you,' he said. He sounded casual, which she didn't like.

'You need to retire,' she said. 'Get out of the business, go travel, buy a boat, sink it, whatever. You need to stop working in the business and you need to stop living in Challaid.'

He smiled at her. 'I'm a little young and a little poor for retirement.'

'There's more than one way to stop living in a place,' she said, almost bored by her own threat, she had made it so many times. 'On your terms or mine, you're going to stop.'

Sorley smiled and reached into his pocket. Viv tensed and he smiled again, more broadly. 'Just my phone,' he said, and took it out of his pocket. He tapped the screen a couple of times and a recording began to play.

'She's going to come after you,' a local accent said, a muffled voice. 'She wants rid of you, I want rid of her. Easy-peasy, we work together. You get her in place and I'll take care of the rest. Get her to the multi-storey that fell over, down in the basement, that's a good spot.'

Viv looked at the phone. She didn't want to speak because she didn't like being boxed into a corner.

'You know that was MacPherson,' Sorley told her. 'He came to me, I didn't go to him. He wants you out of the way because he thinks he can take your share, and he wants me to help him. Thing is, the offer he's put on the table for me to help is not one I like. I don't trust him. Once he's done with you I become his next target, I know that. So my question is, what's your offer?'

'Why would I need to make you an offer? You've already told me that MacPherson is working against me, what else can you do?'

'I can get him into the right position for you.'

Someone stopped living in the city, but it wasn't Sorley. It was the young man who had worked under Viv and hated her and her family. The young man who had been in a fight with her brother and had been blamed for it just because his punch bag was related to someone senior. He watched her get rich from his efforts and he wanted what she had. His plan to kill her hinged on someone else being the lure, and Sorley was the man he wanted for the role. Instead Sorley lured MacPherson into place and the young man disappeared while Viv grew stronger than ever.

They had another meeting, a couple of nights later. She told him that the job had been a success and their deal would be honoured. He would be allowed to continue to work, and the Creags would break the habit of a lifetime and avoid stamping on him. There were conditions. He declared his loyalty to the Creags so that he couldn't declare it to anyone else. Not that there was anyone else, but the Creags were always wary of outsiders coming in and getting help from people like Sorley. He wouldn't have to kick a cut up to her, though, and she would let them continue to operate so long as he didn't expand.

'You stay the size you are now and work the places you work now, nothing more,' she told him.

'Deal.'

They drank to it, and they drank some more. It was two in the morning when they left the bar and got into a taxi. Sorley's memory of it was blurred, but it was his flat they woke up in. Viv naked on top of him, him tucking her hair back to see her peaceful face.

She got out of bed and walked across the room to pick up her clothes. She started to dress, her face hard again. When she was finished she stood at the foot of the bed and looked down at him.

'Remember what I told you. No expansion. If I think you're building your own little gang, you will have violated our agreement and I will remove you from the city. Remember that.'

She walked out of the flat.

46

DARIAN WENT THROUGH the blue door and down the dark concrete stairs to the basement. It was cold in there, and there wasn't much light. He opened the door at the bottom and stepped out into what had been the underground level of the car park. It was a square of bare concrete, flat and empty, no cars allowed in since the collapse. There was one light on, an industrial spotlight that looked like it had been left behind by the engineering team that made the place safe and must have been stealing its electricity from one of the buildings next door.

Viv stood in the circle the light made, dropping the cigarette she had been holding and crunching it under the heel of her boot.

She said, 'I'm glad you came, Darian.'

At the mention of his name there was movement. The blue door opened and shut behind him as a man stepped in, blocking his exit, leaning back against the door and crossing his arms. The ramp up to the ground floor was covered by the arrival of a young woman in shadow, something glinting in her hand. It looked like a screwdriver.

It wouldn't be a gun, possession of one carried a mandatory seven-year prison sentence so only morons, the desperate and the very professional dared carry. Being caught with a knife was a year in The Ganntair, not worth it when you could arm yourself with something else, like a workman's tool. You could walk down the street with a screwdriver in your pocket and the police would have to prove you weren't heading home for some DIY. It was a soon-to-be-closed loophole.

The two new arrivals both looked like a fight with Darian would be a small piece of cake to them. And there was Viv, standing facing him in the circle of light, her expression unchanged.

Darian said, 'I'm not.'

'No, I thought you might change your mind pretty quickly. You've been annoying more people than just me, it seems, and you were bloody annoying for me. Important people are angry with you, and do you know what happens when the VIPs get huffy?'

He looked right and then back over his shoulder. The threats around him, none of them with even a hint of reluctance. It was a question of how far they would go, whether killing a man provided any of them cause for moral concern. It didn't look awfully likely.

He said, almost in a whisper, 'Bad things.'

'Yeah, bad things. It's a shame, but it's a shame that you brought on yourself.'

Viv stood and stared at Darian, a long ten seconds of silence before she finally took a step forward. Her people tensed, the one on the right stepped forward and closed the circle around Darian. He looked quickly left and right, searching for an escape to run to. His chance of getting out was slim, but it was no chance at all if he stood where he was.

There was movement behind the woman on his right, someone who had presumably just come down the ramp.

Darian looked away, assuming it was another of Viv's people, looking to the left where he still thought his best chance of escape lay. There probably wasn't an exit there. Surely Viv would have had someone to cover it if there was, but turning this into a race was his best hope. Then he heard the voice.

'That's probably enough.'

It was a familiar voice, and when Darian turned he saw a familiar face move into the edge of the light. Sorley stood and looked at the brutal people looking back at him. He didn't flinch, and didn't look to have a single drop of the nerves Darian was suffering from. The reason for his calm became clear when the other shadows around him moved into the dim light by the bottom of the ramp. There were two of them, two young men, both as ready and willing to embrace violence as their saviour as Viv's people were. The former wrestler TLM stood on one side of Sorley, both of them looking positively dwarfish beside Gorm MacGilling. Supposing the seven-footer had been the only person Sorley had brought for backup, he would have looked enough to even the odds. There would be no guns there either, but they would be tooled, and they had bulk on their side.

Viv looked at Sorley and said, 'I remember when your gang was too small to stand in a fight like this.'

Sorley said, 'This isn't a fight yet, just a get-together that doesn't know how it'll end.'

Viv turned to Darian and said, 'I told you to remind your brother about the last thing I said to him.'

'I haven't seen him since we last spoke.'

Sorley, his voice bouncing across the large space, said, 'It's a hell of a thing when me and my wee brother see more of you than we do of each other, isn't it, Viv? There's a solution, though. I'm going to need you to give me your word that you'll leave Darian alone.'

Vivienne moved across the no man's land to stand in front of Sorley. Gorm flinched when she moved, waiting for someone else to start the defence before he joined in, the sort of hesitation that had marred his basketball career. Viv stood what would have been nose-to-nose with Sorley if she hadn't been five and a half inches shorter than him. In silhouette they would have looked like lovers, going for a kiss.

She said, 'Why would I give you my word?'

'Because I did ignore the last thing you said to me.'

'And why would you trust my word?'

'Because I'll always enjoy checking up on you.'

She smiled at the idea he would be checking on her instead of the other way around. The smile disappeared and she turned her back on him, walked past Darian and over to the safety of her people. Darian had already taken a couple of short steps towards his brother, and moved a little more quickly now. This could still turn nasty and he didn't want to be standing halfway between the two sides if it did.

Viv said, 'What good timing you have, Sorley. And what wisdom your little brother has, to call you for backup. We'll see how well that wisdom serves you both.'

She led her people through the blue door and up the stairs. They had come to beat someone up, not to fight. Viv wasn't going to let this turn into something she might not walk away pristine from, big fights needed planning this did not have. The woman with the screwdriver shot a dirty look in the direction of the ramp, empty hatred for people she wasn't sure why she despised. The door shut behind them and Gorm breathed out the hurricane he'd been holding in, TLM laughing nervously.

They waited a few minutes to be sure they didn't bump into Viv's lot on the way out. Wouldn't do to dodge battle in the basement only to collide with it at the exit. Sorley's two went up the ramp first to make sure it was clear and he and Darian walked slowly up behind them.

'You're gathering an interesting collection of enemies in a short space of time.'

Darian said, 'I didn't upset her that much.'

'You're right, that wasn't about Viv, that was about someone else. My guess is you've upset someone who's leaned on Viv to try to scare you off. She's good at scaring people is Viv.'

'Except she didn't want to scare me, did she? You turned up just in the nick of time and she tells her colleagues there that I called you for backup. I didn't, so I'm starting to think she did.'

Sorley smiled and said, 'Viv's a decent person, except for most of the time. Her letting you go doesn't give you a free ticket; you still have to be wary of her. It just means she didn't want to do the bidding of the dirty cop, that we'll call DI Corey for simplicity's sake, who sent her here in the first place. You be okay to get home in one piece?'

They were out on the street, Sorley's thugs eager to leave. Darian said, 'I've got a car, I'll be fine. Thanks, Sorley.'

'No bother, but, remember, I ain't the fourth emergency service so don't expect me to turn up on a rescue mission again.'

Sorley and his gang walked up Letta Road to the corner and disappeared round it. As Darian walked down to the Skoda he heard the sound of a car and a motorbike starting up. His big brother, still looking out for him, and then he thought of Corey. This dark business had moved onto another level, more vicious than before, and while it felt like he'd stepped out of a trap he knew this had to be the endgame. Corey had made a desperation play, a last resort.

47

DARIAN FELT EXHAUSTED and decided to go home. He dumped the food from Mr Yang's in the bin, but he didn't go to bed when he got back to the flat. Instead he sat at the living-room window and looked out at the lights of the city and the darkness of the loch, the lights of a single boat snaking through the water towards the southern docks. There was often a squat boat out dredging the loch in the darkness, keeping it clear for larger shipping than the first people to dock there had dreamed possible. It was a view that usually soothed him. His mind was racing and he was feeling frustrated, the overwhelming sense that the end of this investigation was close but wasn't in his grasp. Corey still had the power, so he could dictate events while Darian had to sit and wait for things to happen to him.

As he ran his finger over one of the many fissures in the table he closed his eyes and tried to line his thoughts up in a neat row. He had wanted to destroy Corey from the moment he met him, and he still believed he could. Going to Viv for help just showed how scared he was, how much he had to hide. All of this because of the Moses Guerra killing, and Corey's devotion to covering it up. The cop knew more about what had happened than anyone, and it was another secret he would have to be forced to spill.

It was a pathetic and selfish feeling and he shook his head when it ran through him, but he couldn't help resent the fact it wouldn't be him who got the credit for bringing Corey down. Whatever cop led the investigation into their colleague would get most of it; Sholto would be sure to gather up whatever crumbs were left, and Darian and Maeve would be left with little but a pat on the head for their efforts.

Darian took a look at his watch and tried to work out where Corey would be right at that moment. Viv would have been in touch with him by now, would have told him she confronted Darian, but that Sorley and his gang showed up and forced them out of the building. Corey would hit the roof, accuse her of chickening out and blame her because his last resort was closing down. Viv would probably shrug it off, a smart enough woman to know that Corey had reached the end of his rope and might be out of her hair if she could play for time just a little longer. Hard to know what a man like Corey might do next.

Darian looked down at the street where Gallowglass had been sneaking around stalking him. Darian wanted to do something, to break the inactivity and quieten the voice telling him he needed to be out in Challaid making use of the dark hours before someone else did.

The heavy silence was chased from the flat by the shrill ring of his phone, lying on the table. He was guessing it would be Maeve, Sholto or Sorley, and wasn't expecting any of them to be calling with good news. He picked it up and looked at the screen. A number with no name was showing, someone who had never called before. That made him nervous, but he pressed green anyway.

'Hello?'

'This is finishing now, Ross, it's finishing now. I'm not letting him get what he wants, I'm going to get that bitch of a girlfriend of yours and you're all going to tell the truth about it, you understand me?'

The phone cut off. It had been the angry voice of a young man spitting with emotion. Young in that he was younger than Corey, but not as young as Darian was at the time. The sound quality had been poor, but he was sure it was Gallowglass, ranting into his phone as he drove. That had been the background noise, the drone of an engine moving fast and needing a gear change that a driver with his phone in hand couldn't execute yet. A man barely in control of himself and his car.

The threat was to Maeve. Gallowglass was going there and he was going to get her, and his reasons made little sense in the few seconds he'd spent shouting them. Gallowglass was driving to Maeve's flat. He called Maeve, growling for her to answer as the phone rang through to voicemail. He tried again with the same result.

Darian sprinted out of the flat, the keys to the Skoda in his hand, pulling the front door shut behind him with a slam. He jumped down the stairs two at a time, almost falling down them, and ran out into the street. It was the one time he drove the Skoda and didn't notice the smell, pulling out into the middle of the road and racing east through Bank. There were still plenty of cars on the road – there are at every hour in this city because there's never a better alternative – and the city didn't race past nearly as fast as he wanted it to. It felt like the longest drive up the east side he'd ever made, despite the fact he almost lost control a couple of times when he clipped the kerbs, calling her again on the phone and getting no answer. He turned onto Sgàil Drive and stopped with a screech on the street outside her flat, parking between the car he had seen Gallowglass drive when Maeve took him to see Gallowglass's house and the car in which Corey had taken him for his nocturnal chat after their unexpected encounter in Moira's house.

CONFIDENTIAL INVESTIGATION INTO CONDUCT OF DC RANDULF GALLOWGLASS, CONDUCTED BY DI ADOLPHO PUGA, BAKERS MOOR STATION

SUMMARY OF CONCLUSIONS –

- DC Gallowglass did attack [redacted] on Fair Road in Earmam, breaking his nose and a tooth and then refused to call for medical treatment before questioning him. There was insufficient evidence to suggest [redacted] was a suspect in reported crime.
- DC Gallowglass repeatedly pursued suspects in cases that were not assigned to him, interfering in areas of investigations and districts of the city where his work obstructed other officers, despite multiple warnings.
- DC Gallowglass, in at least one provable case, suppressed evidence against a suspect he considered a source of information, and in so doing prevented a charge and likely conviction being brought against that suspect.
- DC Gallowglass used his position to pursue vendettas against several individuals who had angered him, either by refusing to work as a source for him or by proving investigations of his to be wrong. These vendettas included threatening the individuals and harassing them by informing neighbours and employers that the individuals were under investigation by Challaid Police when they were not.
- DC Gallowglass did attack [redacted] in a corridor of Cnocaid police station. DC Gallowglass had gone to the cell in which [redacted] was being held and attempted to force her to talk to him without a lawyer present. He did become violent when

304

she refused, dragging her out into the corridor and striking her twice about the head.

In the course of investigating the conduct of DC Gallowglass I have found evidence of seventy-one clear breaches of conduct and twelve criminal offences of varying severity on his part. His colleagues have repeatedly stated that they no longer feel safe working with him, and his behaviour towards fellow officers, witnesses and suspects has routinely fallen far below that expected of a serving officer. For the sake of the dignity of the force and the trust of the public, it is not conscionable that DC Gallowglass should remain a serving officer.

Further to the investigation into DC Gallowglass's conduct, I recommend that those working most closely with him, particularly his direct superior officers, be investigated. In light of the catalogue of misdemeanours carried out by DC Gallowglass, it is improbable that none of his direct superiors could have been aware of his conduct. Several officers have informed my inquiry that they reported DC Gallowglass to his superiors and yet not only was no action taken, no record of the complaints was kept and the complainants were made to feel intimidated within the station.

Challaid Police continues to suffer low trust ratings among the public, and it is the actions of officers like DC Gallowglass that are to blame for this. He has been allowed to behave as though the laws he enforces do not apply to him, and not only must that culture end, Challaid Police must be seen to be the ones ending it before an external force does.

48

DARIAN COULDN'T REMEMBER if he locked the car or not as he ran into the flat, and an unlocked car in that area was a vulnerable beast. He sprinted into the building and up the stairs to Maeve's flat, running along the corridor and seeing her front door open. His heart sank; Gallowglass must be in the flat.

He stepped through the front door and saw a glut of people along the corridor in the living-room doorway. Corey was the first he saw, face red and angry, spit on his lip like he'd just been hissing at someone. He turned and saw Darian, his anger touching a new height, and he snarled at him.

'Oh, brilliant, fan-fucking-tastic, look who else is here to join the party. More stupidity to throw on the pile. There isn't one of you with an ounce of sense, not one of you.'

He was trying to say it in a whisper but his rage twisted it into a hiss. Darian stepped along the corridor, getting close to the doorway so he could see what was happening inside. Corey was of little concern to him at the moment; it was Maeve he wanted to see.

She was in the living area, back towards the window, a large kitchen knife in her hand. She was pointing it at Gallowglass, the big ex-cop standing in the middle of the room, staring at her, a concentrating silence. This looked like a standoff that had been going on a while, Gallowglass uncertain about going for Maeve when she had the knife and Maeve unwilling to push past him to the door because she didn't want to have to get blood on the blade. All the while Corey was in the doorway, sniping at the pair of them.

'Come on, Randulf, get out of there. You've lost the plot.'

Gallowglass didn't take his eyes off Maeve as he said quietly, 'You're going to arrest her, gaffer, you're going to take her in and charge her. It ain't going to be me. I'm not taking the fall for this. No way. No way.'

Corey looked quickly at Darian and then back into the room, talking fast and quiet as though Darian might not hear him. 'I don't know where you got that into your thick ugly head but you're not taking the fall for anything. Nothing. Now get out here.'

Darian could see Gallowglass shaking his head. 'No, you're stitching me up. I should have known it from the start. Get rid of me. The pair of you are stitching me up. You hearing this, Ross? Your girlfriend and the cop, stitching me up from the beginning.'

He was shouting the last sentence. He knew Darian was there and he wanted him to serve as a witness. That was the point of the phone call, to bring him here to bear witness to the ending. Darian couldn't affect it, couldn't change what had started without him, but he would be made to see the truth. That seemed to matter a lot to Gallowglass.

Maeve spoke for the first time. 'Don't you come any closer, you're scaring me.'

That prompted Darian to take a step forward and try to push his way past Corey, but the old cop grabbed him roughly and shoved him back. He went nose-to-nose with Darian and said, 'You stop trying to be a bloody hero; this ain't the place for them, this is the real world.'

Darian thought about forcing his way through but he stopped. It seemed Corey wanted Gallowglass out of the room, and there was nothing else Darian wanted more. Corey had a better chance of making their shared ambition happen. The cop looked at him with disgust and turned away to talk to Gallowglass before he thought of another insult and turned quickly back to Darian.

He said, 'You know this is your bloody fault. You sticking your nose in, trying to solve every injustice like a dime-store batman. All you've done is make a bad situation worse. You made this.'

Maeve shouted, 'Don't listen to him, Darian. This is his doing, him and Gallowglass. You were right about them both.'

That provoked Gallowglass, as though it confirmed the fears that had driven him madly here. He took a step towards Maeve, Darian and Corey watching from the doorway, knowing they were too far away to stop it. Gallowglass lurched at her, grabbing out with both arms.

Corey shouted, 'Don't.'

The two men ran into the room but it was over, Gallowglass had jumped at her and Maeve had instinctively stuck out her hand. The knife had gone deep into his stomach, up to the handle, and Maeve had let go. She took a step back so that she was pressed against the window and watched Gallowglass. He stood still, looking down at the knife. His hands reached for it but when he touched it he grimaced and stepped back, scared of the pain he had created.

He whispered, 'I knew it.'

Gallowglass took another step back and stumbled, all of his strength falling out of him as he tumbled. He fell against the wall of the room opposite Maeve and slumped down into a sitting position, the handle of the knife still protruding. He held his hands around the plastic but not on it, fearing it might move. Maeve stood and watched him. Corey stepped towards Gallowglass and stopped, unsure. Darian ran to Maeve and threw his arms around her.

49

HE HELD HER tight and she held him back, both afraid they might drop to the floor if they let go. The fear that had rushed through Darian when he saw Gallowglass move was a new intensity to him, but it was over now.

'Ross.'

Darian turned around. The low grunt of his name had come from the man bleeding on the floor. Corey was standing over his protégé. Darian had expected to see the DI with his phone out, calling an ambulance, but instead he was standing still, looking down with disgust at a man he'd thought he'd known better. Gallowglass was ignoring him, focused on Darian.

'Ross, I'm going to tell you.'

Corey said, 'Shut up, Randulf. Don't listen to him, Ross, he needs help, he's raving. The man has a knife in his guts and a fever in his brain, for fuck's sake.'

It was Corey's tone, the desperation of it, that had Darian walking across the floor towards Gallowglass. If this was something the DI didn't want Darian to hear then it was something he wouldn't allow himself to miss. He stood over Gallowglass, letting the man's fading eyes meet his.

Gallowglass said, 'You need to know because you're the only one that cares about it. Them... They don't care. Since the night it happened they've been lying. Playing games. With you, and with me.'

He grimaced and stopped, looking down at the knife but still not daring to touch the thing that was trying to take his life. He was in pain and breathing fast, but his voice held rising strength and he seemed like he was going to make it. Darian felt comfortable letting him take the time to tell his story. Corey opened his mouth, but Darian spoke first.

He said to Gallowglass, 'Go on.'

'She, your girlfriend, she was supposed to be getting the gaffer, Corey... she was supposed to be getting him information about Guerra's business. Incriminate people. Find out where the money was. He was scared. Lucas, others before him... Other stations are standing up... standing up to him now. He wanted money to get out. She helped him. Then they split up, Guerra, he chucked her... found out, I don't know. She went after him. It was her. It was her that killed him. Went to his flat because there was more she had to get for Corey. He had... that night he had the papers on him. All of it. Got them from the bank. The gaffer's money, Slight, all the details. The bank tipped the gaffer and he told her... told your girlfriend. Didn't want him using them... Chased him and stabbed him. Then she got him in to clean it up for her. Him. Corey. Him and me went round. We took the body away to buy us time. He went... we went into the flat and took away all the stuff about his money. Anything dodgy. Protect the cash so Corey can get it. Then we put the body back... Back in the alley where it was before. The guy who found it, he was our guy, working for us. We controlled the whole thing. Everything. Made sure Corey was in charge of the investigation. It was all up to us, but he was so damn greedy... Wanted everything for himself.'

Gallowglass paused again because his breathing was rapid-fire. Darian looked at Corey, saw the expression on his face change from curious to sickened. He looked back over his shoulder at Maeve, standing by the window. She seemed fascinated, but not scared and not ready to step in and defend herself.

Gallowglass said, 'She's not right, Ross. She's dangerous. Always was. Corey covered up for her because she helped him get the papers from Guerra, that was what he wanted. It told him everything. Everything. He knew where all the money was now... Not just his own, either. He's been scared lately, scared. His contacts are getting picked off. He's not getting away with it anymore. So he wanted to take all the money and run. Use Guerra's papers. Needed to protect your girlfriend for that. Keeping a killer on the streets. A killer. That was when I knew he'd lost it.'

That was as much as Corey was willing to listen to. He shouted at Darian, 'He's talking shite and you're stupid enough to listen to him. Maeve killing Moses? Give me a break. Me letting her get away with it? Not a chance, not a bloody chance. This is insane. The man's losing his wits with his blood; you can see that, you can hear it.'

Darian didn't pay any attention. He turned and looked at Maeve, the person who mattered most to him in that room. She smiled. A little curl of the lips at either side, cheeks dimpling sweetly, her eyes on Darian, judging him. She wanted to know what his reaction was going to be before she provoked it, so they held eye contact for five or six seconds while Corey shouted and she didn't leap in to defend herself. Just smiled.

All the talk of wanting to get justice for Moses, and now she stood there and smiled. The confusion was dizzying. It was Gallowglass that snapped him back to clarity, talking to Corey.

'All that talk about doing the right thing, that was bullshit. You said we were going to help the city. You said I was going to still be doing police work. I was intimidating people for you to make money from them. I was covering up for a murderer. A murderer... You made a fool out of me. Well, I put a stop to it, didn't I, gaffer? I put a stop to all your lies. That's what a good cop does. Now you got to face the music. You and me together. I'll tell them every damn thing.'

Corey said nothing. He stood looking down at the man he had trained and considered a worthy apprentice. This was betrayal, a failure of priorities the DI couldn't comprehend.

Darian turned fully to face Maeve. She had been dumped by Moses when he found out she was feeding info to Corey. She waited outside the flat and she went for him, cut him. Moses ran but he was carrying the paperwork that shone a light on his work, so he tried to be careful, tried for escape without looking for help. She killed him and called Corey to cover it up. He covered up a murder because she got him into the flat to clean out the rest of the paperwork that would tell Corey where mountains of dirty money were. That trail of soiled wealth led him to Moira Slight and Durell Kotkell.

Darian looked at Maeve and said, 'Why did you hire me? You could have been clear if you hadn't brought me in.'

The smile spread. 'I didn't want to be clear. I told you, I wanted justice for Moses. You know what really surprised me? I went to his flat and I didn't know what I was going to do, but when I did it, it was perfect. I've never felt anything like it. The excitement, Darian, there's nothing in this world like it. The power of life in your hands, running on the edge of death. You'll never experience the thrill of it, and I wanted to keep that going. It was fun. Don't pretend you didn't have fun with me, because I know you did. You loved it, and I loved it.'

He didn't know when it had happened but the window behind her was wide open. It was uncharacteristically still out there, the curtain hardly moving. Maeve still smiled, looking Darian in the eye. This had always been her plan. Ride the thrill all the way to whatever ending it arrived at, and here it was.

Darian said quietly, 'Don't.'

She shook her head and laughed. Then she stepped backwards and perched on the windowsill. She dropped back into the dark Challaid night.

50

IT TOOK TWO steps for Darian to reach the window and lean out. She fell through the darkness, a shape twisting in the air. Darian could only see the movement, not the person. She hit the ground hard on her back with a crack. She landed in the small circle of light thrown out by a weak lamppost and Darian thought he saw a spray of red burst out of her mouth and fall back onto her. From above she looked like a broken picture, and he wanted to run to her. He stepped back from the window, awed by the moment. It was all instinct for the next few minutes, no considered thought. He turned and ran past Corey and Gallowglass, out into the corridor of Maeve's flat. He heard someone shout after him but he couldn't stop. The front door was still open and he ran, slow and unsteady. He couldn't remember going down to her. He found a large bruise on his knee the following morning that he thought might have come from falling on the stairs, but he didn't remember it happening. One second he was looking out the window at Maeve on the ground, the next he was on the pavement beside her.

If it wasn't for the speckles of blood on her face and the pool forming under her head it would have looked as though she had walked to the lamppost and lay happily down there. Her left arm was by her side, her right arm across her stomach, her legs together. Her eyes were half-shut, and that same smile was still on her lips. She looked like a woman who had achieved what she had set out to, who was content with the ending she had chosen.

Darian dropped to his knees beside her, careful not to touch the blood. Under the shock wasn't a sense of grief but of embarrassment. Later he would be angry with himself for feeling that way as he knelt beside the body of a person he had been close to, but you can't suppress your true feelings. He was humiliated. He had been so close to Maeve and she had fooled him absolutely. He wasn't accustomed to being made to feel stupid, and this moment was crushing. It changed how he saw himself.

He didn't know about time. He might have been on his knees beside her for ten seconds or ten minutes, he had no idea later. No cars came along Sgàil Drive, nobody approached on the pavement. He snapped back to the real world, and pulled his phone from his pocket. He dialled 999 and gave them the address, told them he needed an ambulance fast because a girl had fallen out of a window and a man had been stabbed. He gave little detail, and, even though they asked him to stay on the line, he hung up. That call served its purpose, making sure Corey couldn't so completely control the aftermath of this situation in the way he had Moses' murder.

Next he called Vinny, the first honest cop he could think of. It wasn't his patch, but Darian couldn't think of a cop in Earmam he knew and trusted like Vinny.

Vinny answered his phone and said, 'Darian, mate, what colour of trouble have you got for me tonight?'

'Vinny, I'm sorry, I really am, but you need to get to

Sgàil Drive, under the hill in Earmam. A girl's dead. Maeve Campbell. She jumped, and Corey is here and he's involved up to his shifty eyes. He's here, and Gallowglass has been stabbed. Corey's here and he'll try to get his cops involved in this to protect him and I need people I can trust.'

There was stunned silence before Vinny said, 'Wait, what the hell are you talking about? Is this real?'

'Please, Vinny, I need help here. Sgàil Drive.'

He hung up on his friend, because there was one more call to make. His hand was steady, he was feeling calm now, calling Sholto and expecting to have to wait for an answer. Sholto liked an early bed, and a late-night call would be met with a grumbling, sleepy, delayed answer. Not this time. This call was answered on the second ring and Sholto was talking before Darian had the chance to open his mouth.

'Darian, good, I was about to call you. I'm at the docks, watching Murdoch Shipping. I've got them, Darian, I have. I got a hold of all the shipments they're registered to receive this week and there's an extra one being made right now. Something coming in without being registered. That alone is enough, but I bet what's being...'

Darian interrupted him, saying, 'Sholto, listen to me, you have to come to Sgàil Drive in Earmam. Maeve's dead. It was her who killed Moses, and she's stabbed Gallowglass and killed herself. Corey helped her cover it up, and now he's here and he's going to try to save himself again, I know it. I need you here.'

He hadn't been frantic; his voice sounded calmer than it had when he'd spoken to Vinny. Still, Sholto understood that this was no joke because he didn't pause before he said, 'I'm on my way.'

Darian slipped the phone back into his pocket and looked at Maeve again. Seeing her happy and peaceful, a smile on a pretty face covered in blood. It was hard to look away from her, as it always had been. He forced himself. This long night wasn't over just because Maeve had left, there was dark work lurking ahead.

51

HE RAN BACK upstairs, emotions packed away. All of what remained ahead involved Folan Corey, a man capable of slipping through gaps left by hotheads. Darian remembered going back up the stairs, his mind clear enough now to take in every detail. The front door of the flat still open, but no sound or sight of the neighbours. All that had gone on and nobody in the building had taken an interest, hiding until they understood the consequences.

He walked in and along the corridor to the living area and stopped in the doorway. Corey was on his knees beside Gallowglass, the reddened knife on the floor beside him. Blood was pulsing out of the wound and rolling thickly down his side, and Gallowglass was lying with his head slumped sideways, eyes shut. Darian took a step closer as Corey stood up and looked at him.

Corey said, 'The knife fell out. Have you called an ambulance?'

It was only later that Darian thought how revealing it was that Corey hadn't used the last few minutes to call an ambulance himself, relying instead on a man who wasn't even in the building to do it for him. Instead, Darian was thinking about the knife, about how firmly planted in Gallowglass's stomach it had been before Darian left. It had stood upright without being touched, Gallowglass lying back against the wall and letting it rest there, settled and waiting to be removed by a medical expert. He wouldn't have pulled it out, and it couldn't have worked itself loose.

Corey seemed to read his thoughts in his expression, and said, 'It was his breathing. He was breathing faster, coughed a bit, and his stomach pushed out the knife. He's losing a lot of blood. Have you called an ambulance?'

'Yes, I called an ambulance.'

Darian dropped down beside Gallowglass and put his finger to his neck, trying to feel for a pulse. There was nothing, but his own nerves could have been causing him to miss the target. He jumped up and ran to the kitchen area, coming back with a towel. Corey was still standing in the same spot. Darian dropped down and pressed the towel against the wound, trying to stop bleeding that had finished its escape, trying to keep a dead man alive.

Corey said, 'It's too late, he's gone.'

He was right. Darian left the towel where it was but he stopped pressing it, stopped fighting a battle that had passed by without him. Death always walks a little faster than life. He stood up and glared at Corey. 'Why didn't you try to stop the bleeding? Why didn't you help him?'

'I did help him. Jesus, I've been helping him his whole working life, long past the point where he deserved it. I've carried his deadweight longer than any man should and as long as I could. I did nothing but my best for him. It was too late, Ross. It's over.'

They were both silent for a few seconds, staring over the body at each other. Corey almost smiled when he said, 'I take it your flying girlfriend landed hard. Is she dead?'

It was an attempt to bring mindless anger into a conversation that Corey didn't want to be mindful. Darian said, 'She is.'

'Probably just as well, a trial would have been embarrassing for you. An evil woman like her, getting you under her thumb and into her bed. Tricking you like that, tut tut. No, this is the best thing that could have happened for you. A truly evil woman.'

Darian could see where this was going already, and he thought he knew where it had come from. 'He said you were going to set him up, make him the scapegoat. He had sussed you out, Corey. He knew you were only in it for yourself. If he didn't know it before Moira Slight's house then he knew it after. That's why you pulled the knife out. Making sure he couldn't repeat what he told me.'

'The only people left who heard him are you and me. You, the son of a murderer and employee of an unregistered private detective agency who appears to have been in a seedy sexual relationship with a double killer. Murder seems to hang around your family like a noose. And me, the decorated DI, head of the anti-corruption unit whose protégé died trying to stop that evil woman. He was like a son to me.'

The smile on his face as he spoke said as much as the bloody knife on the floor beside Gallowglass. Darian wanted to lash out because he knew Corey was right and knew he was going to get away with it. There might be consequences for him, but they would be no more than a single drop of the bottle of poison he deserved. It was a stark reminder of the futility of truth.

Before Darian could say something in response he heard the first distant scream of a siren in a hurry. Things began to happen more quickly now. From the still of death to the energy of life racing to confront it. It could have been an ambulance or a police car; it didn't matter to Darian which; he just wanted to be the first to meet them. He ran out of a flat that contained no one he could help, and back down the stairs. He was standing next to Maeve when an ambulance careered round the corner, the driver enthusiastic about the freedom his siren gave him.

Darian told the medics what had happened, both to Maeve and to Gallowglass. He repeated the story again thirty seconds later when a police car screeched to a halt, half on the pavement, and Vinny spilled out of it. He had PC Sutherland with him, but the young cop stayed pale and silent in the background. Darian told Vinny everything quickly, and Vinny wrote it all down.

In seconds the place was throbbing with people, cars and ambulances choking the narrow road, all the neighbours rushing out to form a gawping crowd now authority had shrilly announced its arrival. At one point Darian was sure he spotted DC Vicario talking to Vinny, reading from his notebook on the pavement near where Maeve had fallen. She was from Whisper Hill station, this shouldn't have been her patch either, but Vinny must have called her. Then Sholto was there, a hand on Darian's shoulder, trying to comfort him.

He watched them cover Maeve and her dead smile with a blanket. He watched the police debating among themselves who should speak to who. Corey left with a detective Darian didn't recognise, but was later told was Lee Kenyon from the anti-corruption unit, and MacDuff. Sholto made sure Darian was left alone for a while by marshalling former colleagues away from him. After half an hour of empty movement and light, Sholto drove him to Earmam police station. Above them, on the crest of Dùil Hill and lit by moonlight, the Neolithic standing stones, An Coimheadaiche, looked down on human folly. It's a cruel moon that shows you all the night can hold.

52

DARIAN IS ONE of a rare group of people who couldn't legitimately complain about the way they were treated by Challaid Police. They questioned him politely, diligently took down all the details from the recorded interview and didn't accuse him of anything. The process was professional and respectful. It seemed as though they were eager to get as much muck on DI Folan Corey as possible, and make some of it stick. They didn't seem confident.

The same questions, over and over, followed by the same uncomfortable answers. There was no way of telling the story that didn't make him seem like a little boy, led with ease by the wily Maeve Campbell, and he had to keep repeating the tale. He blushed more than once as he told them every damned thing that had happened, but he didn't hold back a bad word of what had been said or a grim detail of what had been done. They seemed less interested in Maeve killing Moses, that had been settled and they had no punishment to give a dead woman. Their interest was Corey, and what his role had been.

Darian didn't know how long he was questioned for, but it must have been hours. He walked out into the corridor when they were done, Sholto still sitting there waiting for him, several paper cups that had contained weak coffee at his feet. They shook hands, but Darian paused before he thanked his boss, looking towards the voices that were drifting down the corridor.

At the other end, just outside another interview room, was a gaggle of people. There was some laughing and joking among the group. It was MacDuff he noticed first, standing on the edge of the circle looking tired and annoyed, like a teenager waiting for a lift from a parent who hadn't turned up yet. The female detective who had arrested Randle Cummins, DC Lovell, was there, and DC Kenyon who had taken Corey away from Sgàil Drive, and presumably at least one lawyer, and in the middle of them all was DI Folan Corey, the star of the show, relaxed and happy.

Darian stood and stared until Corey noticed him and there was eye contact. Corey gave his slyest grin, said something to the people he was with and made his way along the corridor alone. Sholto sighed loudly, but Darian stood his ground.

Corey said, 'I hope they weren't too hard on you, young master Ross, but it might be the only way you'll learn.'

'No harder on me than they would have been on you.'

'Me? Oh no, they've nothing to be hard on me for. I was a cop working with a former colleague to try to catch a killer. I've suffered a devastating loss. You're the one that was rolling around on top of a murderer; I would think they'll have a few questions for you about that, even if they haven't fired them at you yet. And you, Sholto, running an unregistered detective agency and working a case on behalf of a killer. Dear oh dear, that won't go down at all well. No, I worry about the pair of you, I really do. What future is there in this city for two men like you?'

He smiled and walked away down the corridor, back to the group at the other end. Darian could see that none of it was bluff. His word against Darian's and that was a duel he could win with a blindfold on.

Darian said quietly, 'He's going to get away with it.'

Sholto said, 'He's probably not going to prison, which is where he belongs. But he won't go unpunished, there are too many people who want rid of him and will see this as their best chance. That pal of yours from Whisper Hill, Vinny, he brought a lot of colleagues with him. They want Corey's head on a stick, but they'll settle for pushing him out of the force and defanging him. Don't underestimate them; there are still some cops with actual talent and a will to point it in the right direction in this city. He thinks he's so smart, but the problem with always being a step ahead is that it tends to leave a lot of people standing behind you. Corey's been helping criminals stay prison-free for a long time and it's been annoying them, but Ash Lucas was one of the last straws. A violent sexual offender and Corey walked him out of the station like he was a VIP. They didn't like that at all up at Dockside station. He might get away with his freedom, but he won't get away with his job.'

It was a small victory for decency, as decency's victories usually are. Darian said, 'He's going to come after you and me, try to shut down the office.'

Sholto laughed and put his arm around Darian's shoulder as he led him towards the front door of the station. 'I'm not worried about that guy. We have more friends in the police than he does, and we have some powerful backers now as well. How about that, us with influential friends. Kotkell would have made sure we had a tremendous reputation at

Sutherland if this had broken his way, but as it turns out his successor will have a lot to thank us for and I'll be sure to point that out in a firm but politely worded letter that hints at what we know about the bank's business. And now that I've got the evidence for Murdoch Shipping taking illegal deliveries we'll have another hulking bodyguard in Glendan. Having some corporate bullies in our corner might not be the most noble way to keep our heads above water, but it's better than drowning.'

They stepped out into the cold at half past three in the morning. It was dark and the streets were empty. They got into Sholto's car and he drove them back to the scene so Darian could pick up the Skoda. They stood together on the pavement near the lamppost that marked the spot and they were silent for almost a full minute.

Sholto said, 'You sure you don't need a lift home?'

'No, I'll be fine. I'll see you at Cage Street tomorrow.'

Sholto understood that he'd done his bit and Darian now wanted to be left alone. What he really wanted, as Sholto drove away, was to lie down on the pavement and go to sleep. He was tempted to go to Misgearan and find amnesia there, but even drinking was too much effort so he drove home instead.